AN AYAH'S CHOICE

PRAISE FOR AN AYAH'S CHOICE

'A rare jewel, beautifully contrasting the vivid world of turn-of-the-century India with the gray skies of pre-war England through the eyes of a fiercely independent young heroine.'

Kate Quinn, New York Times bestselling author of 'The Rose Code'

'An unforgettable journey from turn-of-the-century India to England…I was completely riveted, utterly spellbound, and sorry to see it end.'

Julianne MacLean, USA Today bestselling author

'A page turner exploring how the central character, Jaya, navigates to find her own agency against a backdrop of sex, class and colour based discrimination.'

Dr Helen Pankhurst CBE, author of 'Deeds not Words'

'A journey of love and self-realization, Shahida Rahman's latest novel is utterly transportive, both tender and thrilling.'

A. J. Gnuse, Author of 'Girl in the Walls'

'An odyssey of Britain's complex relationship with India at the height of the Raj. This is a tale of love, broken promises, murder and revenge set against the backdrop of the fights for female suffrage and Indian independence.'

Dr Sean Lang, Anglia Ruskin University

AN AYAH'S CHOICE

BY SHAHIDA RAHMAN

ONWE

First published in Great Britain in 2022 by Onwe Press Ltd. This
paperback edition was first published in 2022.

1 3 5 7 9 10 8 6 4 2

eBook ISBN 978-1-913872-10-6
Paperback ISBN 978-1-913872-09-0

www.onwe.co | @weareonwe

This story is dedicated to the women who fight for a voice, strength and freedom.

As a woman, us women will not be pinned down nor weighed down by anything, no matter how hard that 'anything' tries.

-Aminah

PART I: INDIA

CHAPTER 1

Khesar India Bihar State, 1900

Maji's voice faded as Jaya sprinted toward temporary freedom, her satchel thudding against her back, sweat pooling at the base of her neck. She turned the corner and ran away from the village to her secret spot by the river. Once she could no longer hear the shrill sound of her mother's voice, she ducked under the branches of the tree that blocked her hiding spot from those passing along the dirt road. She scrambled over the forest floor, taking care not to put her foot down on a snake, and climbed down to the thick curved root where she rested her feet as she sat, relieved, on the sun dappled boulder. When she set her satchel on the rock a bit too hard, she saw silver flashes of a school of fingerling fish dashing off through the ripples of the clear river. She sighed as she pulled out her drawing book and her stick of charcoal.

At the river, Jaya became who she wished to be. Not the daughter of a woman disappointed with her own life, living in a village where nothing ever happened. Not a girl destined to a marriage and children and dreary days of cooking and cleaning and saying yes sir to a man who didn't deserve it. Here, with the river singing softly and the forest holding her in an embrace, Jaya was an artist. She spent her days creating the world as she wanted it: putting people where she liked, adding a tiger, making a man's eyes wide with wonder or thin with anger. In her drawings, Jaya found a new life – lives where she decided where a tree would be, and whether a girl would become a warrior on a horse, or the horse itself.

Jaya wanted so many things and, in a life prescribed by a mother who resented her, and a village filled with people who continued to think the thoughts everyone had been thinking forever, it was only inside her drawings that she truly felt free. For freedom was what she wanted. Freedom to make different choices, freedom to say no or yes or maybe. Freedom that was not available to a poor girl in a remote village in India.

She'd find her mother quietly steaming when she returned to the house, but she didn't care. Today had begun normally, like a hundred mornings before. Maji asked her to hang the clothes in the bushes to dry, which she had done. As usual her mother commented, never able to keep her words in her head, always allowing them to tumble out of her mouth in any way they liked when it came to her daughter.

'Why put that red dress in the sun? As if it is not so faded already,' she'd said. 'You are either stupid or stubborn, Jaya. In either case, you are useless. Why can't you be like your brother? Krishnan was always good. Now he works in the town, brings home money. You? You'll never amount to anything.'

Jaya learned the best way was to keep quiet, but this morning that was not an option. Some days something inside of her would not keep quiet, could not. It insisted that she stand up for herself.

'If I'm so useless, it's better I go.'

Just as her mother tried to respond, Jaya reached for her satchel, knowing already where she was heading, and dashed out of the yard. Her mother chased after her, with her ever-present cane, to beat her daughter if ever she could catch her, screaming every insult she could find at this daughter that caused her such anger.

Jaya easily left her mother far behind. Besides being good at drawing, she was an excellent runner, even beating most boys in the village.

On the warm boulder, Jaya took up her charcoal and positioned her drawing book on her lap, her legs crossed as she liked, and not in the prim and proper way her mother insisted upon. She sketched a black and yellow oriole as he flitted among the reeds, collecting strips of building material to carry to his nest in the tree. He took time expertly weaving the strips into the half-finished structure.

How Jaya wished she were a bird and could fly far away! Away from the mundane household chores and the prison her mother attempted to lock her inside. She'd fly away and build her own little house high up in a tree. If Maji passed underneath, she'd poop on her head. The thought made Jaya smile. And then, almost immediately, she felt sad.

Two nights before, when she was in her bed not quite asleep, she heard her mother outside, crying as softly as possible. Jaya had heard her mother cry like this before, but this time she knew the reason. She'd seen the incident that caused the tears. It was a public humiliation, the most recent in a series of humiliations that began so many years before when she was left a poor widow with two young children.

The daughter of Maji's childhood friend was getting married. Maji had raised the girl as much as her own parents, and she had been happy to help with some of the pre-wedding preparations at her friend's house. Early, on the day of the wedding, when all the village women gathered at the bride's house, Maji put on her best clothes and went to join them in the celebration.

When the young bride saw her, she screamed. The friends and neighbours rushed forward and watched as Maji's oldest friend said, 'You must go. You know a widow is bad luck. Do you want this marriage to fail?'

Jaya was in the crowd that witnessed her mother humiliation, and they'd all watched as she'd turned, said nothing and walked, straight-backed and dry-eyed, to her tiny hut down the dirt lane.

A poor widow was the near bottom of the social hierarchy. Pain and humiliation had been part of her mother's life for as far back as Jaya could remember. Maji's only relief was that she was Brahmin, and her first-born was a hard-working son, Krishnan, a brother to Jaya.

What Maji wanted most was for Jaya to grow up quickly and be married off to a good husband. Jaya was beautiful, and that helped, but her way of wandering around in the forest, daydreaming about a life she could never have had caused rumours in the village that were limiting her chances of finding a good match. This infuriated Jaya's mother, for it was something she knew her daughter had control over, but seemed not to care about. Jaya was already nineteen, with no husband

and she'd soon be too old for the best prospects. Then what would they do? A widow and an unmarried daughter would starve to death in poverty.

Jaya cared nothing about a good match, or the rumours that swirled around the village that she spoke to tigers and swam naked in the river. She preferred people think such things about her. Better reasons for them to leave her alone with her thoughts and her drawings.

Jaya dreamt of the day that she would run even further, run away from Khesar, and the life she had there, forever. She would miss nothing and no one except her brother Krishnan. In her heart, she knew that day, her day of freedom, would come, but the only question was when.

In some ways, Jaya felt compassion for her mother, but not enough to love her. It was impossible to love someone who beat you daily, who forced you into a life you could not endure and who tried to hold you prisoner until she could marry you off. No, when Jaya left this place, she would not miss Maji.

The oriole alighted on a reed, so near Jaya could have reached out and touched him. Instead, she stayed still and looked closer at the way the light reflected in his round eye, how the feathers on his wing overlapped each other so perfectly, as if arranged by God. She shifted slightly and the clatter of her bangle scared him off. She looked down at her wrist, running her finger over the engravings on the ivory bangle Krishnan had brought for her when he'd visited the month before.

'I bought it in the market at the edge of the city. When you visit, I'll take you there,' he promised.

'Will you take me there, Krishnan? Really?' Jaya asked.

Her mother had made a big scene shortly after her brother had arrived. She shouted her usual insults about how no man with sense would marry an animal like Jaya. She'd stormed off to her room to lie down, and Krishnan took Jaya's hand and led her out to sit in the shade of their favourite kadamba tree. Its sweet scent surrounded them, reminding Jaya of how they'd play for hours there when they were children. She immediately felt better.

'I will, I promise.' He took Jaya's arm and pointed out the elephant on the bangle; it was his favourite among the many carved into the ivory. Jaya agreed it was the best one.

'I wish you would try harder to not make Maji so angry. She'll kill you one day with that cane. I could not go on if that happened.'

'Don't be silly. She can't kill me. I only let her beat me a bit, to get it out of her system. If it becomes serious, I run to the forest for a while.'

Krishnan laughed. 'You run very fast.' He let go of her hand. 'I know you're different, and special. I want your dreams to come true. As soon as I can, I'll bring you to the city. I'm still an apprentice, sharing a room with three other men. But once I'm a qualified blacksmith, you'll come and stay with me.'

'But that is two years away! She'll have me married by then!'

'Is marriage the worst thing? At least you would be free of her. I can't protect you when I'm not here. Maybe a husband is a good idea.'

'Free of her, but given over to another who will likely beat me too, and worse. I'd rather die.'

Krishnan reached into his leather bag and took out something wrapped in lots of brown paper. 'I was saving this for later. But have it now.'

Jaya opened it to find gulab jamun, her favourite sweet. She smiled up at her brother and then dove in.

'Don't think this will bribe me. I'll marry no one. And you have promised to get me free from here. I know once I'm in the city with you, I'll find a way to be the artist I want to be.'

Krishnan put his arm around his sister. 'I'll try. In the meantime, maybe I can look for a post in one of the British houses for you. They always need nannies and housemaids. Would you agree to that?'

'Yes, I'll do anything to leave this place.'

A visit from Krishnan was always a beautiful relief even if it meant he had to return to the city. She would be left behind with an even angrier Maji, but it was a price Jaya was willing to pay.

Perhaps not surprisingly, Maji even blamed Jaya for being born. During the pregnancy, Jaya's father had died, crushed by a carriage at the port in Calcutta where he'd worked as a porter. The grieving Maji went into a gruelling labour a few weeks later, bringing forth another child that she had no way to support. Besides taking a long time to recover from the difficult labour, Maji's in-laws took everything she and her husband had managed to buy and save. They kicked Maji and her two small children out of the very house she and her husband had built in their village. Though sati had been banned, backward in-laws like hers still believed that a good wife jumped into the flames and joined her husband. If she did not do so it was proof that she was evil, and likely the one who had prayed for her husband to die. The stress of all of that, along with her recovery, meant Maji had no interest in the beautiful little girl from the very first moment she saw her.

Krishnan was the one who placed Jaya on their mother's breast to nurse while Maji slept, trying to regain the strength she was sure Jaya had stolen from her. Krishnan was Jaya's real parent. He was the one who loved her unconditionally, and who wanted the best for her. He was the one who told her stories.

One of Jaya's favourite things was to listen to Krishnan tell her stories about when she was a little girl. 'You started to draw before you could walk,' he'd say. 'You used to create designs and faces in the dust with your small fingers. I taught you to use a stick to draw. Maji hated to see your fingernails full of dirt.' Krishnan would laugh then. 'It seemed that even without fingers or a stick, you would have drawn with your toes, or your nose. Something inside of you simmered with energy. It seemed that if you didn't release it, the heat would grow, burning you from the inside out. Drawing helped. I knew you were special even then. You were a girl who would not accept things as they were—you wanted to make the world bend to your visions.'

She smiled thinking of that little girl drawing with sticks in the dirt. Her thoughts had wandered while waiting for the oriole to return, but he never came back. She paged through her sketchbook. On the first page she had drawn their neighbour, Arjum, grinning up at her: Dark lines rounded his belly and cheeks, his eyes mere slits from the laughter coming through his wide lips. His deep laughs were heard from morning until night when snores replaced his chuckles. The portrait seemed to conjure up those sounds, too. Next was Pia, a child from the village. Jaya had been attracted by her halo of curls. She was proud of the way she'd captured their shine and bounce with just a few swift strokes.

Krishnan featured in many of the sketches: deep in thought,

twinkly eyed and teasing, and one that captured his pure joy, his head thrown back in laughter.

She turned the page and smoothed her palm over the clean space. She grasped the charcoal. Her first strokes were tentative, but as her mother's face appeared, the lines grew bold and thicker with intent. She soon lost sense of time and place. Her fingers cramped, and she flexed her hands looking at her work.

Her mother stared up at her. Harsh judgement filled her eyes, and an admonishing finger obscured part of her chin and cheek. Piles of laundry and stacks of buckets towered behind her. With one finger, Jaya traced the chain that crept around Maji's thin neck. She considered the drawing while pulling her thick rope of hair over her shoulder to rest on her chest. Its silkiness soothed her, and she stroked it for comfort. The sun was sinking and, regrettably, she closed her drawing book and carefully stored it and her charcoal in her satchel. Reluctantly she made her way back to the road, the oriole singing out its praise for the day.

CHAPTER 2

The letter arrived two weeks after Krishnan's visit. Maji
collected the letters from the post office in the next village,
which was a mile away, and there was one addressed to Jaya.
Maji opened it and read it before arriving back home.

'Your brother has written you, I see,' Maji said tossing the
letter on Jaya's bed.

Jaya took the letter outside to sit under their tree and read in
peace:

Dear Jaya,

*I have news. I asked around for positions as we had spoken about when
I was there. A friend works at a large house, one of the big men in the*

British government. They need a woman to look after their children. I have managed to get you an interview. You must be here by next week Tuesday. That is the day of the interview. Bring all that you require in case you get the job. They will likely hire you straight away. You'll not have time to go back to the village to collect your belongings. They will give you a room in the big house if you are hired. It's a good position. Come quickly.

I can't wait to see you.

Love,

Krishnan

Jaya knew her mother had read the letter and was waiting for her to go back in the house. She would certainly have something to say about the new developments. But Jaya was not ready for her criticism and comments. She held the precious letter in her hand, the key to leaving her prison. She would walk away from this place and never return. She smiled, dreaming of the future that was waiting for her. This letter was the first step towards that future.

She laid her head against the trunk of the tree and thought of all that the letter promised. She would have her own room, food and money on top. She would save her money, for she knew the more money she had, the more control she would have over her life. She could feel the quiver in her heart, and heard the small whisper that told her, 'It is beginning.'

She got up and went into the house. The Tuesday of the interview was three days away. She needed to prepare.

Her mother was sitting at the table on one of the crude wooden stools. She held an empty metal cup in her hand, spinning it this way and that on the table, looking as if she'd been doing it for some time. She kept her eyes on the cup when she spoke to Jaya.

'So, you will get a job in the city? Who will hire a lazy girl like you? Don't get your hopes up. Krishnan might think you have a chance, but I know you do not.'

'We will see.' Jaya had no energy for a fight. She knew her mother would not stop her from going, no one could.

'I'll send you a letter when the negotiations are finished,' her mother said.

'Negotiations?'

'We are near to having a husband for you. When the negotiations are finished, I will send you a letter. You must come home immediately. The husband will not wait for you.'

'I'm going to the city to meet Krishnan. I'll not be here.'

'When I call, you come. Don't start your stubborn ways with me. Only a lazy, evil woman refuses marriage.'

Jaya said nothing more. Maji could do what she liked. It had nothing to do with her. She would not return for this man, no matter who he might be.

***

Jaya approached the large iron gates of the property and explained to the man at the gate that she was there for the interview for the ayah job.

'Like the rest of them,' he said, pointing through the gate.

Behind the ornate gate was a lush garden full of all the colours the earth could muster, and yet Jaya noticed none of it. She only had eyes for the long line of women; all here for the single post that, in Jaya's mind, was already hers.

She'd learned more about the job after talking with Krishnan. An English family with two small boys needed a nanny, an ayah, and Krishnan had procured an interview for Jaya with the master of the house, a British man who was high ranking in the Colonial Police in Banka. Jaya hadn't understood that half the women of Banka and the surrounding villages had managed to get an interview as well. Jaya had no experience with children, and wasn't even sure what a nanny was meant to do, but she knew how to read and write and, of course, to draw. Maybe these skills would help her find success. So, she tried not to be discouraged by the many women who looked at her as she joined the end of the queue.

The grand house, two stories high, stood on a large piece of land surrounded by manicured grass, which was bordered by an immaculately cut hedge. In the sunlight, the white walls of the house seemed to glitter. Lush and colourful, the pink and red bougainvillea that grew up one side were swallowed whole by Jaya's artist's eyes. There were outbuildings at the back of the property, and though Jaya could only see the edge of them, she assumed that must be where her room would be, the room she would have all to herself.

Before arriving, in Jaya's mind, the job was already hers. But now, looking at the women in the queue, her courage wavered. Dozens of women just like her waited, hoping for a different future than the one that they'd been offered at birth. One by one, they were called. They climbed the stone steps and disappeared through an open door at the top. Each returned, passing the women still waiting in line, their heads bent and eyes downcast in disappointment. Each one who failed was one less for Jaya to worry about.

Time passed slowly in the hot sun. Sweat trickled down Jaya's spine and she licked her dry lips. Her stomach growled with hunger. When only one woman waited in front of her, Jaya bent down to her dusty feet and tried to clean her sandals.

The woman ahead of her turned and watched her cleaning her feet; her weathered face was in sharp contrast to her clear brown eyes.

'Who have you worked for?' she asked.

Jaya stood pulling her thick braid forward. 'No one, chaachi.'

The woman leaned forward, her keen eyes taking in Jaya's face, body and clothing. 'I have worked for seven families just like this one. I was an ayah before you were born,' she said. 'I will get this position. You've wasted your time coming here.'

Jaya straightened her sari and ran her hand along her braid. 'Yes, chaachi.'

Jaya tried not to let the woman's words affect her. Who knew? Maybe this colonel and his wife wanted an ayah with no experience, someone they could train as they wanted. She would not let her hopes fall. Nothing was decided until she was told she did not get the job. Until then, there was still hope.

A movement in a window above caught Jaya's eye. Two little faces peered out. Jaya smiled and raised a hand thinking those must be the children the chosen ayah would care for. The two faces disappeared after giving Jaya tentative waves.

The door opened and a servant stood at the top of the steps, her sari draped across one bony shoulder. 'Next.'

The woman in front of Jaya marched toward the house, and Jaya stood alone. She dragged her foot through the dust, creating a large circle, two eyes and a wide smiling mouth. She glanced up at the window where the boys had been. One had returned. He patted his head in a silly way and Jaya laughed.

Heartened, she shook her braid at him and he smiled down at her.

'Hmph.'

The experienced ayah returned. She stalked past; her head held high despite her obvious disappointment.

'Go,' she barked. 'Good luck to you.'

The long queue of woman was finished, and now only Jaya remained. Her hopes rose knowing that all of the women before her had been unsuccessful. It was up to her to show them that she was the best person for the job.

'You ... come,' the servant called from the steps.

She wiped her palms on her sari and headed up the stairs.

'The Colonel is waiting,' the woman said. 'Follow me. Be quick.'

The servant swept through the kitchen allowing Jaya only a glimpse of the stone benches and the row of shiny copper pots dangling from the ceiling. Something delicious bubbled on the stove, and Jaya's stomach reminded her how hungry she was. The kitchen had a tap right inside of the house; she had never seen anything like it before. How her life would change if she lived in a house like this one.

Jaya stepped lightly on the beautifully tiled floors so as to not make a noise as she followed the thin back of the servant, past a curving staircase and towards a closed door at the end of a hallway. Jaya could barely keep up with the woman she was so busy looking around at all the amazing sights. The servant stopped and tapped on the dark wood of the door.

'Yes,' a rich, deep voice answered from inside.

The woman opened the door and stood to the side. Jaya looked at her.

'Go in,' the woman said, a hint of kindness in her voice that surprised Jaya after her previous abrupt manner.

The door swung open and Jaya stepped inside. Colourful rugs covered slate floors, and a plush leather sofa and chairs circled a knee-high polished teak table. A man sat at a large wooden desk and indicated that she should sit in the straight-backed wooden chair in front of it.

She approached as instructed, noting the man was younger than she expected, maybe just a bit older than Krishnan. He had fair hair and penetratingly sapphire eyes, which distracted Jaya who was not used to such things. He wore a sharply pressed white uniform. She'd seen British people before, of course, but she'd never encountered one so close before. The people she had seen from afar always seemed so bland. Often they wore a pinched look on their face as though they had smelt something rotten. She felt her blood boil at the memory. She hated that look.

Jaya thought it odd that a man who was so important would

have eyes that looked ready to laugh at any moment, and a soft mouth with full lips that did not seem used to giving orders. He did have a strong chin though, and a defiantly straight and purposeful nose. She was not familiar with such faces.

'Please sit down. Your name?' the man said.

'Jaya,' she whispered, shifting under the weight of his stare. She glanced around the room searching for her breath. Her skin pricked. She felt so exposed. She took a step back. Where was his wife? Surely, she should be here. Jaya knew if his wife were here, her heart wouldn't be pounding so fast. If his wife were here, she might be able to pull Jaya away from his stare. Her stomach twisted as something sour settled on her tongue. Wife. He must have a wife.

On the dark wooden surface of his desk was a stack of paper. A few pieces had been carelessly crumpled and tossed aside. Jaya was surprised at such careless abundance. She struggled to buy her own paper for drawing; it was often a hard-earned gift from Krishnan, so to waste paper in this manner seemed indulgent. She thought of all of the paper she might have if she lived in this house, this house of shiny pots and water that ran like a stream in the kitchen.

'Jaya,' the man said, pulling Jaya's mind back to the task at hand. Her throat tightened. He seemed to caress the name in his mouth. He looked at her and smiled slightly.

'Do you write, Jaya?' Heat flashed across her face as an image of that stupid pinched expression sprang into her mind. *Do I write? Probably better than you.*

'I can read and write, yes, sir.' She squirmed under his close inspection and placed both hands in her lap to keep them still. 'I draw too, Colonel. Quite well. I can teach your boys.'

'I see.' He smiled at her confidence.

Jaya stared at her feet. The colonel cleared his throat. 'What experience do you have, Jaya?'

'I clean and cook and sew, Colonel. I have done that my whole life. I am strong and a fast learner.'

'This job is for an ayah. What kind of experience do you have with children?'

'None to speak of, Colonel, except for playing with the children in my village.' She considered the question further. 'It's not been long since I was a child myself, you see. I know how they think. That might be helpful. And I'm a very fast runner. Your boys will never be able to escape from me.'

The man laughed at the unexpected answer. 'Yes. *I see that you are young, but you are not a child anymore.*'

His tone made Jaya look up. The Colonel's strong gaze bore into her soul. She felt a shockwave ripple through her heart; an unfamiliar feeling. It disturbed Jaya how much she liked it. She blushed with embarrassment, hoping that the Colonel could not detect her rapid heart rate pulsing in her chest. He was a boss, a man from a completely different culture who would only ever view her as a lowly servant. Part of her wanted to despise him, to spurn all those who yielded such power in a country where they were visitors rather than natives. Yet another part of her harboured a yearning that she had not experienced before.

Seconds past and Jaya's discomfort did not ease. His eyes studied every section of her face. What did he see? Was he judging her like so many before him? Her back straightened at the thought. Let him, she thought furiously. It was bad enough being picked apart and ridiculed by her own people, but she'd be damned if she would give that power to him. Yet another part of her harboured a yearning that she had not experienced before.

A sharp breath drew from her mouth as she watched the corners of his mouth lift. He wasn't judging her, no; he seemed … curious? A warm feeling spread in the pit of her stomach. I see that you are young, but you are not a child anymore.

Jaya pretended not to have noticed him looking at her. She felt her breathing become heavy and overpowering. She was in the spotlight. She flicked her hair over her shoulders.

His prolonged eye contact forced Jaya to glance down. She was not used to such scrutiny.

'Do you think you can handle two boisterous boys, Jaya?

Clearly you have a playful nature and a sense of humour, which I would regard as essential qualities. Professional qualifications and experience are useless if you are unable to connect with children on their level, which I believe you can.'

Jaya lifted her chin, keeping the paper and ink in sight. 'I can look after your children, Colonel. I promise. Please give me a chance. You'll not be disappointed.'

A lock of flaxen hair escaped from the Colonel's carefully slicked back hair as he looked up. It fell over deep-blue eyes that cut into her beating chest. Jaya's itch to smooth it back startled her. What was she thinking? She'd thought she was immune to such inappropriate intentions. But then she'd never been near a man such as the Colonel. She laid some blame for her odd behaviour on the house, and its wonders. She was not herself. At that moment she did not know that she would not be herself again for a long time.

'Right.' The Colonel slapped his palms onto the desk. 'My name is Colonel William Edmundson. You will address me as Colonel from now on. Do not disappoint me, Jaya.'

She stood up. 'I ... I have the job then?' Jaya stuttered. She should have felt relieved. In truth, she did, but there was something else bubbling up in her core that filled her with excitement.

'You do. Sayida will show you to your room.' The Colonel's

eye sparkled as he smiled a genuine smile. 'I hope you'll be happy here'.

Jaya thanked the Colonel and left the room. She tried to find her way back to the kitchen where she hoped she would find the servant woman who had led her to the Colonel's office. The house was so big, with many twists and turns leading into large rooms or other passages, but finally she saw the kitchen and walked towards it. The servant woman was standing in the room when Jaya entered.

'He has hired me. I am the new ayah,' Jaya said.

'Yes. I know. Call me Sayida,' she said. 'We must get you cleaned up first.' Jaya followed Sayida outside as she led her to the rooms at the back of the main house.

As she followed Sayida, she wondered how she had known so quickly that she'd got the post. Had she been told while Jaya had been lost in the innards of the house? Who knew what went on in a house such as this?

They walked to the last small room in a line of adjoining rooms.

'This is your room. Mine is next door. Go inside and wait for me. I'll bring bath water.'

Inside Jaya found an iron bed with a thin horsehair mattress and a blanket. Next to the tiny window with only shutters,

was a simple wooden chair and desk. Jaya's mind already saw
the hours she could sit drawing at that table, looking out the
window at the vegetable garden and trees, alone and at peace.
Even if everything else about this position was horrid, this room
would be enough to compensate.

Sayida returned with a bucket of warm water and a bar of
soap that smelled like roses. She also carried a sari, not new but
in better shape than the one Jaya wore.

'Wash and change. Then come up to the kitchen. You'll find
me there.' She looked at Jaya staring at the small bottle of oil
she'd brought with the soap. 'It's for your skin. You'll see. It's
good.'

Sayida had been kind and understanding, so she washed
quickly and applied the oil. Sayida had been right. The oil
made her light brown skin glow, and it smelled of the forest.
She finished her ablutions and put the sari on. It was dark and
light blue in a beautiful pattern. Already Jaya felt her new self
appear. She tossed the dirty water at the back of her new room
and then walked quickly to find Sayida.

Up in the kitchen, Jaya found a white woman standing beside
Sayida.

As she was about to enter, Sayida said, 'Take off your
sandals.'

Only then did Jaya realise how dusty they were. She'd been

too caught up in the excitement of her new room and new clothes to notice. She lifted her sari to remove the sandals when a hand reached out and slapped her bare leg hard.

Jaya looked up at the white woman, her face contorted with disgust.

'Have you no shame, girl? Don't flash your bare legs around.'

Jaya looked at her, confused. Had she left her mother's beatings in Khesar only to come to this grand house and be beaten by this woman?

'I'm sorry, Memsahib,' Sayida said. 'She's young, she'll learn.'

'Well, teach her some decency, Sayida. I will not have her swanning around here half-dressed like some wild native. She'll learn to control her natural urges, or she will leave my house.'

Sayida nodded. Memsahib walked off saying nothing more. Jaya was suddenly relieved, happy now that this wife had not attended her interview. She was sure the woman would not have hired her.

Jaya stepped outside to place her sandals on the wide veranda. When she looked up, she saw the Colonel watching her. He smiled and she looked away. When she looked back, he was gone.

Inside, Sayida took Jaya to the side. 'You must take care. That was Sara Edmundson. She is the Colonel's wife. You must learn how to manage yourself around her. I've known her a very long time, and still her moods can catch me off guard. Please take care. Sara is not … well. It is not talked about, but I have known her since she was a small girl, and she has some sort of madness disease that makes her behaviour unpredictable.'

The words 'madness' and 'unpredictable' made Jaya feel uncomfortable, not because they made her fear Sara, but because this was Sayida's opinion. There was always a reason for poor mental health, and Jaya preferred to judge people for herself. She'd merely lifted her sari to remove her sandals. Was that incorrect? She would have to watch, and learn quickly.

CHAPTER 3

'Sit still.' Jaya spoke softly, her gaze darting between her sketch pad and the small faces in front of her. 'Edward, face this way. Yes, good. And Christopher, smile. You look miserable.' The shrinking piece of charcoal moved feverishly over the rough paper.

Christopher squirmed. 'Are you done yet?' He pulled at his collar with chubby fingers.

'Not long now.'

Jaya finished drawing Christopher's eyes. 'Yes, I'm finished.'

She looked down at her drawing. Christopher had his father's eyes. He had his father's playfulness, too. The Colonel tried hard to appear serious and stern, but it was not his nature, his eyes told the truth.

Edward, the older boy, was the serious one. Sometimes Jaya felt sorry for him. He seemed to carry the weight of his family's problems on his slim shoulders; and the problems were many. Jaya had only been in the house less than a month, and she could see that there was much unhappiness in this family. Problems escalated when the Colonel was not around, and he travelled a lot. Even Jaya felt happier when he was around; she tried not to examine that feeling too much. She was trying her best to take Krishnan's advice.

He had visited on a rare day when the Colonel was at home. Jaya and Krishnan were in her room, and the Colonel had come down from the house to ask Jaya about something. She went out to speak with him, but Krishnan must have been watching though the open door.

'How are you getting on with the two rascals? They seem happy, so they must like you.' The Colonel smiled and placed his palm lightly against her upper arm.

Jaya felt flustered again, but scolded herself for reading too much into the gesture.

'They are … so different,' she stammered, 'but both lovely. Christopher doesn't let anything bother him, but Edward …'

'Ah, yes, Edward,' interrupted the Colonel. 'Edward cares too much … about everyone and everything. It's just his way. Don't let it trouble you.'

The Colonel patted Jaya's arm and, as he moved his hand

away and down, his fingers brushed lightly against the back of Jaya's hand. She instinctively moved her hand away. Something sharp shifted in the air. Jaya stole a glance at the Colonel and her breath caught in her throat. His lips were pressed together and the slightest of creases had formed on his brow. It almost looked like…like he was in *pain*? As quick as it had come, that expression vanished from his face, yet it remained ingrained in Jaya's mind. Was it one of rejection, hurt, disappointment, or was it just wishful thinking on Jaya's part? She couldn't tell. She felt a flush creeping across her cheeks and the heat on her ears.

The Colonel quickly straightened himself up and said coolly, 'Right, I'll leave you to it. I have business to attend to.' He turned and strode toward the house.

When she came back into her room, her brother looked at her for a bit and then said, 'You are here to take care of children. That's it.'

'Yes, I know that.'

'You mustn't become confused,' he warned. 'You are here all of the time, and you can become confused about your place in this house. Or someone can make you confused.'

Jaya knew exactly what he was alluding to. She shifted under his stare but raised her chin all the same.

'Don't worry about me,' she said. 'I can take care of myself now, big brother. I'm not a little girl anymore.' Krishnan said no

more, but the conversation shook her. Had she been too quick
to dismiss his caution? He knew things that she did not, and
perhaps she should take advantage of his wisdom.

As Sayida had warned that first day, Sara was like a
tropical storm. She could move in amidst the sunshine and
drown everything in seconds. Whereas Christopher took no
responsibility for his mother's moods, Edward seemed to think
it was his duty to help his mother, and allow his words to soothe
her hateful words and actions.

Already Jaya found herself drawn to Edward. She tried her
best to alleviate his burdens. He was a child; he should not have
to be responsible for his mother. Jaya had too much experience
with a problematic mother. She would do all that she could to
protect Edward.

'Let me see,' Edward said, sitting next to Jaya on the floor of
the nursery. Jaya held up the drawing of him and his brother.
'We're very different. Do you think people know we are
brothers?'

'Look at your mouths.' They had their father's mouth, his full
lips. 'They're the same.'

Edward looked more carefully. 'Yes, maybe.'

Neither of them heard Sara entering the nursery. 'What is
that?'

Jaya jumped to her feet. She'd learned already that Sara felt sitting on the floor was dirty and 'native.' Sara grabbed the drawing pad from Jaya's hand and looked down at the drawing of her sons. Jaya's heart thudded in her ears. *Don't turn the page. Please, please do not turn the page.*

'This is good.' Sara carried it over to the light coming in from the large sunny window at the back of the room. Her features softened. 'You must do a more formal one – on the stone steps at the front of the house. We could have it framed.'

She dropped the drawing pad on the table, said nothing more and left. Jaya released the breath she had been holding. She pressed her lips lightly to stop smiling. Sara would not have been pleased if she'd turned back a few pages and found the drawings Jaya had made of the Colonel. His face filled her imagination and came out through her charcoal when she was alone in her room and her mind was quiet.

Two days later, Jaya and the boys were on the stone steps at the front of the house in the full glare of the sun. Sara insisted the boys should be in their formal suits despite the heat, and that they sit on the hard steps. She passed by periodically to check on the progress, so they dared not disobey their mother.

'My bottom is sore. I can't do this another moment,' Christopher insisted.

'Please, every time you move it takes me a little longer. Sit still for five more minutes and I promise I'll set you free,' Jaya begged. She reached forward and wiped both of the boys' sweaty foreheads.

Edward took a coin from his pocket and handed it to his younger brother. 'Jaya said we'll go to the park today. You can buy the sweets you like. Sit still so we finish quickly.'

Christopher smiled and put the coin in his pocket. Jaya's heart warmed at the sight.

'Let me see,' Sara insisted, sneaking up on Jaya from behind. Jaya held the portrait up for her to view. 'Yes. This is good.'

Sara carried it away and, like that, they were free. Jaya stood.

'Quick, let's get you two into your play clothes and then we'll run to the park.' Jaya knew they must escape quickly before Sara got another idea in her head.

The nearby park was full of towering trees that created welcome shade. Edward pushed Christopher on the swings, while Jaya sat down on a near-by bench and closed her eyes, enjoying the coolness from the nearby river.

Had she fallen asleep? When she opened her eyes, she couldn't see the boys at first. Her heart plunged. The swings were now empty. She stood, her head spinning until she found Edward at the tall slide, and a staggered breath escaped her.

'Where is your brother?' She tried to keep her voice light but it sounded strange and high. She was being silly. She knew Edward would always have an answer to that question.

'He's on the swings.'

'No! He's not. Christopher is not swinging.' Jaya attempted to slow down her breathing as she grabbed Edward's hand. *Do not panic,* she chanted in her head as they rushed back towards the river. Christopher was always keen to be close to the river. *Do. Not. Panic.*

Just when she was sure he was dead at the bottom of the river, she saw him standing on the riverbank, next to a man. Tears welled up behind her eyelids but she banished them away as she and Edward ran over to him.

'Christopher! Why did you run off? I've told you never to do that,' Jaya said.

The man standing next to Christopher said, 'He's fine now. You can calm your heart.'

Jaya looked at the man, so insightful and kind. 'Yes … I see he's fine. Thank you.'

'You fell asleep,' Christopher said.

'I closed my eyes only.' Jaya looked at the man. What would he think of an ayah who fell asleep while watching her charges? 'You should not run off. I've told you the river is dangerous.'

Christopher had already forgotten. 'Look Edward! I put a boat in the river.'

Edward stood and watched a stick, Christopher's boat, float lazily along.

Jaya turned to the man. Now she noticed he was not as old as she'd thought at first, the white beard had given the wrong impression.

'Thank you for your kindness,' she said.

'You're most welcome.' He looked at her and smiled. 'I know small boys. I was once one myself; they can be quite wily.'

Jaya laughed. 'Yes, I looked down for only a moment and he was gone.'

'I can only imagine the stress that caused you, and I'm sorry for that.' He stepped forward and held out his hand. 'I am Rafik. I work in the bank, a senior clerk. I came out for some air, it's such a beautiful day. I'm thankful that I could be here to be at your service.'

'I'm Jaya Devani.' She shook his hand. He was an odd sort of man. Being near him made her calm. What was it, she wondered? He was dark in complexion with kind large eyes. His smile, she decided, was compelling. It was serene. She tried to imprint his face in her memory to draw later.

'I work for the Edmundsons in that big white house up the road. I must get back. We've been here longer than I had expected. They will be looking for us.'

'Yes, of course. It was a delight to have met you, even if under such circumstances. If it's not inappropriate, may I accompany you some of the way back, as I am going in that direction anyway?'

Jaya hesitated, as she was not sure what Rafik's intentions were, but then saw no harm as it was such a short distance and, besides, she was in the company of two young charges.

'Thank you, Rafik. That is kind of you.'

She turned to the boys and held out her hands for them to each take one.

Rafik commented about how well-behaved the boys were and how fortunate they were to have such an attentive ayah. Jaya smiled coyly, feeling embarrassed, but said little.

'In the distance, Jaya noticed Sara waiting at the gate. She mumbled her apologies to Rafik, explaining that she had to get the boys back to their mother quickly.

'Of course, I understand. Goodbye, Jaya. It was a pleasure meeting you.'

'You too, Rafik. Goodbye.'

When they reached the gate, Jaya could tell from Sara's expression that she was enraged.

'Where have you been all of this time?' she snapped.

'Jaya fell asleep and I went to the river and floated my boat,' Christopher said, excited to tell his mother of his grand adventure.

Before Jaya could speak, Sara's hand flew from her side and slapped her face. The force was so hard that Jaya fell to the ground, gravel scraping her knees underneath the thin fabric of her sari, her nose dripping blood. As she got to her feet, she glanced behind and her stomach hardened when she locked eyes with Rafik. Heat raced up her neck. He had witnessed the altercation. She looked away quickly. She simply couldn't bear it.

'I'll look after my sons for the rest of the day,' Sara declared, dismissing Jaya with a filthy look. Christopher ran off toward the house, but Edward lingered, hoping to help Jaya. But Sara would not have it. She grabbed his hand and dragged him toward the house. 'I will be sure to tell the Colonel to dock your pay for today.'

Jaya walked to her small room. She needed to wash the blood from her face. She hoped it would not bruise and, especially, she hoped the cuts from Sara's rings would not leave scars. Everything was made worse by knowing Rafik, and the boys, had witnessed what had happened.

Sayida was coming out of her room when Jaya arrived. Jaya tried to duck into her room before the older woman could see, but Sayida grabbed her hand and stopped her.

'What's happened?' Sayida asked. 'What happened to you?' She reached toward Jaya's face, but Jaya jerked away. 'Memsahib did this?'

Jaya nodded.

They went into Sayida's room. She pulled out a wooden chair for Jaya and held out a cool, wet washcloth. 'Come. Sit.'

The chair creaked as Jaya dropped onto it, suddenly so very weary. She lifted her face and closed her eyes, allowing Sayida's firm fingers to work their way over her skin. She realised that Sayida's comments on her first day had been correct after all; Memsahib Sara was not well in her mind.

Sayida lowered her voice. 'Memsahib has had a temper since she was a little girl when her mother hired me to watch her, to be her ayah. She has never known limits, that one.' She shrugged. 'But it's not for us to say. We're here to keep her happy, and her children warm and fed.' She removed the washcloth and patted Jaya's skin with a soft flannel. She leaned closer. 'You'll live.'

Sayida's eyes searched Jaya's and she stepped back. 'Don't let those boys run roughshod over you. They need to learn respect, the kind of respect their mother does not have for others. Their father might teach them a bit, but you're the one who spends the most time with them. Who better to teach them than you?'

'Why didn't they want you to be Edward and Christopher's ayah?' Jaya asked Sayida. 'You have more experience than me.'

Sayida laughed, though with a bitter edge. 'How can I be the ayah to those boys when I still need to be the ayah to their mother. You know she's ill. The Colonel insists I watch her, try to stop her from doing her worst.'

'You could try harder with her when it comes to me,' Jaya said teasingly. 'Anyway, maybe I won't be with them that long.'

Just saying the words brought relief to Jaya. The constant threat of Sara's moods sometimes, like today, proved too much. They reminded her too much of Maji. Jaya would not return to her mother's place, though. She would stick it out here until she found another plan. However, she was growing attached to the boys, especially Edward. Then there was the issue of the Colonel; why was he always at the front of her mind in her quiet moments? She would not admit it out loud, but leaving this house would bring sadness, too, if she were honest with herself.

'What are you saying? You're with this family now. Like me. I've been with Memsahib Sara for a long time. There are few days when I do not think of leaving, yet I'm still here. She's a difficult woman, a troubled woman. I brought her up, and now I have a hand in helping you bring up her children. This is perhaps why Shiva brought me to Sara so long ago. Few would have stayed this long. I must accept his will. You must accept it, too.'

Jaya knew Sayida was from the Ahir caste and, under British rule, she would have found it difficult to find other employment. The British thought all Ahirs were criminals, and their view had become widespread. Jaya thought it was unfair, like so many other things.

Sayida might not have choices but Jaya did, even if right now it did not look that way. So much about the world is first decided in our minds. In Jaya's mind, everything was there. Everything was possible. Despite Maji's efforts, and now Sara's, she did not put a fence around her imagination. For now, she was here, she was an ayah and a servant to a mad woman, but it would not always be like this.

CHAPTER 4

The next day, Jaya stopped at the hall mirror to inspect the damage Sara had done to her face. She touched the cut along her jaw and winced. Sara had scraped and bruised her cheek, but they would heal. The cut by her eye, though, would have to be kept especially clean. The sooner it closed, the less chance there'd be of scarring. She knew it was vain to be so concerned about her face, but she was proud of her smooth brown skin and didn't want Sara to leave her angry marks on it. She didn't want any memory of Sara on her body for as long as she was living there.

She turned and walked down the hall. Somehow, today, the Edmundson compound felt lighter and warmer. Jaya knew the source of the feeling before she could see it herself.

Colonel William was home. She felt better knowing it was so. Jaya would see him at dinner when she served the family meal. The anticipation lightened her heart. The Colonel's presence always made things better for her.

She thought about him the entire day as she floated through her duties, though she knew she should not. Sometimes she wondered if she was just imagining that the Colonel saw her as more than an ayah to his boys. Was all of this just in her head?

Then she remembered when Krishnan had seen them together. He'd seen it too.

Since she moved to the house, whenever she and the Colonel were in the same room, the electricity was there. Would anything come of it? *Did she want it to?* She knew the answer to that question, and she also knew it was not right. She would never disappoint Krishnan by behaving in a way that would make him think less of her. She needed to stop these feelings in herself. Hopefully, once she did, the Colonel would see that there was no opportunity for him to pursue anything.

'Wake up, woman,' Sayida snapped. Jaya stood in the middle of the dining room daydreaming. 'Set the table for dinner. We don't have all day.'

Jaya pulled four heavy plates from the corner cupboard and arranged them on the linen tablecloth. The fine silver would be used, as was the custom when the Colonel was home, and she was careful to line the forks, spoons and knives with precision. She laid the place setting at the head of the table with more care than the others. She rested her hand on his chair.

Just then, William's large frame filled the doorway. 'So, here you are.' His broad smile reached his intense eyes, forming crinkles at the outer edges. He seemed genuinely delighted to see her.

Jaya's face flooded with heat. She turned away from him. Her hands trembled as she adjusted the fork beside his plate and knocked it in her surprise.

'I'm sorry, Colonel.' She dropped her gaze and hurried off to the kitchen.

For a large man, William moved with the grace and speed of a cat. He skirted the table and caught her arm before she could disappear. He looked at her and Jaya tried to read what his eyes were saying, but before he could speak and make things clear, there was noise in the hallway.

'Daddy!' The boys tumbled in. 'Daddy, Daddy, Daddy!'

William squeezed Jaya's arm gently and released her, turning away from her and looking at his children as they raced into the room.

'Boys!' He laughed holding his arms open. 'You're so quiet! I didn't even hear you coming. You must speak up!'

Jaya escaped into the kitchen with the warmth of William's

hand still on her upper arm. She stood in front of the sink to calm her nerves and to remind herself that she must maintain her resolve to let nothing happen. Thankfully, Sayida was busy with the gravy and did not look her way.

'Christopher, Edward, stop dancing around like monkeys.' Jaya heard Sara arrive in the dining room.

'Well? Are they seated?' Sayida asked turning toward Jaya. The food was ready and the gravy had been poured into its ceramic bowl. She went to the soup still simmering on the stovetop.

Jaya peeked into the dining room. 'They're seated.'

'Come then, don't idle. You know how she can change. Get the tray.'

Fragrant steam filled Jaya's nostrils as she placed the bowls of soup on the tray. She lifted the tray and backed through the heavy door into the dining room. She placed the tray on the sideboard and turned, folding her hands in front of her, waiting. Her demure stance masked what she was truly feeling.

The Colonel paid Jaya no attention, despite the intimate moment they'd had only minutes before. He stood and went to a soft chair in the corner where he had dropped his satchel. She scolded herself for imagining that a man of such status could ever have any feelings for her. After all, she despised everything he represented.

'Come. Boys, I've brought you something.' Christopher and Edward climbed down from their chairs and ran to their father.

Sara said, 'I hope you've not bought more toys for them. They're spoiled already.'

The Colonel ignored her and bent down to his sons. 'Look at what I have for you.'

From his satchel, William produced a pair of stout wooden statues, each one of a Hindu god. Jaya knew the pair on sight, but listened as William explained what they were.

'This is Brahma,' he said, handing one of the statues to Edward. 'And this one is called Vishnu,' he said as he gave it to Christopher.

Christopher was delighted by the gift, but Edward eyed his with a touch of scepticism. Whispering to his father, he said, 'Mother says the Hindu gods are born of filth.'

A laugh burst from William. He glanced quickly at Jaya and then said, 'Jaya and Sayida are of the Hindu faith.' Edward looked briefly at Jaya and gave a small smile. 'No Hindu I've ever met is filthy, and neither are their gods,' William declared.

Jaya was not astonished by Edward's comment, as she recognized them as Sara's words. Born of filth. *How dare she!* Jaya was finding it harder and harder to keep her tongue. If they were all like Sara, Jaya thought, Mangal Pandey had been right to fight against the British being in India. You should not insult the person that you are visiting, but Sara had never learned that simple lesson.

There was much about her life that Jaya had discarded before moving into this house, but her faith was not one of them. Each morning, before anyone in the house awoke, Jaya climbed out of bed and made her way onto a worn mat in the corner of her room. There she performed her morning ritual. It was a series of meditations, quiet chanting, mudras and mantras. The entire ritual lasted about forty-five minutes. She always did it privately, not because she wanted to hide it, but because she revelled in being alone with her spirit.

After William corrected Edward, he looked at Jaya. He opened his mouth to speak but seemed to have decided otherwise. He blinked back at her wordlessly. She knew it was then he noticed the wounds on her face. He looked at his wife and then back at Jaya. His jaw had hardened but a soft wetness brewed behind his eyes.

Jaya's jaw throbbed as she gave him a small smile and straightened her spine. She turned to Sara. 'May I serve the soup, Memsahib?'

After serving the family, Jaya returned to the kitchen with her empty tray, and she took a lungful of air. She hadn't realised she'd been holding her breath as she set the soup bowls in front of each member of the family. Sara was especially observant this evening, following Jaya's every move. Jaya attributed the tremor in her hands to this scrutiny, not to the soft purposeful tap of William's toe on hers as she served him.

***

Half-way through dinner, Sara pushed her plate away. 'I'm too exhausted to eat,' she said. 'I'm going to bed.'

William looked at Jaya standing near the buffet, waiting to be told what the family might need. 'Jaya, please tell Sayida to make some tea for Mrs. Edmundson.'

'I don't want tea,' Sara said. 'I told you, I don't want that tea anymore, William.'

Her husband ignored her and repeated calmly, 'Jaya, please tell Sayida to make madam's tea.'

'Yes, sir.'

Jaya went to the kitchen. She wondered why Sara squandered her life sleeping, for at every chance she got, she would go to her bedroom and be asleep in minutes. Jaya knew that she would go off to bed now and not re-emerge until past noon tomorrow. Her fatigue had to be due to more than missing England and her sister.

If she had this life, this house, that husband, she would use every opportunity she had. If Jaya were in Sara's shoes, she would use her position to do so many things – what those might be, Jaya was not sure, but she certainly would not waste her life sleeping. To give her credit, perhaps it was not a conscious choice for Sara.

In the kitchen, Sayida was sitting in the straight-backed wooden chair at the end of the row of shelves in the corner, snoring, her eyes firmly closed. Jaya knew how hard Sayida worked. She was up each day long before sunrise and often not in bed until midnight. Jaya didn't like to disturb her brief naps, but she had no choice. She cleared her throat and pretended to be just entering the kitchen.

Sayida was up and on her feet at the sink clanking dishes. She turned to Jaya. 'What? What do they want?'

'The madam wants her special tea,' Jaya said.

Sayida sighed. She put the tea in a porcelain cup and covered the leaves with boiling water from the kettle always at the ready on the hearth. Using a small steel dropper, she squeezed three yellow drops of costly laudanum into the hot tea.

It was an unspoken rule that no one spoke of the drug Sara was addicted to. It was what was required. Jaya wondered how much more unpleasant their madam might be if she was not medicated daily. She was glad that Sayida made Sara's tea because there were days, days such as today, that Jaya could easily put a higher dose in the hope that Sara would be in a constant state of drowsiness. *Could she do such a thing?* Jaya was not sure, but she certainly dreamt of it often.

On the rare occasion, Jaya felt pity for Sara. She'd been forced to leave England and move to the small town of Banka because of her husband's work. At least in Calcutta, where Sara's father had worked for a large import-export firm, she had had friends and a life. Once she was married to William, her life became subordinate to his. What she wanted was irrelevant. From Jaya's viewpoint, a rich British woman had the world at her feet but, in the end, Sara, too, was merely a woman. Women in India and women in England were the same – neither had real choices in life. Instead, everything was decided for them when they were born, and their sex discovered.

In a sort of protest, Sara refused to show any interest in Indian culture, life or customs, especially the culture and life in Banka, her new home. She hated the climate, the constant rain, the endless poverty, the aromatic food and the many religious conventions. She wanted to be in Calcutta and, if not that, in England, where her sister now lived, a sister she missed desperately. She hated Jaya because Jaya stood for everything she despised; her bronze skin, long-lashed eyes and charm. What's more, Jaya stood for this place that held her captive.

Sayida put the tea on a tray and handed it to Jaya. 'Hurry, you know how she is when she needs her tea. Don't let her wait. It's better the Colonel is there; she will drink it if he is there.'

49

Jaya carried the tray to the dining room only to find Sara's chair empty. William looked at her. 'She couldn't wait. Jaya, please could you take it to madam in her bedroom? That would be such a help. Thank you.' He gave her one of those smiles that ignited emotions she couldn't explain. She broke eye contact with William and felt her body flush.

Jaya said nothing, simply bowing her head, and then left to deliver the tea. Upstairs, in the passage, Sayida was waiting for her.

'Let me come with you. You know how she can be sometimes when the tea is late. You don't need another beating. She's better with me.'

Jaya knew it was not just to keep Sara from beating her. She'd watched Sayida with Sara on the bad days. The Colonel had instructed that madam must drink the tea, but sometimes she refused and had to be coaxed. Jaya hated to witness those times, hated to be part of it, but Sayida explained that the tea was crucial, as Sara's addiction made her a danger to herself and others. Missing a dose could have dire consequences.

'Let's do it quickly. You know it will be upsetting,' Jaya said.

'Not to worry,' Sayida said, her voice entirely composed.

They entered the bedroom. Sara's eyes were wild, and Jaya knew immediately that things would go badly. Colonel William said Sara had 'nerves,' but Jaya knew that was not correct. She certainly had something, but it was not nerves.

'I will not drink it,' she said, looking at the tea Sayida held out to her.

Sayida's voice remained calm. 'The Colonel insists. It will ease your mind. Don't you want to sleep?'

'It does everything *except* ease my mind.' She looked at Jaya. 'What is it you are looking at?' Jaya lowered her eyes and started to fiddle with the end of her sari.

'That's right; avert your eyes, you coward. Carrying out his unjust orders.'

Jaya did not know what to do. If she kept her gaze away from Sara, she would be unable to help Sayida. If she dared look again, she would be struck. There was no way to win.

'The Lord made you pretty, but he also made you weak,' Sara spat at her. 'Your weakness will swallow you.'

Jaya dismissed madam's words. They were nothing more than the bitter ravings of a woman caught in a net from which she could not escape. She took a deep breath.

'Drink, please,' Jaya said, trying to help Sayida. 'You'll have lovely dreams.'

'What do you know of my dreams?'

Jaya said nothing. Indeed, Sara's dreams were probably very often nightmares. Whatever went on inside her head was no doubt of the dark variety, if her conscious time was anything to go by.

'I wish to speak with the Colonel first,' said Sara. 'Go and get him. I will drink it down if you bring him to me.'

'He is eating his dinner,' Sayida said.

'I don't care! Bring him! Bring him to me immediately, you stupid cow!' Her small fist pounded the blanket in frustration.

'I'll bring him,' Jaya said to Sayida. The older woman neither nodded, nor said a word; all she wanted was for the tea to be finished so she could go back to her work. She was so tired.

Jaya moved toward the door, seeking the temporary freedom on the other side.

'Oh yes, I'm sure that's an errand you're most grateful to run,' Sara said, as Jaya opened the door to leave.

She left the bedroom, shutting the door gently, not wanting to hear another word.

Sara's words echoed in Jaya's ears as she hurried down the stairs. What did she mean? Was she aware of Jaya's feelings for her husband? Had she noticed his foot touching hers under the table this evening?

She shook her head. What would an established British colonel want with a young girl from the village? She must hide her adoration more carefully if even Sara, with her drug-filled mind, could see them. She could dream about more than a touch, more than a look, but these thoughts must be locked away, and she must never act on them. This job was a step on her way to freedom. She would not ruin it.

When Jaya entered the dining room, William smiled at her.

'Jaya, is there something?'

'Memsahib wishes to see you, Colonel.'

He scowled and pressed a napkin to his lips. 'Did she take her tea?'

'No, not yet. She wants to speak to you first,' she replied.

He put the napkin down on the table and pushed his chair back, suppressing his irritation. William gave his boys a wink, 'I'll be right back and I want clean plates when I return, my fine little gentlemen.' Then he got up from the table and faced them again for the punch line, 'Except for mine, of course.'

The boys laughed. Jaya's tight lips melted into a smile. As William walked past her, he grasped her fingers and tugged her into the hallway. Her skin tingled under his touch as she followed his straight back and slim hips.

Once the door was closed behind them, he stopped and faced her, his fingers encircling her slim wrist. Pale stubble roughened the Colonel's strong jaw, and she ached to reach out to touch it. His musky scent drew her to him and she could feel her heart beating wildly in her chest.

'Who are you, Jaya?' He said her name like a caress.

'I am your ayah, Colonel.'

'You are so much more than that, my dear.' He reached forward and gently stroked her wounded cheek.

Jaya was silent, not trusting herself to speak.

'Will you do me the honour of coming to my study later?' He raised his eyes to the floor above them where his wife lay in bed. 'After I finish with *all of this?* After you've put the boys to bed?'

All of this? Jaya was disturbed by the coldness in William's reference to Sara, as though she were an inconvenience.

Jaya nodded. 'I ... I ... Colonel ...' Jaya wrapped the end of her sari around her hip, fidgeting with it, not knowing what to say.

'Jaya!' Edward called out from the dining room. 'Christopher's under the table!'

William laughed. 'Go.' He jerked his head toward the dining room. 'Go be an ayah for a little while. Then come to me, and you can be a woman.'

***

'Time for pudding, boys,' Jaya said, carrying the desserts into the dining room. Sayida had not returned yet. Jaya flicked her gaze to the ceiling and a tingle formed at the base of her neck. She wished she could see through walls. See exactly how things were going up in Sara's bedroom.

Edward looked up at her, and Christopher popped out from under the tablecloth where he'd been hiding.

'You sound funny,' Edward said.

Jaya laughed, but knew what he meant. She was unable to keep the excited anticipation out of her voice no matter how hard she tried.

Just then Sayida charged into the room. 'I'll do this.'

She grabbed the tray from Jaya. 'You go. When he's finished in there, she'll be in a state, and I dealt with it last time. Please, can you go?'

Jaya could see the bruise forming on the side of Sayida's face.

'Just stay well away from the bed.'

Jaya placed her hand on Sayida's arm. She did not deserve this. 'Yes, I'll go.'

'Pudding, pudding, pudding.' The boys rapped the table with their palms.

Jaya climbed the stairs to find Sara's door cracked open. She peeked in. The teacup rested on Sara's chest.

'Why do you feed this to me, William?' she asked. 'What have I done that is so wrong?'

'It always helped you sleep, my dear. Dr Jameson gave it his confident recommendation. My only concern is your wellbeing. You know that.'

'It gets worse each night.' Jaya could hear madam begin to

cry.

'Maybe you just think it's worse, my darling. The dosage is the same; we've changed nothing.'

Sara lowered her voice, so Jaya had to strain to hear her. 'I despise this place, William. Why can't we go back to England? I ache with longing to see Victoria. If you loved me at all you would take me to her. I fear I'll die in this godforsaken country.'

'I'm at His Majesty's service. I have no choice. Unless you want me to resign,' William said. 'Would you rather live here, in a compound the size of a palace, or in England begging for bread?'

Sara was silent. Jaya could see Sara bring the cup to her lips. She took a small sip.

'There's a good girl,' the Colonel soothed. 'Drink it down, my darling. You will feel better once you do.'

Jaya stood frozen, her knuckles clenched, anticipating a protest, but Sara finally gulped down the rest of her tea, and then rested her head on the pillow.

'I'll see you in the morning, my love.' The Colonel kissed her pale forehead and turned toward the door.

'You may go in now,' he said softly to Jaya as he left. He stroked her shoulder as he passed, before heading down to the dining room to finish his dinner. His touch made her skin tingle, and a heaviness settled in the pit of her stomach.

Inside Sara's bedroom, Jaya sat on a chair near the bed and pressed a cold towel against her perspiration-drenched forehead. Finally, she closed her eyes and submitted to the pull of the drug. Touching the woman with gentleness was strange; it was usually Sayida who nursed Sara. Jaya couldn't miss the stark contrast between her own firm, brown hands, and the pampered, near-translucent skin of the Englishwoman. She studied her mistress. Sara's features were clean, regular, pretty in their way. Jaya could see why the Colonel had fallen for her youth and beauty. Dressed in rich fabrics and jewels, she would have been magnificent.

Jaya was surprised when Sara's eyes opened, searching through a narcotic fog. She muttered something.

'Pardon, Memsahib?' Jaya leaned closer, turning her head to listen.

Sara lifted her head from her pillow and with force grabbed Jaya's thick plait.

'Swine!' she hissed.

Instinctively, Jaya pulled her hair free and backed away, the colour draining from her lips and her chest tightening as she struggled to catch her breath. Not wishing to further aggravate Sara, Jaya tried to maintain her decorum.

'Go to sleep,' she said in a soft voice. She stepped away from the bed, and remained still until she heard Sara's breathing deepen. Finally, she was asleep.

***

Jaya knocked softly on the study door. She hoped the Colonel would be inside, and that he would not be, her conflicting emotions struggling to compete with each other. She'd considered not going to the study, but the pull was overpowering. Her only hope was that the Colonel would realise his actions were inappropriate, and would choose not to meet her after all.

That hope was dashed when she heard his deep, mellow voice. 'Come in.'

Jaya hesitated before opening the door and then silently stepped inside the room. Her heart was racing again, and she was visibly trembling. The Colonel sat at his desk, in his shirtsleeves, his muscular forearms exposed. His head was down, and he was writing. Unsure whether he knew she was there, Jaya waited, biting her lip, her back pressed against the door.

William put down his pen and pushed the paper aside. He looked up and smiled, his cobalt eyes penetrating her soul. He said nothing for a few moments; he only looked at her, his gaze moving down her body and then back to her face. His lips parted slightly and she heard him inhale sharply.

'Come closer.' Was he toying with her, or simply deriving pleasure from the power he could exert over people? Jaya's feelings of desire and repulsion battled furiously.

Jaya moved nearer to the desk, dragging her feet and swallowing repeatedly. She ran her tongue across her lips. Her mouth felt unpleasantly dry.

The Colonel stood up, removed his glasses and placed them with precision on his desk. 'Sara, is she sleeping?'

Jaya cleared her throat. 'Yes … Memsahib is finally resting. The boys too.' She had trouble formulating her words, which were punctuated with pauses.

The Colonel crossed to where Jaya was standing and touched her waist.

'Let her rest, then,' he whispered. He stepped back from her and held out his hand. 'Come. Sit with me, Jaya.'

She took his outstretched hand and let him lead her to the dark leather sofa. They sat beside each other close, but not touching. Jaya pressed her hands into her lap and sat rigidly, inwardly questioning her integrity.

'Does it hurt, much?' William asked, tenderly tracing his fingers down her face.

'A little. It will be better soon.'

Jaya paused for a moment, then poured out the words quickly

before she had second thoughts. 'Sir, I don't feel comfortable watching Sara being persuaded to drink her tea. It clearly distresses her. Why does she have to drink it if she doesn't want to? I don't want to be part of it, so if you feel that is unacceptable then please feel free to dismiss me.'

The Colonel grimaced, then leaned towards Jaya and placed his hand on her knee. 'She hasn't always been like this, you know.' The Colonel's eyes widened and he raised his eyebrows, turning away from Jaya momentarily and staring out of the window.

Jaya suspected as much. Life can turn people into someone they never expected to be.

The Colonel leaned back into the sofa and clasped his hands together, resting them on his thighs. 'Years ago, when we first met in Calcutta, she was such an exciting and clear-minded soul. Something changed when her sister married and moved to England. Their parents had been cold people, and she and Victoria were close. Sara grew to hate India. The move here to Banka made it worse, and I feel guilty about that. She's frightened all the time. She misses her sister. Can you understand that? Does it explain her awful behaviour to you at all?' He knitted his brows together and looked at Jaya like a lost puppy.

'There's something else. Once, I actually tried to stop her

taking her tea, but she flew into a hysterical rage. I ignored her and left the room, thinking she would calm down and fall asleep, but she didn't. She tried to kill herself, and unfortunately it was Edward who found her.'

'I am sorry to hear that,' Jaya said, a dull ache spreading across her chest, 'you are very patient with her.'

'I have no choice. I must treat her like one of the children. Any argument would simply escalate to the point where she would begin breaking expensive vases and threatening murder. I can't have that sort of behaviour. We're part of the colonial government; we must maintain a certain standard, a certain decorum. Life would be much worse for Sara if we did not do so.' Jaya regarded the subtle darkness that sat under his eyes so often hidden beneath his quick smiles.

'But I think it is hard on you, Colonel.'

William touched her jaw again. 'It's hard on you, too.' William's voice cracked and his eyes glistened.

He moved closer so that the length of Jaya's thigh was warmed by his. Beads of sweat appeared on Jaya's upper lip, and the racing adrenaline caused conflict between the fight or flight response. Instead, she remained immobile, longing to gasp for air and feeling lightheaded and almost helpless.

William cupped her face in his hands and explored her face fervently. He fixed his gaze on her swollen lips and leaned in.

Jaya retracted her head slightly, but William moved his hand around to the back of her head and gently drew her in. It felt as though this was the moment she had been waiting for her entire life. His lips were as sweet and soft as she had dreamt they'd be. Her own stirred in response and she lifted her hand to feel his evening whiskers.

Too soon, he pulled away and Jaya glanced down awkwardly. He stood and went to the door. He produced a gold key from his pocket and used it to click the lock into place. He returned to Jaya. He took her into his arms, and she did not resist. She didn't want to.

'You're so beautiful,' he said. 'I've been thinking of nothing but you since I first saw you that day of the interview. I saw you at the end of the queue. I knew I would hire only you.'

'Is that true?'

William leaned away from her so he could see her face clearly and she could see his. They stood close.

'I'll never lie to you, Jaya. I know this is not ideal. I'm married, I'm your employer … those are things I cannot control. But I can control what is between us. I can control what is in this room. I will always be honest. Here, I want us to be just two people, a man and a woman, *equals*. You're the most beautiful woman I have ever seen.'

Jaya smiled. 'So here … like this … we are equals?' She could hear the sound of her breathing become faster and heavier.

'Yes.'

Warmth infused with every part of her body as she let his words sink into her. Equals. Did William know what he'd given her? Had she ever wanted anything more? *You are not a child anymore.* His words echoed in her mind and her stomach lightened. Jaya held William's gaze. His eyes were dark as they roamed over her face. The air was so thick, she wasn't sure if she was still breathing. It was strange. She expected that she should feel exposed under such a stare. Ashamed, even. She should be thinking of her mother's scolding, the whispers of her neighbours and the honour that they hung around her neck, ready to be tightened if she took a step too far. Jaya heard none of that. All she heard was her breath as she drew closer to William. She put her hand on his cheek and without thinking, she kissed him. She could tell that he was surprised that the quiet, demure ayah was taking control.

'I like you like this,' William said.

'This is who I am, this is who I want to be,' Jaya said, looking into his azure eyes to see if he objected to her words. He did not, and that made her even happier.

And like that they were the only two people in the world. That's what Jaya told herself; and with no fearlessness she gave herself willingly to him.

CHAPTER 5

Time passed in a glorious love-filled fog for Jaya. She spent her days looking after the boys, waiting for the evenings, which she spent with William in his study. He kept a stack of paper and pencils on his desk and, after they made love, he worked while she perched on the edge of his massive chair, engrossed in her artwork for the rest of the evening.

Jaya drew trees and flowers and captured animals so well they looked ready to walk, slither or fly off the page. But her favourite subjects were people. She sketched an outline of the face first and then focused on the eyes. She drew William in his many moods – pensive, light-hearted, loving and even angry. Sayida was a stern subject, but that spirit in her eyes refused to be extinguished. Jaya made sure to always capture it.

She had stacks of drawings of both boys. They were so different from each other: Christopher so full of life, always ready for the next adventure no matter the danger; Edward more pensive and hesitant, but more caring too. Edward and Jaya had grown very close. She sometimes lay in her bed fearing what might happen to him if she should ever leave the house. She tried her best to take on the many burdens he carried, telling him more than once they were not his to bear. He was getting better at letting his parents' problems remain with them, but he still saw Christopher as his responsibility. He even worried about her welfare. He suffered when Sara attacked her even though she tried to explain to him that it was nothing, that his mother was unwell.

Edward was turning into quite a fine artist and that made Jaya happy. He was meticulous with detail; whether it was a hibiscus flower or the front veranda, he took so much care. Just like with Jaya, drawing gave Edward some time to relax and melt away inside himself. In some ways they were quite similar, and perhaps that was why Jaya felt so close to him. She loved Christopher too and, though she was also quite courageous, she usually thought more before acting. In his unthinking exuberance, Christopher often seemed like a completely new type of human.

Each night, when she reluctantly left the study and returned to her room in the building at the back, Jaya hid her sketches of William under her mattress. Later when she wanted to feel again what she felt each night in the study, she'd take them out to study William's face and body.

The happier Jaya felt, the more abusive Sara became. Though she and William were always careful, Jaya knew that her new contentment could not be completely concealed. She soon found that her secret was open knowledge to Sayida.

One evening, Jaya snuck quietly around the corner heading to her room when she heard a noise in the darkness.

'Foolish girl,' Sayida said.

Jaya adjusted her eyes to see Sayida sitting in the shadows outside her own room. Normally Sayida was fast asleep by this time.

'It's late,' Jaya said. 'Why are you still up?'

Jaya moved closer to look at the older woman, to see what troubled her so deep in the night. Also, she needed Sayida to be sound asleep because Jaya had another mission that night. A message whispered and passed along through a series of servants in the British quarter informed her that she was to meet Krishnan at midnight. Krishnan struggled to get away from his job during the day since he was an intern and, as such, he was expected to be ready to be called for work at any time. At midnight, he hoped his boss would finally be asleep.

Jaya might find herself in trouble, as well. The Colonel had ruled no one should be out after dark. There'd been rumours of servants in the area joining the Congress. In their bid for Indian independence, servants everywhere were being recruited and taught how to kill their masters in their sleep, and the British feared they would succeed. Slipping out at midnight would be Jaya's own personal act of rebellion.

'It's late, you should go and sleep, Sayida.' Jaya cared about Sayida. She'd taught her a lot and had made her transition to this new unknown life much easier, and Jaya was grateful to have her. She did not want to argue with her about what she and William did in his study, for Jaya assumed that was what she was referring to.

'What if you get pregnant? What then?' Sayida asked.

Jaya shrugged. 'I've not thought about that.'

Sayida winced. 'I don't want to hear such things. It is wrong.'

'You're the one who began the conversation. I was only explaining.'

'You give yourself to that man,' said Sayida, 'and you become a slave.'

'I am not a slave,' she replied. 'We're equals in that room.'

'And what does Sara do to you?'

'What Sara does to me is not what William does to me.'

'So? And it doesn't trouble you that William turns a blind eye to the way Sara treats you?'

It was true. William treated her with respect and gentleness when they were alone, but he never spoke a word against his wife when she belittled Jaya in his presence. He'd never been tested as to how he would react if Sara slapped her in front of him. She seemed to know where to draw the line when he was around. Jaya could only hope that, if it happened, he would step in.

'What do you expect me to do?' Jaya snapped. 'Resist the only pleasure my life provides?'

'Pleasure has a close and intimate neighbour, Jaya,' Sayida said.

'Yes, I know. Pain. We've discussed this before.'

Sayida never voiced it, but Jaya gathered that the older woman knew intimately about the harsh pain that deep love could inflict. Jaya suspected she was only trying to protect her from what she'd experienced herself.

'Yet the message has failed to get through. The young want to learn everything themselves. I fear this will end badly, Jaya.'

Jaya sighed. She didn't want this talk now. Her body still sang from what she and William had done, and her heart was happy with the anticipation of seeing her brother.

'Goodnight, Sayida.'

She went into her room, leaving Sayida out in the cool night.

Dropping back onto the thin mattress, Jaya waited and listened for any movement outside. Soon she heard Sayida go into her own small room next door. Jaya would wait to be sure the older woman was sound asleep, and then she would sneak out into the night to see her brother.

***

The moon was high in the sky, a tight, white ball of light, when Jaya slipped out of her room and dashed down the path to the fence surrounding the property. Jaya walked barefoot. It was cold, but her sandals would have made noise that might put her at risk of being discovered. Not even Sayida seemed to be on her side at the moment, so no such risk was worth taking.

Inside the perimeter of the property, she hid in the bushes and cupped her hands around her mouth. She blew into them and created the twittering sound of the nightjar. The sound went out into the night air.

After a moment, a fellow 'bird' called back. Krishnan popped his head in between two fence bars near where she stood. Jaya ran to the gate and let him in. They hugged and he lifted her up and twirled her around.

He set her down and pushed the hair back from her face to take a look at his lovely sister.

'You look good, Jaya. Happy,' he said. 'This position is good for you, I think.'

'I am content, more so now that I'm seeing you.' She took his arm to lead him to the far southwest end of the property where no one would hear them. 'Come.'

'No,' he protested. 'Outside.'

'I can't leave, Krishnan. They'll have my job if I'm caught.'

'You're already risking your job by being here with me. Another several inches can't hurt. It's important.'

Jaya looked back at the house, dark and still, then back at her brother. It was easy to choose, she missed Krishnan so much. She followed him out of the gate, wedging a large stone in place to stop the gate from slamming shut and locking her out. He held her hand and led her a short distance away. He stopped and pointed to a bicycle leaning against a tree. He smiled at her.

Jaya was confused. 'A bicycle? I don't understand.'

'It's yours! I got it for you.'

It was dented, scraped and bearing traces of rust though very recently polished. The tyres were nearly new. To Jaya it looked perfect. She could not believe what Krishnan was telling her.

'It's mine?'

He laughed, a sound she realised she'd missed so much. 'Yes, it is yours.'

She had no idea how she would explain having a bicycle to

people in the house, but for now it hardly mattered. She'd make up something. The important thing was, it had been years since she'd had her very own bike, and she could not wait to ride it. It smelled of freedom.

'Where did you get it?' she asked.

'Around.' Jaya didn't know what the odd look on Krishnan's face meant. Was he hiding a secret from her?

'You didn't steal it, did you?' she asked.

'No. Never.'

'Good! Thank you,' Jaya said, as she climbed on the bike. 'And how is Loki?'

Loki was Krishnan's girlfriend.

'It's over,' he said, shaking his head. 'The yogi said the match was inauspicious.'

'But you love Loki,' Jaya said.

Krishnan's face fell and Jaya could see the parting had been difficult for him. 'That's true. I gave her my heart.'

'What does Maji say?'

'Oh, you know our mother – she believes in these traditions. Whatever the yogi says must be followed.'

Jaya's expression softened, and she lifted one of her hands from the handlebars and reached out to squeeze her brother's arm. Her eyes moistened as she looked at Krishnan's incredible gift and then back at his drooping shoulders and joyless eyes. It was unfair that he should be parted from Loki, and she wished she could alleviate his pain.

They sat on the grass by the bicycle and talked. Krishnan spoke of his job training as a blacksmith. He perked up as he told a funny story about the gardener there, who got his thumb caught in the water tap in the garden, and how it took four men, a donkey and a fair amount of lard to free him. Jaya told him about Edward and Christopher and about her paintings and drawings. Krishnan did not avert his attention once as his sister animatedly relayed stories from her new life.

'What will you and Loki do then?' Jaya asked, tilting her head and drawing her eyebrows together. She hoped they could find a way around their problem.

Krishnan sighed and gazed into the distance. 'If it is meant to be, we will be together.' He could not conceal the wistful tone in his voice. He turned to face his sister. 'And you, Jaya? Will you marry? If a kind, good man who could understand your need for freedom and space could be found? Would you agree to marry him?'

Jaya threw back her head and laughed, for she knew such a man could not be found. 'If he is found, my brother, I will marry him. In a second, I would marry him.'

Jaya smiled at Krishnan and remembered again how it felt to be a cherished little sister. When the eastern sky lightened, she clung to him tightly one last time, mentally bestowing good luck upon her brother, before slipping back in through the gate with her new bicycle.

***

Jaya's eyes were closed for what felt like a moment, when suddenly Sayida was shaking her awake. 'Get up, girl! The boys are already shouting for their breakfast.'

She struggled to sit up, her lids heavy. Sayida's bright, freshly ironed sari testified to the fact that she must have been up for hours. Jaya swung her feet heavily over the side of the bed and looked around groggily. 'The boys … are dressed?'

'Dressed and ready for the day. I tried to wake you, but you were dead to this world, and it wouldn't do for the children's wails to wake Memsahib.' She tossed Jaya her clothes. 'The Colonel has already had his breakfast. I'll feed the boys. Come quickly, before she realises you are late.'

Jaya's breathing became fast and shallow as she fumbled around and hastily enrobed herself, the folds of her sari swirling to the floor. She thanked the gods for a friend like Sayida. Her face flushed, and still hyperventilating, she rushed to the house and headed for the stairs and the nursery, but paused for a moment to catch her breath, the veins in her neck bulging. Out of the corner of her eye, a movement in William's study caught her attention. Jaya glanced through the doorway at William's broad back as he bent forward, looking at papers on his desk, and was reminded of the night before.

'William?' She spoke breathlessly, using his name, sure that others couldn't hear.

He stopped ruffling through the papers, but didn't turn around. He was in his master role, not his lover role. 'Yes?' His response was abrupt and devoid of emotion.

Jaya shuddered. 'May I have Sunday off, Colonel? To visit my mother. I haven't seen her in many weeks.' Yes, she planned to visit her mother, but a touching reunion was far from her mind. She had something else in mind.

'Alright,' he said. He still had not looked up. Jaya bit her lip and began to walk away, but then she hesitated and turned back.

'Are you angry with me?' she asked, twisting a lock of her hair.

Something was going on and she wasn't sure she wanted to know what it was. The wording of the question was purposeful. If she had asked him something more personal, he could remind her of her rightful place, even after their nights together. She did not want that reminder. William had yet to exercise such displays of power, but that didn't mean the hierarchy did not exist. Jaya wasn't ready to find out exactly where she stood in his world. Their affection was too tender, too young to thrive under such scrutiny. The equality she felt each night in his study would not stand up in the light of day.

William turned to face her, and Jaya caught her breath. Something was very wrong.

'The Memsahib is with child, Jaya.'

'But how?' Jaya asked.

William walked behind her and closed the door. 'We *are* still husband and wife.'

Jaya shook her head. 'It's not that,' she said. But it was, only she would not let him know it. 'It's ... I'm just surprised.'

Jaya was surprised at the sharp feelings she felt, realising that William still lay with his wife. Did he touch her softly too? Did he whisper in her ear and tell her she was beautiful? Jaya shook her head and the visions fled. She lifted her chin and clenched her jaw. She would not let him see what she was feeling.

William invited her to sit next to him on the leather sofa. She did not anticipate the conversation that ensued. As she pressed her thigh against his and leaned forward to kiss him, testing his true loyalty, he pulled back and said, 'Wait. There is something important I must discuss with you.'

Jaya was taken aback and scolded herself again for being too presumptuous.

'Jaya, I hate to raise this topic, but I… we… haven't talked about protection – you know, from pregnancy. Are you using anything? The last thing I need is for you to become pregnant. How would I explain that to Sara… to anyone?'

Jaya's face and neck flushed. 'Um, err… no. I thought…'

'You thought what? That you wouldn't get pregnant, or that you wanted to have a child?'

'No, I… I hadn't really thought about it. I'm sorry. I suppose I thought it wouldn't happen. I feel so stupid.' Jaya was close to tears. Sayida's previous warning rang in her ears. Why hadn't she listened?

'Well, we can't change what has happened, but we can do something to prevent future problems.'

Jaya was shocked to hear William imply that a child was a problem, but she tried to understand his concerns.

'I will sort something out for you so that we don't have to worry about any unexpected surprises.'

Sara's pregnancy had been an 'unexpected surprise' for Jaya, but she wasn't ready to give up what she had with William so she agreed.

Soon Jaya would have yet another youngster to look after, a child whose existence would be a testament to the fact that Jaya alone did not own William's heart. Moreover, Jaya recalled Sayida's description of Sara's even more unhinged depression following her previous two births. The months ahead would be difficult.

William hadn't finished destroying her world though.

'We're going home. I've asked to return to England. Having another child here would kill Sara and, despite everything, our children need their mother. She needs to be with her sister.'

The children needed their mother? The children rarely saw their mother! Would they even miss her? They'd miss Jaya and Sayida. They were the ones who played with them, fed them, dressed them and told them stories. Sara had given them life and then she'd given them away. Jaya cooled the small feverish bodies when they were sick, she rocked them to sleep when they were afraid and she knew every detail of their faces, she could draw each from memory. She loved them. Sara didn't, or if she did it was in a way that was of no use to them.

William said something Jaya hadn't heard. 'What did you say?'

'Come to England with us,' he said softly.

'England? But I can't go to England, I know nothing of that country,' Jaya said.

William ignored her words, and his voice gained energy as he imagined a scenario that Jaya was sure would never materialise.

'We could have more time there. There would be less travel for me, more freedom. Freedom to be with you.'

He touched her arm and a familiar warmth rushed through her. She softened. She wanted to be with William. She wanted to see what kind of men his boys would grow into. But could she leave India? Could she move to England, away from everything she knew, away from Krishnan?

'But how could I manage the household alone?' Jaya asked.

'I'll bring other servants,' William said. 'Anything you want … you will only care for the boys … and the new baby.'

Perhaps this was an opportunity for Jaya; she needed time to think. There was also the option that she could remain in India, and at last be free of Sara. But to be free of Sara meant losing William. She traced the tips of her nails across her teeth and gazed at her feet, her eyes out of focus. Sadness engulfed her when she thought of that possibility. She yearned for the courage to forge her own future, not one linked to her mother or William or even her brother. But she was realistic enough to understand that it was nearly impossible, at least for now. Maybe William taking her to England was her way out.

'I must think,' said Jaya, subconsciously rubbing a hand across her heart as she moved away from William, forcing his hand to fall from her arm. 'The boys are waiting for me, Colonel.'

He flinched and his lips parted before his posture stiffened and he held his head high. Perhaps he thought he had complete power over her, or else he was too used to getting his own way.

***

That morning was fraught. The boys were hot and irritable, and Jaya could not settle her mind after what William had told her. The boys played at writing their letters, but Jaya felt claustrophobic and longed to get out of the house.

'Come! I want to show you something,' she urged.

She held out her hands and they each took one. They walked out to the courtyard to a line of shrubs that grew along the inside wall at the front of the property.

'Close your eyes.'

'What is it you want to show us?' Edward said, squeezing his eyes together.

Christopher peeked through one eye. Jaya warned him to close his eyes or he'd not be surprised. Jaya reached behind the bush and retrieved her bicycle. She pushed it in front of them and stopped. 'Open!'

Christopher spoke first. 'What is it?'

'It's a bicycle, silly.' Edward reached out a tentative finger and touched a large crack in the seat cover. 'It's old.'

'It's old, but it's mine. I'll take it on adventures all over the country.'

Christopher skirted the bike and stood behind Jaya. She felt a tug on her sari. 'You won't leave us, Jaya, will you?'

Jaya looked down into his large blue eyes and said, 'I won't leave you, Christopher.'

But you might leave me, she thought. Everything came flooding back. England was so far away. If she went, how would she ever return to India if she needed to? She'd heard stories of women, other ayahs, going with British families and never returning. To their families and friends, it was as if they had died. She would be so far from Krishnan and everything she knew. She imagined tall stone buildings, hurrying masses of people and rushing carriages. It would all be so strange to her. At least William had said he would bring other servants. Perhaps Sayida would go as well. That would help.

'Jaya! Lunch is ready. Bring the boys in.' Sayida stood in the doorway as the boys raced toward her and ducked under her arms.

Jaya gave a small wave and hid her bike in the bush again. She looked up and saw Sayida still staring at her even though the boys had already run into the house. *What that was about?*

At lunch, once all of the Edmundsons were at the table, Jaya began to think again of being in England with them, all alone. When she leaned down to serve Sara her hands shook.

'Heavens, girl,' Sara said. 'This is our finest china. Do not treat it as you would your own clay plates.'

'I'm sorry, Memsahib.'

'Jaya has a bike!' Edward said, and Jaya froze.

'An old bike,' Christopher added.

William looked at Jaya. 'She does, does she? And where did she get this bike?'

The question was directed at Jaya.

'My brother left it outside the courtyard for me, Colonel.' It was almost true. 'He found it and fixed it up as a gift. It's so I can travel home faster, and have more time there. He left a message with one of the delivery men that it was there.' Her lie spilled out with hardly any effort.

'A gift, you say?' Sara wiped the corners of her mouth with a linen napkin. 'Stolen property, more likely.'

'My brother does not steal, Memsahib.' Even Jaya could hear the steel beneath her own quiet words. Who did Sara think she was, making such accusations about Krishnan?

'Maybe you stole it,' Sara said.

'My dear,' William said. 'It must be a gift. I sincerely doubt our dear Jaya plucked some poor rider off his bike and stole it herself.'

'Jaya says she can ride it all over the country,' Edward said. 'Is that true, Papa?'

'I suppose it is, Edward.' He put down his fork and flexed his fingers. 'Unless she's too busy looking after you two.' He looked at Jaya as he spoke, an action not unnoticed by Sara.

After lunch, the family went their separate ways, and the afternoon took on a sleepy mantle of quiet. Sara disappeared into her room, and Jaya soothed the boys to sleep with an Indian song Krishnan used to sing to her as a child.

Just before Christopher drifted off, he said, 'You won't ride away on your bike, Jaya, will you?'

She leaned over and kissed his curly head. Before she could answer, she heard a sound and looked up, and there was William. From the doorway he said, 'You won't, will you, Jaya?'

'How long have you been standing there?' Jaya said. She looked down and saw both boys were asleep.

'Long enough to know you are torn between us and India,' William said.

Jaya stood and they walked together out of the room, closing the door gently behind them.

In the hall, she turned to him. 'I am torn. It's true.'

'What can I do to convince you to come to England?' He stepped closer, but Jaya moved away.

'I need time to think,' she said.

William put an arm on each side of Jaya and leaned towards her recklessly, not caring who might see. 'And now you want to ride away from me on your new bicycle.'

'I do want to ride my bike, but not away. And never away from you.' She looked up at him with her large dark eyes. His need for her beat between them, one careless move and it would all come crashing down, neither able to stop it. Jaya ducked under his arm and stood away from him to save them both from themselves.

'You are my servant, Jaya. What if I forbid you to leave?'

There it was – *the first threat of power.*

'I must do as you say, only while employed by you. I'm sure your wife would be pleased to find you another ayah. Then I can be off on my bicycle to live my own life, where no one forbids me from anything I might want to do.' William could speak as he liked, but so could she.

William winced. She'd hit a soft spot. 'I don't want to lose you, and neither do my boys. How can I make you stay? How can I convince you to come to England with us?'

Jaya saw an opportunity and took it. 'By allowing me the freedom to go if I choose to.'

William raised his eyebrows. 'You want to be able to leave here and ride through the country on your bicycle?'

Jaya could feel her courage rising. The scent of freedom was giving her strength. 'That would do for a start.'

'Then go. Ride. Take the afternoon off and return because you want to, not because you have to.'

Did he know how much that answer drew her to him? He gave her freedom; he let her decide her own destiny. This she would remember.

CHAPTER 6

Jaya pushed all thoughts of the Edmundsons from her mind as she cycled through the streets of the neighbourhood, getting a feel for her new bicycle. What freedom! Her hair flew out behind her while her sari whipped back and forth in the wind. Everything disappeared except the cool wind on her face, and the passing scenery zipped by in a beautiful blur. Sara, the boys, and even William seemed a world away.

She recorded everything in her mind for later when she could sit and recreate it in her drawings and paintings. Two boys played in a stream, their splashes sparkling like gemstones in the afternoon sun. A pair of young women balancing taut bundles of grass upon their heads as they walked, their slim necks straining under the weight. Near the edge of the road, a man walked a greying, ancient donkey attached to a leash. The donkey was too old for work however, touchingly, it seemed to be the old man's friend.

As she rode, she wondered about these people. Everyone had a partner or a friend, even the old man with his donkey. Who did Jaya have? She knew she'd never really have William; that was only a fantasy she conjured up in the deep night when such things were allowed. William's partner was Sara – pregnant Sara. There was nothing special between Jaya and William, despite the words they spoke to each other in his study. It was all fantasy, magic with smoke and mirrors, nothing of substance. Frustrated by her thoughts, she pedalled faster and faster.

She thought of her brother and her mood changed. Seeing him the other night had felt so good. His kindness by giving her the bicycle was an added benefit. She would try to pay him back. Despite her wish never to go back home, she would do it for him. He had always been her champion, and now it was her turn to help him. She would see her mother and she would get her to change her mind about Loki. Her brother's happiness was at stake.

Though she vowed not to think about it, her mind went to her indecision about going to England. She might go as William and Sara's servant, but that didn't mean she must remain in that position. England was a different place than India. Jaya suspected women there would have more say about their own lives; she hoped that was the case. And if it was, saying yes to going to England could mean that her boat passage was a ticket to freedom and a life as an independent woman. *Isn't that what she'd always wanted? Why was she so hesitant now?*

Maybe London was an opportunity to find a life as an artist too. Jaya thought of a life of art, drawing and painting, free of all other obligations. What a wonderful life that would be!

She had heard talk about the women over there, strong, independent women who lived without men. Once she'd heard Sara and some of the women who visited talk of women in England fighting men for the right to cast their vote. They spoke of a brave British woman called Emmeline Pankhurst who led the women. It seemed to Jaya that women in England thought like her, that a woman should be able to choose her own life.

She'd once mentioned such women to her mother, women who wanted more from life than marriage and children.

'They think they don't need a man,' she'd said. 'They try to think for themselves. But tell them to ask me about it. I will tell them about life without a man.'

Jaya did want a man; she wanted William, but he was taken. Maybe there was an alternative in London. In India, her life provided few choices, and none of them were good ones.

She remembered stopping by a field one time and watched

the men ploughing, their oxen straining against the heavy plough. Women followed the men throwing seeds onto the upturned soil, covering them over with bare feet.

Would that be her life if she stayed in India? Married to a man she did not know and, surely, could not love, spending the rest of her days doing back-breaking work in the fields and, even worse, raising endless children at the same time? The thought crushed her.

William was offering something else, but at what cost? He would be everything to her in England, as she would have no one else, and she would be merely a small part of his life, never anything more. She would have to reconcile her mind to that fact if she decided to go with him.

And, of course, leaving Krishnan would be heart breaking, only made tolerable if she knew she left him behind happily building his life with Loki. She vowed to get Maji to change her mind on their marriage.

Realizing it was getting late, Jaya pedalled home. She had much to think about.

***

Sunday arrived. Jaya woke up early and prepared to leave for Khesar. She packed a few pieces of clothing, her charcoal and a stack of paper, and set off on her bicycle just as the sun came over the horizon. She sped through the countryside, her tyres crunching as they threw up dust and dirt. She'd not been home since she'd got the job at the Edmundsons, and she was surprised she felt no apprehension about seeing her mother. She'd changed in the few months away, that was true. But it was also because she had a mission, a plan, and the mission concerned Krishnan. She cared too much about him to allow any room for doubt. She would be successful today.

She arrived at her village and rode her bicycle into her mother's yard sending chickens scurrying. She got off and leaned it against the wall.

'Maji!' she called while entering the house.

She breathed in the scents she'd taken for granted when she'd lived here; sandalwood incense, the nutty aroma of Desi ghee sweets, and the familiar, comforting smell of the masala box – a blend of traditional, homely Indian spices. An avalanche of memories filled her mind. She was surprised that the house looked so much smaller, cruder and dirtier than she'd remembered it.

She heard a noise and turned to see her mother coming out of her room. Jaya took a sharp intake of breath. Her mother's face was etched with deep furrows, the skin hanging loosely from her jaw and peppered with dark brown patches. Her cheeks were sunken, and she appeared so much shorter and more fragile than Jaya remembered. She reflected on how every wrinkle told a story of struggle and survival, sadness and joy.

'Hello, Maji.'

'You're home.' Maji's sunken eyes widened and she held a hand to her mouth as she shuffled forward slowly. She looked Jaya up and then down. 'Have you lost your job?'

'No. I have the day off. I've come because I need to speak with you.'

Her mother looked her in the eye while wringing her hands. A look of jealousy altered her features yet again. Jaya had saved enough to buy a new sari – blue, the colour of William's eyes. She bought it to wear today, specifically to see that look of jealousy in her mother's eyes.

'I see you live well. You never think to spare a few coins for your mother,' she said scathingly.

Jaya did not flinch and remained silent.

Her mother lifted the kettle from the fire and poured water into the chipped enamel teapot. She pulled down cups and saucers from the cupboard and put everything on a tray.

'Come, we will sit and have tea,' she said, kinder than Jaya remembered her. Then she remembered how her mother often used kindness to lure Jaya into a trap. She would need to tread carefully. Her mother carried the tray outside to a wooden table where they often sat.

Jaya took the chair opposite her mother and watched as she poured the tea.

'I want to speak to you about your refusal to allow Krishnan to marry Loki,' Jaya said.

'It is done. The yogi saw the truth. We must follow his wise words.' She sipped at her tea as if the issue were over.

'They love each other. Don't you care about your son's heart?' Jaya asked.

Maji smiled. 'And what of my own heart?' she asked. 'It beats with faith. I listen to our yogi. And so should you.'

'You cannot do this to Krishnan. He is the best part of this family. He deserves happiness more than you or even me.'

'Drink your tea. It's getting cold,' her mother said.

'I'm not here for tea. I want my brother to marry Loki.'

'Relax,' she said. 'Your brother will marry Loki.'

'He will?' Jaya was confused. Had she been successful in her mission so quickly?

'The yogi said his first marriage will fail, but his second one will endure. So, his first marriage shall be to a tree.'

'You can't be serious,' Jaya said.

Maji nodded. 'Are we not Hindus? Do we not honour our faith?'

'A tree?'

'Yes, that's correct,' her mother said. 'And it shall be chopped down to conclude the marriage.'

'Does Krishnan know about this?'

'He will. He is coming in one week. It will be done then.'

Using tradition against tradition. Jaya enjoyed this sort of thinking. She sat back, content that her brother would soon find his way back to Loki.

Maji looked at Jaya's bicycle. 'So, I see Krishnan gave you the bicycle.'

'You knew about his gift to me?' Jaya asked, surprised.

'Of course. He got it in this village.'

'Where did he get it?' Jaya's jaw tightened. Why had Krishnan failed to tell her that detail?

Maji looked over her shoulder. She was suddenly evasive, as if she had spoken out of line. 'The bicycle?'

'Yes, isn't that's what we're talking about?' Jaya said. What was this all about?

'The bicycle came from Rafik.'

'Rafik? Who is Rafik?' Jaya asked.

'Rafik is from the next village.'

'Why did Rafik give Krishnan the bicycle? Is he too old to ride it?'

'He is only thirty-nine years old.' She placed her cup on the table with a clank. 'He gave the bicycle to Krishnan as a gift to you. He wishes to marry you, Jaya.'

Jaya kept silent. She could feel rage building inside of her. Krishnan had to have been aware of what was going on. Why had he lied to her and let her think he had bought the bike as a gift for her? Did he also think that his sister was little more than an object to be bartered?

Jaya had concluded the business she came for. She drank the rest of her tea and stood up.

'I don't want this bicycle. I need to return to work,' she said.

'You'll not stay overnight? I could take you to Rafik, so that you could meet him.'

'That won't be necessary. Please return the bicycle to Rafik,' Jaya said. She gently put the bicycle down in its side, turned around and started to walk away without another word.

CHAPTER 7

Jaya arrived back at the big house in the dark. She wondered if she would find William in his study. She wanted to see him. She was upset about the trip, and her brother's betrayal. She quickly washed, dressed in her clean sari and went looking for him.

She moved through the quiet house. Sara would have fallen into her drug-induced sleep, and the boys would have been put to bed by Sayida. When she got to the study door it was closed so she knocked gently. He called for her to come in.

He lay on the leather sofa, his feet up, shoes off, in his shirt, reading a book. He looked up and when he saw her, he smiled. He put the book down and held out his arms to her. He stood when she came to him and hugged her, kissing the top of her head and then her lips.

'I was just now thinking of you, wondering how you were getting on at your home. Was your mother happy to see you after so much time?'

'We don't have a relationship like that.'

He said nothing more on the topic, but looked at Jaya more carefully. 'I didn't know it was possible, but you look even more beautiful.'

'Thank you.' Although flattered, Jaya was still feeling angry with Krishnan, which in turn made her feel irritated with William, knowing that any feelings he had for her were not exclusive.

'Why did you return early? Did something happen? I thought we agreed you could spend the night and come in the morning.' William tilted his head, adopting a look of concern.

'Yes, but I don't want to speak about it.' Jaya paused to study William. Was he just feigning empathy? Only interested in his own carnal desires?

He sat back on the sofa and pulled her to his lap. He kissed her again, running his hand down her hair, holding her around the waist.

'I missed you, Jaya.' William moved in for a kiss, but Jaya pulled back.

'Did you? I wonder. Sometimes I think I'm just some toy. A toy like the ones Edward and Christopher use to amuse themselves. Liked today and forgotten tomorrow when a new one comes along.'

She could see her words hurt him, just as she intended. She wanted him to know that she was a realist. She knew the terms between them, no matter how he tried to paint them or cover them with sugar.

'Jaya, no, please don't say that. I think it was our destiny to meet. There was something about you; I saw it that first day. Of course, I saw your beauty, but there was something else. There was defiance in the way you held yourself; it set you apart from all of them. I should have dismissed the lot when I spotted you, because I knew I would hire only you. And when you walked into this room, I knew my heart was yours. You are not a toy, never a toy.'

She liked his answer, but she was not done with him yet. 'You say that your heart is mine, but still you sleep with your wife. I don't like being second. I'm a woman who wants position one, or nothing.'

She knew the dynamics were changing. They'd been equal in this room, but now she was ensuring that she was the one in control. If she were to travel overseas, she needed to fix a few things into place.

'Jaya, if I stop sleeping with Sara, she will know that something has changed.'

'You can make a story of some sort. You are sick … you don't want to disturb the pregnancy. You are an intelligent man. I'm sure that you can think of something. I will not travel all the way to England to be number two.'

William smiled. 'So, you have decided to come with me … with us?'

'I did not say that.'

'Oh, Jaya, please do not do this to me. I can't sleep or eat for fear that you will refuse me. I need you with me.' Jaya noticed William's eyes moisten, but still wondered whether it was an act.

'Then?'

William sighed. She had him in a corner. His lust, and perhaps love – Jaya was not decided on the latter – left him no choice.

'Yes, yes! I will come up with something. I will only have you.' He sounded frustrated, and Jaya began to wonder whether she'd been too demanding.

Jaya smiled and looked lovingly into William's eyes to placate him. 'Then I will go to England with you.'

'You have made me very happy.' William's voice softened and his relief was evident. Jaya saw a vulnerability that had never been evident before.

Feeling the need to justify her request, Jaya said, 'I could have made worse demands, that you divorce her for example. But I didn't because I care about Edward and Christopher.'

'And what do you feel about me?' William's blue eyes widened as he gazed into Jaya's, like a small boy pleading for a favour.

Jaya ran her hand up his leg from his knee and up to his thigh. 'Let me show you.'

William placed his hand firmly on top of Jaya's, preventing her hand from moving any higher.

'Jaya… remember our conversation about contraception?'

William presented her with a contraceptive sponge.

'You must use this. I'm sorry, but we must stay safe.'

The sight of it made Jaya's stomach turn. 'It's just a sponge!'

Would it hurt? Would she be able to feel it inside her with the netting around it? The thought of washing it and reusing it also seemed repulsive, but what was the alternative? The thought made her uncomfortable. She said no more.

***

Since Jaya told William she would accompany them to England, he'd changed – he was more patient with the children, he laughed louder and more often, and Jaya often heard him whistling as he moved through the house. Was his return to England the source of his happiness, or was it his unborn child, or was it her?

Jaya quickly adapted to using the sponge, even though she found it messy, inconvenient and awkward at times. It didn't, however, prevent William continually asking her whether she was 'safe'.

Jaya climbed the stairs with Sara's breakfast tray. At the door, she could hear Sara arguing with William.

'She will not come with us! *Never!*' Sara shouted.

'Quiet, dear,' William said. 'You must take care, remember the baby.'

'When we get home, we'll hire a proper nanny, not that ... that uncultured beast.'

William's voice was calm. 'The "beast" is cheaper. All ayahs are, Sara.'

The words from William's mouth sliced like a sword in Jaya's heart. How could he speak of her in that way?

'Oh yes, cheaper! Cheap like a whore, I bet?' Sara snapped. Jaya could imagine her upper lip curling derisively.

'Don't you ever make accusations like that!' Jaya could hear the ice in his voice. 'Understand this, I negotiate with extremely powerful men and yet they do as I command. If you think for a moment you can stand up to me, Sara, you must seriously think otherwise.'

'I'll bet she does as she is commanded as well.'

'Enough, I'll not discuss this further, and you will not speak of it again. You are my wife, Sara. It is you and only you whom I love. Yet, at every instance, you fail to accept that my love is real. It exists just as this chair exists. You trust the chair to break your fall. Why will you not trust me in the same way? I'm tired of this constant battle. I am your husband, your master. You will do as I say. I know what is best for this family.'

William loved his wife? He didn't seem to even think of Sara when he was holding her close, when he caressed her skin, when he whispered in her ear.

'You negotiate with the men at work,' Sara said. 'And you deceive them, too. That's why I'm depressed, William. I know with whom I live.'

'And you shall live with Jaya as well! The decision is made. Jaya stays with us. She will travel to England with us. Perhaps, when the child is older, we shall discuss it again.'

'Oh, yes, of course. For how long, William? Twenty years? Thirty? What happens when we have no more children under our roof? Will we still need her then? Perhaps to aid me in my old age?'

'I said the discussion is closed and you should mind your words.'

William's footsteps approached the door and Jaya shrunk from sight around the corner. She held her breath until she heard him head down the stairs.

***

Krishnan had sent a message saying that they must meet in the park next Sunday, her day off. She had not spoken to her brother since learning the truth about the bicycle, or since she had made her decision to go to England. She arrived as planned and saw him sitting on a bench. Despite her anger, she was happy to see him.

'Jaya, where's the bicycle?' he said as Jaya walked up to him. Her nose flared at the mention of that wretched bicycle. She'd decided to get straight to the point.

'I know the truth about it now.'

'What do you mean?' Krishnan said, feigning ignorance.

'Stop pretending. Maji told me Rafik gave you the bicycle in the hope that it would sweeten the negotiations for marriage. I didn't keep it.'

Krishnan sighed. 'Yes, that's right. I knew you would be angry, so I didn't tell you. But I think you know I would never do anything that I thought was bad for you. I love you, Jaya.'

'So, marrying me off to some man nearly double my age is a kindness?'

'Jaya, you yourself said that if there was a man who would

allow you freedom to be who you wanted, you would marry him,' her brother said.

'Yes! Because I know no such man exists.'

'I know for a fact that such a man does exist. Rafik is my friend. We became friends here in Banka, although he is from our area. He is an intelligent man, a calm, kind man. He was married but his wife died recently. He worked in the bank, but now he will move back to Khesar. He is going to take over his father's bakery. He wants a companion. He wants to marry you.'

'But he doesn't know me.'

'I know you. I know him. I love you, and I think Rafik is a very good choice for you.'

Jaya jumped to her feet overwhelmed with emotion. Why was Krishnan doing this to her? Just then, Krishnan looked around as if expecting someone to arrive.

He reached up and took her hand, guiding her back to the bench. 'Rafik is a good, kind man, an educated Brahmin. He's refined and gentle. He'll not trouble you for children; he has two sons from his first wife. He will care for you and leave you to your art. It will be a good life. It's all I want for you.'

'And what about what I want for myself? Does that not matter at all, Krishnan?' She held back tears of disappointment. She thought at least Krishnan knew her well enough to know that what he proposed would be the death of her.

'Of course it matters. I thought it would be something you would want.'

'Then you don't know me at all!' She could see he was upset that she was not happy with his plan. 'Anyway, I am going to England with the Edmundsons.'

'England?' Krishnan said, surprised. 'But … when will I see you again? You going to England means we will never see you again. Your whole life will disappear. Women who go there rarely return. Jaya, you won't have a future in a place like that. You will be an ayah forever, what sort of life is that?'

'It is better than the life you are offering me, marrying an old man I don't love,' Jaya said.

'You've heard about what they do to ayahs who travel to England,' he said. 'You'll be abandoned on the streets of London. What then, Jaya?'

She thought about this for a moment. It was true. British families often took ayahs with them to help with the children during the journey home on the ship, but once they made it to England, the ayahs were abandoned, with no way of returning to India. Sometimes, once the British family arrived in England, they showed off their Indian ayah until they became bored and then cast her aside. Everyone had heard those stories.

Some women managed to return, others were lost forever. One woman from their village returned after five years in England. Jaya had heard her talk about a special house in London that helped the lost ayahs wandering the streets of London.

Jaya had also heard stories about the perilous sea journey. It was safer now with steam-powered ships, and quicker too, but that didn't make crossing the ocean any less daunting. Jaya had heard tales of seasickness, outbreaks of measles, cramped conditions and far worse.

She'd considered all of this before Krishnan even mentioned it, but she'd pushed it to the back of her mind. Now, his words brought the stories out again.

Would William do that to her? She was fairly certain he would never betray her like that, although the conversation between him and Sara had instilled some doubts in her mind. She shook her head; it didn't matter. Even if she was abandoned in England, there were other reasons Jaya wished to make the journey.

She remembered the great tale of Minnie Green – a strong Indian ayah who had overcome her traumatic voyage, and defeated her employers by taking them to court on British soil and collecting what was owed to her. Jaya knew her story was different. She knew what she was doing, and the decision had been made.

'I'll be fine. I can take care of myself,' Jaya said, with more courage than she felt just then.

Krishnan looked behind Jaya, and then at her again. 'I wanted you to come here to …'

Jaya looked behind her and she saw a man heading toward them. He looked familiar; there was something about the way he walked, straight and confident, distinguished. He was older, but still handsome and strong. He wore a stylish but worn suit. He smiled at them and nodded. And then she remembered. He was the man who had helped her find Christopher when he ran away. He had been so kind to her, and helped her find the small boy. What a coincidence that she should see him again, here.

The man walked to them and held out his hand to Krishnan. 'Good day, Krishnan,' he said.

Jaya was confused. 'Do you two know each other?'

'Yes,' Krishnan said. 'This is Rafik.'

Only then Jaya put it all together. How had she not made the connection? This was the man who wanted to marry her.

Krishnan moved closer to Jaya on the bench to make room for the older man. Rafik sat on the edge and leaned forward so that he could see Jaya clearly. When he spoke, his voice was deep, and he spoke in a slow measured way.

'I know this must be confusing for you, Jaya. That day… in the park … with the boy, it was not by chance that I was there.

I'd met your brother some time before. We became friends. From him I learned about you. I made some enquiries. I suggested to your brother that you become my wife.'

'But why? I don't understand what's going on,' Jaya said.

'Your brother showed me some of your drawings and they touched me. I can't really explain it, but I never stop thinking about them. After that I wanted to meet the woman who saw the world in that way. I was not disappointed when I saw you that day.'

Jaya did not want to be rude to this man who had helped her; he seemed kind and good, but she could not listen to another word. She felt every emotion whirling in a storm around her and didn't know what to do with them. All at once, she felt betrayed and respected and acknowledged and dismissed. She needed to be away from both Rafik and Krishnan. She needed to sort out her mind so she could know what it all meant.

'I must go …' she said, standing. 'My employer will be looking for me.'

She disappeared before anyone could suggest otherwise.

***

She ran as fast as possible to get home. She rushed through the gate and straight toward her room hoping for time alone, but Sayida was outside removing clothes from the line as the sun began to set. She looked at Jaya and left the laundry to follow her to their rooms.

'Jaya? What is it? What has happened?' Sayida said, grabbing Jaya's arm before she could get inside her room and close the door.

'I've been betrayed by my brother. He wants to steal my life from me when I'm just about to make it my own,' Jaya said. She knew her words made no sense to Sayida.

Despite her best efforts, Jaya began to cry. Sayida took her into her arms. 'Let us sit and have tea and you explain what has happened.'

The older woman led Jaya into her own room. She sat her at the tiny table and prepared the tea. She set the tray on the table and handed Jaya a cup. She sipped at it and was surprised she felt better.

'Now tell me,' Sayida said.

'There is a man … a man my brother has arranged for me to marry.'

'Is that not a good thing?' Sayida asked.

'No! I don't want to marry him, I don't know him, I don't love him. He's much older than me.'

'But perhaps that can be better. An older man is more settled, he will provide you with a good home and be able to take care of you.'

How could Jaya explain that she wanted more from life than safety and security? Sayida would remain a servant for the rest of her life for the safety and security that felt like a prison to Jaya. Sayida told Jaya once about the famine in her village that killed her parents and younger sister. She knew deep suffering, so her priorities were different from Jaya's. She could never know how Jaya felt about freedom and independence. For her, they were flippant and unnecessary, for Jaya they were the air she needed to survive.

'Yes, perhaps you're right,' Jaya said. She managed a weak smile for Sayida.

'I know you think I'm an old woman, but I do know some things about love. I was a girl too. Passion fades. This man your brother chose for you, you might grow to like. He might be your friend. That is where love begins and grows and strengthens.'

Jaya thought about her words. Rafik could be the person that Sayida described; she knew this. He would take care of her. And he already respected her art, so he would let her draw and paint. A calm, gentle life could be a good life. The problem was that it was not the life that she wanted. How could she explain that to Sayida? Instead, she didn't and changed the topic.

They finished their tea talking of what the boys had got up to while Jaya was gone. When they finished, Jaya stood.

'Thank you,' Jaya said. Though Sayida had not helped to sort out her thoughts regarding what had happened, at least Jaya was calmer now.

'Oh, I forgot,' Sayida said. 'The Colonel said he wanted to see you when you returned.'

'Let me clean off the dust and sweat first.'

Sayida's demeanour changed. It was clear she had kind feelings for Jaya, but she disapproved of whatever was happening between her and the Colonel.

'He's in the garden,' she said to Jaya's retreating back.

Jaya had not been alone with William since she'd overheard the conversation between him and his wife. The anger still simmered beneath the surface. She did not want lies, he promised they would not have lies. But now it was clear to her that he only patronised her with his commitment to honesty. She wanted the truth, no matter what it was. She deserved that, at least.

She found him at the far end of the garden sitting alone, paging through some papers.

'You're home early,' he said, not averting his gaze from the papers.

'*Is* this my home?' Jaya asked, as though unsure.

'I thought that's how you thought of this place.' He looked at her, seeking confirmation, then glanced around the garden, always wary of onlookers. 'I missed you today,' he whispered, raising his eyebrows to convey a soulful expression.

He held out his hand to her and, despite her best efforts not to, she took it. He pulled her close enough so that he could put his arms around her waist. He pulled her to his lap and kissed her on the lips, throwing caution to the wind, and ignoring the fact that they might be seen.

'I love you,' he breathed. 'My love for you is more real than anything else in my life.' He gazed into her eyes without blinking.

How quickly his words chased away her doubts and anger. William loved her. *He loved her.* He wanted her in his life. He had not lied to her; he had lied to Sara.

William had spoken the perfect words at the perfect time. The confusion caused by the kind Rafik, and his secure offer of a quiet marriage, and a place for her to draw and paint slipped away. Against all sense, now that she was with William, she knew she'd rather accept the possibility of instability because of the deep love they shared.

William removed a slim glimmering box from his pocket.

'What is this?' she said.

He handed her the box. 'Open it.'

Inside she found a fountain pen, shiny, silver, heavy in her hand. It was beautiful.

'A pen?' she asked.

'A new kind of pen,' he said. 'It's called a fountain pen. You fill it with ink and you write until it is empty. And I also got a pot of ink for you. I thought this was cleaner than all that charcoal you use for drawing.' William smiled, anticipating a favourable response.

She looked down at the beautiful object. Indeed, it would work better than her charcoal. It touched her that he had considered her wants and needs. That he had gone to a shop specifically to find a gift that he knew she would love. He could be certain of the perfect gift because he took the time to know her, to know what was important to her. This meant so much to her.

'You're very kind. Thank you.'

'Tomorrow,' he said, 'I will show you how to use it, how to refill it. In my study.' He cast her a seductive glance.

'Oh,' she said, 'in your study. Is that all you will show me?'

He laughed. He leaned forward and kissed her lips. As he did, she felt his passion for her course through her body, uniting with her own passion for him. Together they formed a strong pull – large, wild and dangerous.

She wanted to love this man forever.

***

Jaya pulled the heavy water-soaked sheet from the river. Sayida took the other side and they squeezed it, twisting and twisting to remove as much water as possible before draping it over a nearby branch. They stood for a moment catching their breath in the shade of the tree before going back to the pile of laundry waiting for them.

'Sayida, I must tell you,' Jaya said excitedly.

'What now, Jaya?' asked Sayida. Jaya knew she preferred regularity and calmness, and often chastised her for unneeded drama, but still she was bursting to tell someone.

The words tumbled out. 'William ... I mean the Colonel ... he loves me.'

Sayida opened her mouth to say something but halted as she caught Jaya's stare and looked down with a sigh. 'He said that?'

Jaya immediately regretted having told her, but she continued anyway. 'Yes, he did.'

Sayida went back to the river and squatted down to get back to the washing. Jaya's pulse quickened as heat flushed red hot through her core. Why should Sayida question the idea that an English man like William might love an Indian woman like her? Many British men from the Company had married Indian women. And those women were given more freedom and independence than other Indian women in the country. It was not a wild fantasy for Jaya to think the same might happen for her.

Jaya stood next to Sayida at the river. Sayida looked up at her, squinting her eyes against the sun.

'These clothes will not wash themselves, Jaya. You wanted to help me, so help.'

'You don't believe me. You don't think William said he loved me,' Jaya said, still standing.

'No, I believe he said it. Men will say nearly anything to get what they want. I think the problem is that you believe that the love he is offering is the love that you want.'

'You don't know that it is not.' Jaya grabbed a shirt from the basket and squatted down and dunked it in the water. She rubbed the red bar of soap on the wet shirt and rubbed the shirt roughly against the nearby rock, taking her anger out on the garment.

'Why would he take me to England with the family if he doesn't love me the way I know love can be?'

Sayida sat back and looked at the younger woman. 'Because he want his needs met while his wife is in confinement.'

Jaya tried not to take her words to heart. Sayida knew nothing. William loved her. He did not love Sara. He loved her.

After some moments, when she had her emotions back under control, she said, 'Now I must decide: should I go to England with William, or stay and marry Rafik, the man my brother wants me to marry?'

She wondered if she even had a decision to make. She thought she'd made it; she was going to England. Sayida's words had unsettled her, and brought her own doubts to the front yet again.

There was also a third option. She could make a life for herself alone, under no man's influence. Likely not in India, but perhaps in England. Other women had done it there.

'Well,' Sayida said after a pause, 'having options is a good thing. I would gladly join all of you in England, though it does not seem to be in the family's plans.'

'What are you saying? Sara cannot be without you. William said that you would come too. I was certain you were coming with us.' Jaya was shocked. She depended on Sayida more than she realised, and wasn't ready to think about leaving for England without her.

Sayida just shook her head, looking down at the water.

'Perhaps I could speak to William,' Jaya said.

'Please don't. A new family from England will arrive here. Maybe they will keep me. I'll have to wait and see.'

'Well,' said Jaya, changing the subject. 'My decision about what to do weighs heavily on my heart. My brother likes Rafik. He thinks it's the best option for me – to marry Rafik. Leaving my brother will be very painful if I choose to go to England.'

'And your mother? Will you not miss her?'

'No, not really. But she'll be angry if I don't marry Rafik. He's well-off from his job at the bank, and he'll soon take over his father's bakery. She hopes to gain from that. That is where her sadness will come from, not from me leaving.'

'Perhaps. But whatever the case, it must be hard to bid farewell to one's child.' Sayida's head was bowed, so at first Jaya didn't see her tears.

'What is it? What has upset you, Sayida?'

The older woman wiped her hand across her eyes to remove her tears, leaving a thin line of mud on her face. 'It's nothing. But I have grown close to Edward and Christopher … and you. And too, I worry what will happen if the new family for the house does not need me.'

'But you will come, Sayida. And even if you don't' – Jaya's stomach clenched at the thought – 'you will find new employment, Sayida.' Jaya touched the older woman's bony shoulder, but Sayida shrugged her off.

'I am old, that might not happen.' Her fingers whitened as she squeezed water from a small pair of trousers belonging to one of the boys. 'My legs do not allow me to do what I once did. I have trouble climbing stairs, and I cannot see like I once could.'

'I have learned everything I know from you, Sayida. Surely

they won't leave you behind. It would be so unfair,' Jaya said.

Sayida laughed. 'You are young. Look around you. It is our country, but which Indian lives well besides the ones the British decide are acceptable? I'm Shudra, already barely human in their eyes. I only continue to work here because of Sara. I'll not find another job. The life for most of us in our own country is one of sadness, starvation and strife. The British, some less educated than you and me, step into this country and they are deemed kings, rulers of all they see. They do not have to prove anything to anyone. Their skin decides everything for them. I have no say about it; I have no say about anything. Neither do you. Guided by their whims, and nothing more, William and all of the others will decide our fates.'

Jaya had never heard Sayida sound this bitter. It was clear these were thoughts that lived inside her mind all the time. Jaya could hear the truth in what she said as soon as the words were out of her mouth. If the British were so unfair in India, how much worse must they be in their own country? She tried not to think if it; William would protect her from whatever she found there.

Sayida stood and hung the rest of the washed clothes on the trees along the river. She pulled down those that the warm wind had dried already.

'Wait here,' she told Jaya. 'I'll take these to the house. Bring those when they're dry.'

Jaya watched Sayida leave. She'd come down to the river in a joyous mood, covered by William's declaration of love, and now she felt only suspicion and sadness. Maybe she needed to think further about her decision to go to England.

She thought about Rafik. Krishnan had sent a message that he and Loki would have their engagement party the following weekend at their mother's house. He wanted Jaya there. He also said in the note that Rafik would be there, and if Jaya would only give him a chance, she would see that he was a good man and would make an excellent husband for her.

She decided then that she would go to the party. There was no sense in leaving any options unexplored.

Waiting for the clothes to dry, she sat in the shade of the tree, the river gurgling by, the light breeze touching her skin. She took her paper and her new pen out of her satchel. She looked out over the river, the sunlight dancing on its surface, and a kingfisher in the far tree waiting for his meal to swim by. She began drawing and, as was always the case, her worries disappeared, and contentment surrounded her.

CHAPTER 8

When the day of Krishnan and Loki's engagement party arrived, Jaya donned her best sari and made the long walk to her mother's house. In the days that passed since her time at the river with Sayida, the idea of staying and marrying Rafik began to take root in her mind. It could be a legitimate option. Today she would determine if it really was.

Deep down inside, she hoped Rafik would create within her the very same exciting feelings that William did. Such a thing would make the decision much simpler. For as much as she believed she loved William, there were many problems, and the doubts about him continued to grow.

As Jaya neared Maji's home, she heard drum music in the

distance. Her stomach rumbled and her mouth watered at the smells coming from the special wedding food: dal bukhara, dilli chaat, litti chokha and, her favourite, zafrani pulao. The guests were packed in the house and spilling out into the garden decorated with coloured scarves and beautiful flowers.

Jaya entered the house, pushing through the people. Krishnan and Loki sat on soft chairs in the corner surrounded by flowers and golden decorations. Jaya met her brother's eye when she entered, and he stood and came to her.

'You are here. Now I can be happy,' he said kissing her cheeks one after the other. 'You are so beautiful.'

The happiness was short-lived when her mother appeared.

'So now you are here to embarrass us? A good, dutiful daughter does not refuse a man like Rafik,' she said. 'And now you go off to England without a word to your mother, the one who nearly died to give you life?'

Jaya started to respond but Krishnan stepped in. He grabbed Jaya's arm and pulled her away from the others. 'I need to speak to you in private,' he said. 'We don't have much time.'

Jaya allowed her brother to take her to the back of the house where there were no people.

'Jaya, I have heard rumours. I want you to tell me they are wrong,' he said, uncharacteristically stern.

She wondered what was going on. 'I can't tell you one way or the other if you don't tell me what you've heard.'

'I've been told you lay with Colonel Edmundson.' He looked away from Jaya. It had taken a lot for him to be able to utter those words. 'Tell me it is not true.'

Jaya could not lie to him even though she wanted to. She knew this would hurt him and it might mean even more than that.

'I cannot tell you that,' she said.

She saw on her brother's face something that she'd thought she would never see – disgust.

'What? How could you do that? It makes you nothing but a whore, a common prostitute! I am disgraced by your actions. You have disgraced all of us.'

He spat on the ground at her feet and walked away. Jaya felt as if he had punched her, inflicting a blow so damaging that she could not catch her breath, and perhaps never would again.

Krishnan was the only family she really had and now, thanks to both William and Jaya's choice, she no longer had him. Jaya glanced around feeling the air itself press tightly against her skin. She knew she could not go back to the party; she was not wanted there. She needed to *breathe*. She rushed towards the gate.

'Jaya?'

She looked behind her and saw Rafik. He looked

exceptionally handsome in his gold embroidered kurta. She wiped the tears from her eyes, but made no effort to hide her emotions.

'Hello, Rafik.'

To his credit, he did not comment on her obvious distress. Instead, he said, 'Shall we take a stroll? Just for a little while.'

She was devastated by what had just happened and all she wanted was to be gone, yet she said, 'Yes, alright.'

They walked away, out of the village. To Jaya's surprise, Rafik turned and headed to her secret spot where, as a girl, she went to draw, her spot along the river. She looked up at him and he smiled at her.

'Don't worry, Jaya. I just wanted us to be able to sit somewhere quiet and talk,' he said.

They sat on two large rocks next to each other, facing the river. 'I used to come here when I was young. It was a place where I could be happy,' Jaya said.

'Were you not happy at home?'

How strange that a man such as Rafik would be interested in anything about a young woman like her. Krishnan was right; Rafik was a different sort of man.

'No, I wasn't.'

'I saw that you were very upset back at the party.'

Jaya pictured the horrible look of disgust on Krishnan's face again. She pushed back the tears before she answered. 'Yes. I've disappointed my brother.'

'I'm sure he will forgive you,' Rafik said. 'I've known Krishnan for some time now, and I know him to be a compassionate man.'

Jaya shook her head. 'He is, but I've done something that is unforgivable.'

Rafik chose the kindest path and dug no further. Jaya was grateful for that.

'I had a wife,' he said. 'She died five years ago. We had an arranged marriage. When I first saw her, I thought I could never love her. I found her eyes too small and her ears too large. She often clicked her tongue in an annoying way when she was nervous.'

Jaya laughed in spite of herself, and Rafik smiled at her.

'To my surprise, I soon fell deeply in love with her. None of those things mattered. In fact, now when I think of her, I think of how I loved her too small eyes and her too large ears. And how I wish I could hear her annoying clicking once again. What I'm trying to say is, we don't always know what lies ahead. We might think we know, but we don't.'

Jaya could see that he missed his wife, and that the love he had for her still resided in his heart. 'And you had children?' Jaya asked.

'Yes, two sons. They are nearly grown now, both of them at boarding school.'

He looked at Jaya and she could see sadness in his eyes. 'I am lonely. I needn't hide that from you. I know that you are young, closer in age to my sons than to me, but I know I could give you a life, a good life. And your presence in my life would distract me from the silence I now feel.'

'Even an annoying clicking noise?'

He laughed at the unexpected joke. He was lovely when he laughed. If Jaya had met him before moving to the Edmundsons, she knew she would have married him. He had such a calming way about him and, as he spoke, she could see the quiet, uncomplicated life they could make together. But now everything was different, and that had come into clear focus after witnessing her brother's reaction to her situation. Jaya knew what she and William had done was wrong, but she had ignored it and hidden it away where she might not have to look at it.

Krishnan had pulled that knowledge into the bright light, and showed her the truth. She had committed a sin that she could not recover from. She wished at that moment, as the river sang its watery song in her ear and the birds chirped from the bushes, that she could rub her mistakes away. She wished she could go back in time, and follow the path that led to Rafik. She knew now that would have been her wisest choice.

But it was too late.

Jaya could not allow her misdeeds to rub off on this kind man. He did not deserve that. She stood up. It was important to leave him free of her, unencumbered, so she spoke the next words with a hardness that she did not feel.

'Rafik, I'm going to England with my employer … with *my lover*. I'll never return here. You must find another to fill your silent world. I'm sorry. Goodbye, Rafik.'

She ran through the bushes. It was decided, for good or ill, it was decided. She would go to England. There was nothing left for her in India. Her actions had made certain of that.

PART II: ENGLAND

CHAPTER 9

Somehow her imaginings had not allowed Jaya to anticipate just how relentless the constant motion of the ship could be. She felt every swell of the ocean. Her stomach rolled with the waves, and luckily there was nothing left inside. She'd been up on the deck countless times to be sick. She was surprised to see Sayida sleeping so soundly in the bunk across from hers. The movement of the ship did not affect her in the least.

She looked around the lower deck in the room where the ayahs were boarded. Their wooden beds, one next to the other, ran down the length of the narrow dark room. Jaya had not realised so many ayahs were going to England; they were ten in all. Most British families seemed unable to care for their children without the help of these women. After asking around, Jaya knew most of the ayahs were going to England with their employers for a short time – a home visit – where the families could spend a couple of months with family and then to India. Only a handful were in the same position as she and Sayida – going to England for an undermined length of time, likely never to return to India.

Some of the ayahs had taken this round trip many times. From them, Jaya learned everything she could about England. She learned it was very cold, even in summer. So cold you could never find a place to be warm even in direct sunlight. Their sunlight came from a sun different from the one in India. She was told to be ready to see whites everywhere, and not all were wealthy, some much poorer than people back home. They told her about the food, so bland and tasteless, like eating water. They also warned her that many of the whites could be very cruel, so she must take care. Though others were kinder than any they'd seen before. Jaya compiled all this information and put together a picture of what to expect. It was good to have an idea of what awaited her at the end of this horrid journey.

Her stomach ached and her head spun. She sat up and sipped some water and felt slightly better. She could not imagine how she was going to survive six weeks of this. At least Sayida was here with her. She could not have come without her on this journey, which already seemed like a mistake. Sayida had nearly been left behind until Jaya intervened.

One night, only five days before departure, she and William were in his study. He was trying to convince her to stay with him that night. It had been a particularly difficult day. The boys were over excited by the pending trip, and Sara was in bed for most of the day, but every minute she was up and about she found endless fault with Jaya.

Ever since Krishnan's engagement party, she'd not been herself. She felt untethered and lost, and so very alone. She only wanted to be gone, and she was losing patience with the days of waiting. Waiting meant time for thinking, and that was what she didn't need just now.

William held her hand when she attempted to go off to her room, and he tried to lead her to the fireplace. 'Please, Jaya, my darling, I'll give you anything. My body aches for you.' He genuinely sounded desperate.

Jaya hesitated. Maybe this was the time to ask for what she really wanted from him. 'Anything?'

'Yes.'

'Are you sure of what you're saying?' Jaya tested the waters before getting in.

'Yes. Say what you desire, and it will be done. I am your servant.' William pressed his palms together in a Namaste gesture, as though Jaya were of a higher status.

'Bring Sayida with us to England,' Jaya said, without

hesitating.

William looked surprised and frowned. 'I thought you would ask for a gold bangle or a new set of oil paints. What do you want with that old woman?'

'Please don't speak of her in that way!' Sometimes William was unkind, and Jaya disliked that side of him.

'Sorry,' he said. He gently touched her arm and lowered his voice. 'I meant nothing. I was being silly. I'm sorry. I see now that I've upset you.'

Jaya pulled away. 'Will you take her with us? Will you promise?'

He hugged her closely, kissing the top of her head. 'Of course. It is done. She will come with us to England.'

'You're a man of integrity. Do not act as one who is not,' Jaya warned.

'I will not. I promise, she will come with us.' William looked at her with his now familiar 'trust me' expression, and she knew he would keep his word. She, too, was a woman of integrity who kept her promises.

Jaya sat on the edge of her narrow bunk watching Sayida. She had wondered how she would survive in the tightly packed confines of the ship for so many weeks. The ship had the strange distinction of being quite cold, yet the air was tight and musty at the same time, thick with humanity – thick with this crowd of strangers into which Jaya had been thrust, and with whom she would spend the next eight weeks, depending on the winds and the traffic at the canal. It seemed as if a lifetime stretched before her.

Some ayahs were fortunate enough to dwell upstairs in the luxurious family quarters, yet there had been limited slots for such amenities, and the Edmundsons had made their reservation too late to secure any for her and Sayida. Since ayahs were expected to look after the children on the voyage, it was necessary to have them nearby. Although Jaya had the misfortune of being separated from the Edmundsons, Sara had made it clear that Jaya was not relieved of her responsibilities. Each morning, she would be expected to wake at sunrise and venture four decks above, so that she could look after the boys, while William and Sara occupied themselves with leisurely activities.

It was the third night on the ship, but already Jaya was getting to know her travelling companions and their likes and dislikes. Gossip appeared to be a pastime the women enjoyed and a target had already been chosen.

'Do you know she beats her charges?' one timid young girl whispered.

'With a chain, I've heard,' a hardened sinewy woman added. 'I believe it.'

Stories slithered through the lower berth like snakes on the prowl. Jaya had been content to hold her peace and believed that gossip was merely a way to pass the time. Focussing on a single target fuelled an indignant camaraderie amongst the ayahs.

The target of most of the gossip was a woman named Komali. If everyone was busy speculating about Komali, Jaya knew there was less chance of becoming the focus of unwanted attention from the gossipers.

Komali was from Bhitia, a village not far from Jaya's home of Khesar. Although Jaya had met many ayahs back at home, she and Komali had never crossed paths before.

Jaya ignored the stories, mostly, refusing to reinforce such brutal gossip. The reports of the abuse and torture Komali inflicted upon her young charges could easily have been the workings of jealous minds. She'd seen Komali's children, however. They were timid, slinking about the ship like frightened mice, and cowering when their ayah was close by. Jaya knew that could mean many things. The children might be afraid of the ship and its tossing and turning. Perhaps their parents were the source of their timidity, or even their general nature might be the cause. To blame their behaviour on Komali seemed unfair.

But Jaya witnessed something – she saw the children playing

on deck just as the ship left port. Komali appeared, and she saw her dig her thick, strong fingers into the children's small shoulders, and saw her deep-set eyes flash with fury. The children immediately became frozen in place. It was hard to be impartial after seeing that. Still, she told herself not to rush to judgement because of gossip; that was unfair.

On the first night at sea, Jaya watched her shipmates pick their way down the ladder to their sleeping quarters. She saw their legs first, some sturdy, some as thin as a child's. One at a time, their owners appeared. Quiet conversation rose to chatter once each ayah found their bed, their small piece of the ship that was to be her own for the next weeks.

A slim young woman stepped lightly from the ladder and looked around. She smiled at Jaya who nodded in return.

'Laksha,' she said.

'Jaya.'

Laksha dropped her bag on an empty bunk near the bottom of the ladder and sat down, emitting a tiny groan as she did. She looked up the ladder and breathed deeply. The bunk's location seemed to offer a sliver of prestige, for it was positioned right near the narrow stairwell leading out of the cabin. Jaya was just about to tell Laksha that someone had already claimed that bunk when a shadow loomed over everyone. Alarm shot through Jaya and, before she could speak, Komali grabbed the

young ayah by the back of her dress and pulled her from the
bunk. Laksha's toes barely touched the ground and her eyes
flashed with fear. The chattering among the ayahs stopped and
all eyes watched the brutal assault, but no one moved to help
the younger and much smaller woman. The moment seemed to
stretch into eternity until finally, with a mighty heave, Komali
threw Laksha, and she landed at the foot of Jaya's bunk, her
head knocking against the edge like a coconut.

Jaya held out a hand to the shaken Laksha and helped her to
her feet. Tears glistened on Laksha's cheeks. She swallowed her
sobs while rubbing the back of her head. Her fingers came back
with spots of blood on them. Jaya checked Laksha's head and
then took out her handkerchief and wiped away the blood.

'It's hardly bleeding, but you'll have a bump,' Jaya said.

She looked at Komali who ignored all of them, busy
arranging her things in the metal trunk that was underneath her
bunk. It was as if nothing of any consequence had happened.

'Come,' Jaya said. 'Let me help you find a free bunk.'

She picked up Laksha's bag and walked down the row until
they found an unoccupied bunk. Jaya helped her arrange her
things.

'Thank you for your help,' Laksha said. 'You're very kind.'

Jaya went back to her own bunk. Komali lay on her bed
and watched Jaya as she made her way down the thin passage

between the two rows of bunks. Her glare continued as Jaya folded her clothes and placed them in her own trunk.

It was clear that helping Laksha had been an act of defiance that set Jaya against Komali. She would have to be careful around the woman for the rest of the journey. Jaya had, unfortunately, made a new enemy.

***

If all went well, the steamship was due to dock in London in about seven weeks. From the standpoint of a steamship traveller, this was a lengthy stretch of time, yet Jaya kept reminding herself that, on land, weeks could fly past in the blink of an eye. After the first few days, her body settled down and accepted that this was life for the foreseeable future.

They established a routine very quickly. She and Sayida woke before dawn, bathed, and had their breakfast in the dining room with the other ayahs. Jaya tried to be waiting outside the family's room before they woke so as to go off with Edward and Christopher, and allow William and Sara a few more hours of sleep. Normally it was Sara who stayed in bed, and William often left the room with the boys, and went up to breakfast with them.

Sayida helped Jaya with the boys, keeping them entertained

when they were not taking lessons. William insisted that they continue lessons in writing, reading, French and mathematics on the ship. He reminded them often that in England they would need to be up to the standards of their peers if they were to get into any of the good schools there.

Sometimes, after lessons, Sayida would take the boys to play games on deck with some of the other children, and let Jaya have some time alone to relax.

Jaya brought a single sketchpad and her new fountain pen, but nothing else. He had promised her that once they were in England, he would buy her a new set of paints, charcoal, pencils, and all the paper and canvases she desired. Until they landed, she took care with the paper she had, sketching on the front and back of each page, often dividing the page into fours.

She sat in a hidden sunny spot and began sketching the side of the boat and the sea. With her pen, she tried to capture the light on the water, a difficult task that she was just beginning to understand.

'That's good.'

Jaya looked up and saw Laksha. They'd become friends of a sort since that first day when Komali had attacked her. They had little in common, but she knew Laksha was grateful for Jaya's support.

'Are you free now too?' Jaya asked, as Laksha took a seat on the floor next to Jaya's overturned crate she used as a stool.

'The Cartwrights have taken Emily to the puppet show. I didn't want to go. Those puppets give me bad dreams.'

Jaya smiled. She wondered how Laksha would manage in England since nearly everything new frightened her. At least it was just a home visit. She'd be with the family in England for three months, and then they would return to India.

There was a lot Jaya didn't know about Laksha's previous life. She had mentioned her parents and her three brothers, but never went into any detail. Jaya had no idea what they did, or where they were now and, although curious, decided that if Laksha wanted to talk about them, she would.

'You could be a real artist you know, Jaya.' Laksha looked at the drawing and smiled.

'Thank you for saying that,' Jaya said wistfully. 'I wish I could be a real artist. It's a dream.'

'My Aarush is a bit of an artist. He makes tiny soldiers out of metal, sepoys. The boys love them.' Laksha was engaged to marry a young man from her village, Aarush. He was a blacksmith and, according to her, the most handsome man in the village. Jaya took her word for it, though she suspected she might be overly excited about her future husband. She spoke of little else. Just then, she fished around in the pockets of her dress and found what she was looking for. She gave it to Jaya. It was a tiny kitten made from a scrap piece of iron.

'My Aarush made that.'

Jaya liked the weighty feel of the kitten in her hand. She had to admit, Aarush was indeed an artist. The kitten was bent down at the front, his rump in the air, his tail nearly flicking back and forth in anticipation of a pending attack. Jaya could feel the energy of the perfectly rendered kitten though it was not alive at all.

'This is beautiful. You're right, he is an artist indeed,' Jaya said. She handed it back to Laksha, but she refused to take it.

'Keep it as a small present to remember me by. He can make me another one.'

Jaya was touched by Laksha's generosity. 'Thank you. It's lovely. I'll think of you when I hold it in my hand.'

'Kind thoughts, I hope.'

Jaya smiled, patting her new friend's hand. 'Always.'

***

Part of the daily routine on the ship included Jaya eating dinner with the family in the elegant dining room. This was so that she could tend to the boys, and Sara and William could be free with their friends. The boys always finished early, and Jaya would have them bid their parents goodnight and take them off to get ready for bed.

'Did you like the food, Jaya?' Edward asked as they walked down the narrow passages to the family's rooms.

'I do. Why do you ask?'

'Mother said you would not. She said Indians have no taste for refined food,' Edward said.

Jaya squashed her anger as soon as it rose. She would not blame Edward for the things his mother said. He was only repeating what he had heard; he had no idea how undermining and disrespectful it was. In some ways, Jaya even wondered if Sara realised it herself. For her, all Indians were lesser sorts of human, and all things English were the height of culture and sophistication. No backward Indian like Jaya could appreciate English food or culture.

She got the boys washed and in their nightclothes. She waited in the room even after they fell asleep, that was the routine. Sara would rarely stay late at dinner. Once she and William returned, Jaya would make her way to the ayahs' accommodation, and join Sayida in whatever was going on that evening. Sometimes card games, sometimes singing, other times just conversations of home and the people they already missed after just one week at sea.

Jaya missed only Krishnan. She mitigated her sadness by thinking about how he had treated her the last time they were together, and soon she felt better, at least for a while. He had left no space in his heart for forgiveness, and had not given her any leeway for grace. She'd felt bad that she had disgraced herself and him, at least at first. Then she thought, what was true love if not a place where forgiveness might be given, if not a place where you know people are human and, as such, sometimes make bad decisions and mistakes? Krishnan's harsh, brutal words made her angry now, angry and very sad. They'd left no room for his love to survive. The ache of sadness weighed heavily at times. To manage, she encased it in a protective cover of anger.

As her thoughts wandered, the door opened and Jaya looked up from the chair she'd positioned by the porthole. She'd been looking out at the moon reflecting on the calm sea, her chair positioned in a way that she could keep an eye on the sleeping boys in their tiny room.

Sara threw her small golden bag on the side table.

'You can go, Jaya,' Sara said. 'Don't be late tomorrow morning like today. The boys were up and making noise. I still have that wretched screaming banging in my head. I can't tolerate loud noises when I'm pregnant, I've told you that.'

'Yes, Memsahib.'

Jaya left, closing the door behind her, not looking at William who stood meekly to the side, fearing she'd catch his eye. She found it increasingly difficult to hide her feelings for him so, when Sara was around, it was best to pretend he did not exist.

Jaya left and climbed down to the third deck of the ship. When she turned the corner, William was there. He must have rushed out and taken the ladder at the front of the ship so as to meet her on the way.

'Hello,' Jaya said, surprised. 'What did you tell your wife to allow for your escape?'

'I'm meeting some of the men for poker. I'll be back extremely late.' He looked closer at Jaya. 'Are you seasick again? You're pale.'

'No, I'm not seasick. I feel better now,' she answered. She moved closer to him. 'I miss the study.'

William pulled her into the corner. 'I miss you, desperately.'

His heart beat against her ear. Looking up at him, Jaya allowed her gaze to open with vulnerability. She liked behaving this way in his presence: small and innocent and in need of his strength. It made her feel feminine; it allowed him to rise to his own masculinity, something she suspected Sara did not allow.

He reached for her hand, but he found it clutched something.

'What is it you're hiding from me?' William asked.

'It's nothing.'

'But now I must know. I fear it is a gift from a competitor for your affection.' William smiled, but there was an edge of seriousness to it. William was jealous.

She quickly put her hand in her pocket and dropped the little kitten Laksha had given her onto his open palm.

'It's nothing. I told you. It was just a gift from one of the ayahs.'

'It's good.' He looked at it for a moment and handed it back to her. She slipped it into her pocket. 'Don't hide things from me. I've told you before not to do that,' he scolded, making Jaya feel like a small child being admonished for some wrongdoing.

A stab of annoyance went through her. She didn't like to be bossed around, or reminded of her subordinate position.

'And yet you hide things from me all the time.' She moved slightly away from him.

'I don't. I love you, Jaya. Please don't play with my heart in this way.' In his well-practiced manner, William reverted from being coldly dictatorial to pleading like a lovesick puppy.

Her heart softened when she saw the pain on his face. He leaned in and kissed her, passionately. A surge of desire went through her body.

'I need you,' she said. 'I need to feel you. Alone.'

'I like it when you take the lead.' He breathed heavily and beads of sweat appeared on his upper lip.

'When? When will we manage to be alone?'

'We need to be careful. I must find somewhere we can meet.'

Much as she tried, as much as she knew that onlookers were a very real threat, she could not resist smoothing her hands along his body, down his stomach, up his thigh. He groaned into her shoulder where his head had fallen.

'We'll try … we must try,' he said. 'But it may be dangerous. Many of these families will be part our future life. Gossip could be a destructive force.'

As if Jaya did not know already what the cost of a leak about their relationship had exacted. She suspected the gardener at the house in Banka had told Krishnan, the same man who had told him about the ayah job in the first place. Who else had he told? Jaya had not told William about it though. She did not exactly understand why. Maybe it was just that she didn't want to think about Krishnan's words and accusations any more than she already did.

'In private. We must find a private place.' Her breath softened her voice. 'Someplace where no one else will know.'

'There are the sick bays,' he said to her.

'I don't understand. Sick bays? With a doctor about?' she asked.

He smiled. Clearly, she had failed to understand his meaning. 'I predict that Sara will require constant medical attention at some point. Already, she's complaining of seasickness, constant headaches, and complications from the pregnancy, which I'm sure will soon turn into a full-blown malady. At that point she'll need to stay at the sick bay.'

'And there will be room in your quarters.'

He kissed her and she smiled before a shiver ran through her. Could there be a shred of morality in wishing illness upon Sara? Probably, not. It was wrong from her position, but even worse from William's. She knew, however, that the pact she had made with her own conscience included her own happiness in return for Sara's.

***

When she finally parted from William and returned to her own accommodation, Jaya looked around at the others and wondered if any of the other ayahs held similar affections for their own employers. Naturally, she didn't dare speak to anybody of her personal life. While the other ayahs spent time gossiping, joking and telling tired stories, Jaya was pleased to simply smile politely and say little. She could tell this made some of the women think her strange, particularly the older ones, who seemed keen on talking at all hours of the day and night. But she'd rather be thought of as odd than known for being involved with a married man. She suspected others were in her position too; most of them were quite young and attractive. Surely their employers had noticed.

Sometimes, though, when Jaya looked at the other ayahs who were physically attractive, she couldn't help but worry about whether her love for William was real. If some of these women were in similar situations, wasn't that more a sign of exploitation than actual romance? Did any ayah have the power to say no to her employer without losing her position? Was she deluding herself about the relationship she had with William?

She couldn't let her mind drift down that path. Nothing was ever simple and straight forward when viewed from the inside. From a distance, her affair with William could seem cheap and silly, and little more than abuse, but from her vantage point, from inside the affair, things were of an entirely warmer, kinder and more impassioned nature. Jaya chose to think that what she and William had was an exception. It was easier that way.

CHAPTER 10

A few nights later when Sayida passed Jaya's bed, she whispered, 'She seeks revenge.'

Jaya, who had just been falling asleep, opened her eyes and looked at Sayida. 'Who?'

'That ayah you helped,' Sayida said.

'Laksha?' Jaya propped herself up on one elbow. She spoke so softly she could barely hear her own whispers. 'How? What is she planning to do?'

She was surprised to hear that a woman as seemingly meek as Laksha would have enough pride to contemplate anything resembling vengeance. Perhaps it was just more silly gossip.

Sayida shook her head and spoke again, 'She wishes to use one of Komali's hammers on her.'

Jaya understood this was very serious. 'Are you sure?'

'Some of the other women support it,' Sayida said. 'They're encouraging her.'

'Why does Komali have hammers with her anyhow?' Jaya asked.

Sayida shrugged. 'I hear she's quite handy, which is primarily why her employers keep her. She has a complete set of tools in her trunk.'

'We can't let Laksha do this,' Jaya said. 'Komali will kill her.'

'It's not up to us, dear.' Sayida sometimes frustrated Jaya with her fatalistic attitude about things. It was as if she didn't believe she had the power to act.

'Even if she does succeed, someone could die,' Jaya said.

'Ssshhh ... someone will hear you.'

'It's wrong,' Jaya said lowering her voice. 'We can't sit by and let it happen.'

Sayida paused for a good long while. Then she said, 'Maybe not. Maybe no one will die. It will be just enough to put Komali in her place. She's a bully to everyone. It's better she's sorted out now or it will be a very long trip.'

'I cannot believe you would condone such a thing, Sayida. It's wrong.'

Sayida shrugged. 'It is out of my hands.'

Sayida became quiet and minutes later appeared to be asleep.

For Jaya, sleep was now as impossible as stopping the endless rocking of the ship. She reached across and shook Sayida's shoulder, and the older woman opened her eyes.

'If that happens,' said Jaya, 'there will be investigations in Britain. Paperwork. We will all be in trouble.' Jaya added, 'We could even be arrested.'

Now Sayida's full attention was on Jaya's words. She stared over Jaya's head, no doubt picturing a range of possibilities in her mind. In truth, Jaya did not really believe her own words. She doubted that the murder of a lowly ayah would lead the English to conduct a prolonged or complex investigation. They would find many who would point a finger at Laksha. She would likely be tried and then excused as an imbalanced native, not responsible for her actions. Though it was a stretch, she knew the possibility might frighten Sayida enough to help her.

Jaya's motive for protecting Komali was born entirely from compassion for Laksha. Laksha had been assaulted, humiliated and thrown across the room, for nothing more than a mere mistake. She could have been severely injured. Laksha was a young, hopeful woman with an entire life before her, including a marriage to the artistic Aarush, and likely many children to follow. Jaya held the tiny cat in her hand. Laksha did not deserve to have been treated so badly by Komali, and Jaya believed it would be just if Komali were punished. To achieve that justice, though, would come at a great cost. Laksha had to be stopped from carrying out her misguided plans.

'In the morning,' Sayida whispered to Jaya, 'over breakfast. We will speak with Laksha.' With those words spoken, Sayida turned over and slipped off to sleep.

Jaya may have closed her eyes but sleep evaded her that night.

***

Breakfast was held on the ship's second deck. The difference between the employers' rations and the ayahs' rations was stark. The first-class travellers received beef, bread, butter, vegetables, juice and all manner of filling, tasty options. When the time came to serve the ayahs, the menu grew a great deal slimmer. It consisted entirely of rice and curry, cooked by the lascars below deck. It was decent curry, with a generous amount of salt, but it still left Jaya's belly disappointed. As she got through each spoonful, she simply kept reminding herself that greater pleasures awaited them in England.

Managing to sit with Laksha at breakfast was quite easy for Jaya and Sayida. Her talk about going after Komali was not gaining much support after all. Although plenty of people would be happy to see Komali go, this didn't mean that

Laksha's supporters wished to be her collaborators. Jaya didn't mind being seen with Laksha; she was determined to talk the woman out of her foolish plan.

'I've heard about your plan, Laksha. You mustn't do anything silly,' Jaya said, looking her in the eye and not seeing the faintest trace of madness, or even defiance. She questioned if the rumours were even true. 'Remember, Aarush is waiting for you back home. You mustn't do anything to ruin your future.'

'You don't wish to spend your life in prison, and neither do any of us,' Sayida whispered. 'Revenge is not worth it.'

Laksha listened to her new friends with patience, but after they were through speaking, she surprised them with her reply.

'I'm not planning anything for mere revenge,' she said. 'If I don't do it, death will get us all. I'm trying to save all of us.'

'What do you mean? I don't understand,' said Jaya.

Leaning forward and lowering her voice, Laksha explained, 'Komali does not like anyone to cross her. Another ayah told me that she had taken this journey before when Komali was on board. Two ayahs died from poisoning. They were just dumped over the side of the ship, no investigation. Both had crossed Komali. She keeps poison with her at all times. This ayah warned me because she thought my life was in danger.' Laksha looked at Jaya. 'But Jaya, you've already angered her. She'll likely poison you first if I don't stop her. Then I could be next.'

Jaya couldn't believe what she was hearing. She knew Komali was violent and likely evil, but this was too much. She would not allow Laksha to be the only one to take responsibility for stopping Komali, especially if she had such poison. In that case, they could all be one of her victims.

***

Later in the day, as their ship eased across the Arabian Sea, the hot afternoon sun did its best to warm the decks, but the weather seemed to produce no end of chilly winds. Jaya hugged her shawl tighter and moved into the full glare sun. Jaya and Sayida kept their eyes on Edward and Christopher as the boys took turns skipping with an old, worn skipping rope they'd found inside the ship's toy box. While the boys played, oblivious to the energetic force hanging thick amongst their elders, Jaya and Sayida whispered to each other about the disturbing nature of their breakfast conversation.

'It's a lie,' said Jaya. 'Komali probably spread that rumour just to scare the others. She wants all of us to be frightened of her so she can have her way.'

'I don't believe it,' Sayida replied.

Moving in closer, Jaya asked, 'How can you be sure?'

'Because I know people.'

'Sayida, you've lived your life in the same town, and most of it under the same roof. You couldn't possibly know all types of people. Komali is a rare type.'

Ignoring Jaya, Sayida said, 'I can see the murder in Komali's eyes. A woman who loses her temper so easily, and with such violence, would certainly engage in sinister schemes. I can feel it, Komali is very evil.'

Jaya hugged herself against the cold wind and looked around them at the other ayahs attending to the needs of their own fair-skinned charges. Of most concern to everyone was the possibility of a child becoming too wild or excited, to the point of foolishness and recklessness, and plummeting overboard into the sea. Jaya shivered at the very thought.

No sooner had these thoughts passed through Jaya's mind, than she checked the boys again and Christopher was not there.

'Sayida, where's Christopher?' Jaya rushed to Edward. 'Where's your brother?'

'He went that way. He said he wanted to tell Father something.'

Jaya ran in the direction Edward pointed. She called back, 'Sayida, stay with Edward!'

As Jaya ran frantically down the ship's main deck, calling for Christopher, she tried to remain calm, asking others if they'd seen the boy. She needed to keep her panic at bay. She tried not to look at the worst possible explanation for Christopher's disappearance: the sea. Just when she had settled on the idea that the small boy had somehow gone over the railing and was lost in that massive water, she heard a small voice behind her.

'Jaya!' There he was: *Christopher!*

He was standing right there, at her leg, looking as innocent as a baby.

'Christopher!' Her voice was first sharp, and then when she saw the effect it became soft. She bent to him and hugged him tightly. 'You mustn't run off like that. Where did you go?'

He looked at her, and though it was clear he was fighting tears, he began to cry.

Pulling away from the boy, she bent down and asked, 'What happened? Tell me. You can tell me anything. I won't be angry.'

For a moment, he kept his gaze locked on the wooden boards of the deck. When he finally tilted his neck upward, his face was pink and wet with tears. 'I had an accident. I tried to get to the toilet, but it was too late.'

Jaya nearly laughed with relief. She had him dead in the sea, but he'd only wet himself. She held him to her. 'It's fine. We all make mistakes. Let's go and get you changed.'

They walked together to the family's rooms. They were empty since both William and Sara kept a busy schedule of activities with the other British passengers. They went into the boys' room and Jaya helped him change and get cleaned up.

'I'm scared here, Jaya,' Christopher said. 'I have bad dreams.'

Jaya felt her breath catch in her throat. Her first thought was to share that she did too. She had awful wild nightmares most nights.

'It's just because this is a new place,' she said to him. 'You'll have good dreams tonight.'

Then the boy asked the most unsettling question. He locked his gaze with Jaya's and asked, 'Do you think there's something wrong with this ship? Like ... something bad?'

In her heart, Jaya knew that her most honest answer was to agree with him. There was talk of madness and murder on the ship, so how could she think otherwise?

She ruffled his hair and said, 'Of course not. This is a beautiful and sturdy ship. I think it's lovely. You are perfectly safe here.'

He smiled cautiously. She took his hand and they headed back to the sunny deck, though a foreboding air had fallen over Jaya that would take some while to disappear.

***

The children seemed oblivious to how charmed their own lives were. It would never cross their minds that their dutiful, loving ayahs had their own personal feelings, let alone their own urgent dramas and concerns.

Later that day, when Sayida and Jaya were alone on deck, the boys off with their parents, Jaya said, 'I can't stop thinking about Komali. What should we do?'

'We'll get the poison – steal it from her. Then the threat will be gone,' Sayida said with confidence, surprising her friend with her tone.

They didn't even know for certain that Komali, a violent woman with a case of hammers under her bed, actually had poison, and now Sayida was suggesting they steal from Komali. It would have been amusing were it not so overwhelming.

'It will be simple,' Sayida explained, obviously having given it some thought. 'Like the rest of us, Komali only has a small living space. If what Laksha says is true, the poison won't be in her trunk, but in that bag she keeps under her pillow. I've seen her tuck a bag under her pillow at night. That's my strongest guess as to where she keeps the poison.'

'She might keep it there in the night, but she wouldn't keep it there in the day when anyone might take it. Surely, she would keep it on her person, somewhere on her body,' said Jaya. 'In either instance, it would be impossible to take it from her.'

Nodding with the stoicism of one who has already made a decision that she was not intending to change, Sayida said,

'We'll start with the bed. We shall conduct our search after dinner.'

Jaya knew everything about this plan was flawed, and she felt responsible for dragging Sayida into it. But once Sayida heard that Komali had poison, and that Jaya might be her next victim, Sayida's position changed. Jaya often saw Sayida as a mother figure, and Sayida saw Jaya as her daughter. She would not sit by and do nothing if her daughter was in danger.

CHAPTER 11

The bathing quarters set aside for the ayahs were modest. Essentially, they consisted of a small, dark room – tucked beneath a staircase – where four or five ayahs could bathe at a time. The small room had drains down to the sea. The ayahs collected buckets and water and washed together over the drains. When Komali went to bathe after dinner, Jaya and Sayida would search for the poison.

Jaya thought the poison, if it even existed, had to be on Komali's person, most likely tucked inside her pocket. Sayida, on the other hand, argued that Komali was too calculating to allow it to get wet. Then there was a third possibility: that the poison was hidden somewhere else on the ship, away from Komali's sleeping area all together. For now, there was no use in entertaining that possibility. The women simply had to do their best.

As soon as Komali left to bathe, they would get to work. Sayida agreed to conduct the search while Jaya stood watch. Their actions could hardly take place in solitude, as not all of the women could bathe as once, meaning others would be lurking about their quarters, some off in other parts of the ship, doing their jobs. In other words, Sayida and Jaya had to be fast and careful.

They told Laksha nothing of their plans. Jaya was not completely sure that Laksha had abandoned her own plans either. This uncertainty worried Jaya. She hoped that if they found the poison they would show it to Laksha, and the matter would be finished. They would throw it in the sea, and all of it would be over. All plans of murder would be gone, and they could get on with their lives.

Once Komali was off to bathe, Jaya stood near Komali's bunk acting as casual as possible while Sayida poked around the area. Moving fast and exuding the air of a woman who absolutely belonged where she was, Sayida checked under the blanket and the lump of rags that served as a pillow. She also checked inside the pillowcase, then began to rapidly and carefully pick through Komali's clothing.

'Quickly!' Jaya hissed.

'Hold on.' Sayida was focused and she didn't seem to fear

Komali at all, which was certainly different from the way Jaya felt about the woman. She knew if Komali found them searching through her things, they'd get a severe beating or worse.

Fortunately, Komali was known for being selfish during bath time. Most women washed quickly to make sure that everyone had a chance and the water lasted. Komali took her time with the water, making sure to get more than her fair share. Nobody argued with her about this, for they were far too fearful of her.

Sayida held up a bag before Jaya's eyes, smiling.

'No ...' Jaya said, in disbelief.

Eyes sparkling with the rush of victory, Sayida answered, 'Yes.'

Sayida opened the bag and inside was a brown paper packet with 'rat poison' written on it. Jaya knew such poison was extremely dangerous. Even having it under her pillow might have killed Komali if the packet had opened. So, it was true! Komali did keep poison to kill her enemies. Jaya could not believe it. For a moment, she considered that maybe Komali had left it in a relatively obvious place as a warning, and that the bag may have contained an innocuous substance, but was marked 'rat poison' to scare the other ayahs. If it was rat poison, and her intention was to kill others, would she make it so obvious? Regardless, they couldn't take any chances and they certainly couldn't test it.

The air thinned to nothing. Komali's deep voice thundered through Jaya's chest. She was just around the corner! Sayida's hands shook as she put the poison in her pocket. Jaya forced her limbs to move as they rushed back to their own beds. She held her breath when Komali entered the room. The large woman looked around and sweat formed on Jaya's forehead. She watched unblinking as Komali went to lay on her bed, and Jaya remained like that even as light snores escaped Komali's mouth.

They needed to get rid of the poison but the thought of leaving their beds made Jaya's head light. She didn't dare look at Sayida, who sat silent and rigid at her side. Jaya couldn't shake the feeling that even the smallest gesture would alert Komali to what they had done.

Deep in the night, when movements in the room had long ceased, and the snores of sleeping women filled the air, Jaya leaned over to Sayida, 'We must get rid of it, tonight … now.'

'I've decided … I'm keeping it,' Sayida whispered.

'Why? What would be the point of that?'

'Because it's a weapon.'

'Who will you use it on?' Jaya couldn't believe what she was hearing. What was Sayida thinking?

'Who do you think? Komali.'

'You wish to poison her? How has it come to this?'

Sayida shook her head. 'No. But we can toy with her mind. She'll panic when she finds it missing. We could use this to our advantage.'

'You're playing foolish and dangerous games!' Jaya hissed.

'So?' Sayida replied. This was a Sayida that Jaya was not sure she knew. 'I did not start these games.'

'It doesn't matter who started them. You've no need for that poison. You must throw it away,' Jaya insisted. Why was Sayida being so recklessly stubborn?

Within moments, much to her relief, Jaya heard the gentle sound of Sayida's snoring. As for herself, she knew that she would never sleep. And if she did, it would be amidst a raging landscape of vicious nightmares. That poison could cause problems, big problems, for all of them. Jaya was certain of this.

CHAPTER 12

When Jaya woke, after tossing and turning on her bunk, she was surprised that she had fallen asleep. She thought she heard whispers, but when she looked around everyone was asleep. She was wide awake and decided to go out on deck to get fresh air. She stayed only a few minutes as the wind had picked up and it was quite cold. She suspected a storm was coming. Returning to the sleeping quarters, she climbed down the ladder trying to be as quiet as possible. Thinking she heard movement she looked around, but everyone was still sound asleep in their beds.

The ship began rocking hard from side to side – the storm had arrived. Hearing a loud boom, she went to the porthole in time to see a flash of lightning in the dark sky.

She could not rid her mind of the poison. She knew that Komali would soon realise it had been taken, and then something bad would surely happen.

Jaya made a quick decision. She would take the bag of powder from Sayida's pocket while she was still sleeping and throw it overboard. That way, Komali could never prove they had meddled with her belongings. She would tell Laksha what she had done, and all would be fine again.

What was unclear was why in the world Sayida had wanted to hold onto that bag of white powder in the first place – no matter what she said, there was no logical reason for it. It was a magnet for harm.

Moving quickly in the darkness, Jaya knelt beside the sleeping Sayida. She touched her shirt, allowing her fingers to seek the pockets.

Something was not right. Then in a flash, like the lightning outside, she came to a realisation of staggering horror.

Sayida's body was as cold as a block of ice … and she was not breathing.

***

Jaya's scream sounded louder than any ship whistle or thunderbolt.

Within moments, the other women jolted out of their beds, confused about what was happening.

'What's going on?' a woman shouted. 'We're trying to sleep!'

The orange glow of a lantern approached and, in the dim light, Jaya recognised the ageing ayah who held it.

'My dear, what is it?' she asked, shaking Jaya gently.

Unable to speak, Jaya simply pointed at Sayida's corpse. In the lantern light, they could clearly see Sayida's face. Her eyes were open, and the expression on her face told the story: Sayida looked terrified. She had left the earth in a most frightful and frantic state.

More women gathered around, worry and fright etched on their faces. The elder looked at Jaya and asked, 'What happened?'

'I … I … have no idea.' Only then Jaya remembered the poison in Sayida's pocket. Could it have killed her somehow?

Frowning, the elder studied Sayida. A crowd formed around them despite the cold and rough rocking of the ship.

'I think it was the cold,' the elder said, her wrinkles accentuated by the orange light. 'Her age got the best of her. We must grant her a funeral in accordance with her faith. Was she Hindu?'

Trembling, Jaya gave a nod. 'Yes,' Jaya said, barely able to breathe. 'Hindu.'

The elder nodded and looked around at the other ayahs. 'We must tell the family, and alert the ship's officers, as well.'

'We work for the same family, I will tell them,' Jaya said.
'Please, can you sit with her? No one should touch her until the
family is alerted. They will want to see her.'

'Of course,' the old woman said. 'I'm used to sitting with the
dead.'

'What's the noise?' Komali grumbled from her bunk bed.
She aggressively pulled the torn, grey sheet over her head and
grabbed her face, as her muscles tensed. She exhaled a sharp
breath of air, as the room fell silent like a calm before the storm.

Jaya quickly ran out, her pulse racing and her heart fluttering
in her chest, with a pierce in her stomach as she made her way
to the Edmundsons' rooms.

***

'No!' Sara wailed when Jaya told her what had happened.
Sara collapsed into William's arms, weeping and muttering
about how much she had always loved and adored Sayida. As
William held her, he made eye contact with Jaya. Jaya looked at
him for a moment, then looked away.

Sara's display of grief was too much for her to watch,
knowing most of it was all for show. Sayida had been Sara's
own ayah from the time she was a young girl of ten. Jaya
conceded that it was a loss for Sara, but if Sara genuinely
cared for Sayida, why had she not been the one to insist she
accompany them to England? Why had it been up to Jaya to

make that deal with William?

Already Jaya missed Sayida and knew it would only get worse as time went on. Jaya hated thinking selfish thoughts when Sayida had just died, but she knew that her life was now destined to become twice as hard. For one thing, Sara would resent Jaya even more than she already did.

Now Jaya was well and truly on her own, and even the brief snatches of time with William would never be enough to comfort her.

CHAPTER 13

Burn her not up, nor quite consume her, Agni: let not her body or her skin
be scattered.
O all possessing Fire, when thou hast matured her,
then send her on her way unto the Fathers.
When thou hast made her ready, all possessing Fire, then do thou give her
over to the Fathers,
When she attains unto the life that waits her, she shall become subject to
the will of gods.
The Sun receive thine eye, the Wind thy Prana (life-principle, breath);
go, as thy merit is, to earth or heaven.
Go, if it be thy lot, unto the waters; go, make thine home in plants with
all thy members.

The ayahs gathered together on the ship's main deck as the

sun began climbing up into the sky. One of the elder ayahs recited a very moving Hindu prayer to honour Sayida's life. Jaya looked upon the faces of the ayahs and noted how unified they were in this moment. They were all holding hands, heads bowed and some were weeping. Laksha clung onto Jaya, clearly distraught. After all, it was she who had initiated the plan to kill Komali. Komali, on the other hand, stood alone on the edge of the group and was the only ayah not holding hands with anyone. It filled Jaya's heart with gratitude to see both Hindu and Muslim women come together for such a sacred time, but Komali's stance did not surprise her. indicating she was most likely responsible for Sayida's demise. Following the prayer, all eyes looked toward the tossing sea, and they spoke with sadness about how unlucky Sayida had been.

'She was an old lady,' they said.

'The temperature aboard the ship is brutal,' they said.

'Sayida had perished in the cold; it was too much for her,' they said.

They all desperately wanted to believe these things, but Jaya knew otherwise. There was no doubt in her mind that Komali had killed Sayida. Her death was not a cruel coincidence. It was cruelty of human origin.

The ship's surgeon had taken the body and performed some tests. What he'd found was yet to be released, but Jaya knew Sayida had been perfectly well when she'd gone to sleep. Something had happened to her, and she was positive Komali was behind it.

She watched as four of the women lifted Sayida's body to the rail of the ship. The ship's captain nodded his head and they dropped the old woman over the side. Jaya couldn't look; she knew the body was now in the cold sea, the ship already moving away from her. She could not bear to watch that.

Sayida's life hardly registered in the world. Her parents were long dead. Her brother, too. Her sister was a maid to a wealthy Indian family in one of the Princely States, but Sayida could no longer remember where, since it had been so long since she'd seen her. Sayida had no children who would need to be notified, no husband. She was simply a servant to a spoiled, cruel woman who would mourn her only out of selfishness. Did Sayida's life matter to anyone? How could it be that a person could live and die and have no effect on the world? Her muscles tightened at the thought. This would not happen to her. Never. She was more than a servant, more than a daughter hated by her mother and now despised by her brother, too. She would be more. She would make something of her life.

She watched the other ayahs at the railing. As so many do at funerals, some cried, not for the woman now gone, because they barely knew her, but for their own mortality. Perhaps, like Jaya, they cried for their own quiet journey that went unnoticed in the world.

Jaya cried for all of that. But she cried for her friend, too. It mattered that Sayida had lived her life, and that life had mattered. Now her death would leave a space in the world where she had once existed, a space that was hers and hers alone. Her friend's death left another space – a lonely sad space in Jaya's heart.

**

The next morning, Jaya entered the dining area and was starkly reminded of her loss. She could look around the room, but she would not find Sayida. She sat at an empty table near a porthole. After a few minutes, Komali sat down across from her.

'What do you want?' Jaya asked, surprised by her own directness. She was not in the mood for people, Komali most of all.

'There will be an investigation after the doctor's findings are released,' said Komali. 'I heard they want to speak to all of us.'

Jaya's chest tightened. What would they ask her? More importantly, what would she tell them?

Komali wanted to know too. 'You need to get your story sorted.'

'I'll tell them what I know,' Jaya said. 'Sayida died in her sleep.'

Komali smiled and nodded. Jaya knew then for certain that she had killed Sayida. Why else would she care what Jaya told the investigators? Why would it matter to her? Jaya thought of that horrible stormy night. She'd gone up on deck for a breath of air. Was that when she did it? Jaya could think of no other explanation.

But Jaya had her own secret. When she returned to the sleeping quarters after telling William and Sara the news of the death, she found the old woman still guarding Sayida's body. The other ayahs were busy with their own concerns, but Jaya noticed Komali had not been there. Jaya didn't know where she might have gone; it didn't concern her just then. She had more important things to attend to.

'I can sit with her,' Jaya told the old woman who was sleeping in her chair when she returned.

'Are you sure? I can stay,' the woman said, barely able to keep her eyes open.

'Go … go and sleep. I'll be fine.'

Jaya watched her leave. Then she checked again to see if anyone was looking her way. When she was sure they were not, she reached into the pocket of Sayida's nightdress and retrieved the small cloth bag, not considering the fact that if Komali had used the poison to kill Sayida, traces of it might be on the bag. She quickly hid it in her own pocket, the same pocket where she kept Laksha's little kitten.

After the body was taken to the ship's surgeon, Jaya had planned to drop the packet into the sea, but then changed her mind on mere instinct, the exact reasons she could not articulate. She returned to her bunk and as she did so she heard one of the boards creaking near her bunk. Bending down, she found one was loose. She pried it up just enough to slip the cloth bag underneath. She pushed the board back in place, and it was as if nothing had changed.

Sitting with Komali at breakfast, she knew the poison remained where she had hidden it.

'Good, keep to that story and everything will be fine,' Komali said.

Jaya could feel the violence those words promised. She knew Komali had murdered Sayida, but she also knew she did not have the courage to find justice for Sayida. She felt sick knowing she had not been with her friend when she needed her most.

'Now,' Komali said, 'where's my powder?'

Jaya froze. She knew.

'I don't know what you're talking about,' Jaya said, in a voice that sounded far steadier than she felt.

Komali leaned closer. 'You stole it together. She thought she could blackmail me, the fool.'

Jaya's heart was now thundering. In an alternate reality, she would have physically challenged the horrid woman. She'd as good as confessed to having a hand in Sayida's death, yet she exerted her authority. Who knew, perhaps she wanted to use the poison on others. Jaya wanted to stop her. In such moments either heroism rose to the top, or the coward appeared. Jaya was a coward.

'I think you're confused, Komali. Perhaps Sayida knew about this powder you're talking about, but I know nothing.'

Komali took up her plate, her gaze piercing through Jaya, and moved to sit elsewhere. The message in that look was clear – the issue was not finished.

CHAPTER 14

The investigating officer aboard the ship was a British man who introduced himself as Lester. When she entered his small cabin, he stood and shook Jaya's hand. She instantly found him to be polite, even charming. Her mind was at ease right away, and yet she was smart enough to wonder whether his charm was intended to lower her guard, which she had no intention of doing.

Before she was called for the interview, she decided the best course of action was to deny any awareness of a powder, and therefore any involvement in stealing it. She would not suggest anything to incriminate Komali. Perhaps that would be enough for her to leave Jaya alone. All she wanted now was to get to England alive and get off the ship, and as far away from Komali as possible.

'Have a seat, Jaya,' Lester said. He sat down behind a small desk and Jaya took the wooden chair in front of it. He picked up a quill pen, dipped it in the inkwell, and opened a leather-bound book made of thick, expensive paper.

'So, I understand it was you who discovered Sayida, yes?'

'Yes,' Jaya said, trying to keep her voice calm.

'And when had you last seen her, prior to her death?'

'Right before bedtime. We sleep – we slept – side by side.'

His pen produced swift and satisfying hisses upon the paper as he recorded her answers.

'And what was your impression of Sayida's state of mind at that time? Was she agitated at all?'

'No.'

'Nothing had upset her earlier in the day?'

'Nothing. We work for the same family, so we were together all day with the boys.'

'Yes, I know that.' He smiled and looked down at his book for a moment. He looked up again. 'Did Sayida have enemies aboard this vessel?'

'No … not that I know of.'

A pause and then he resumed writing.

'Did Sayida seem unwell yesterday? Tired?'

'No.'

'Seasick?'

174

Jaya felt an urge to lie. Perhaps to paint a deeper picture of a natural death. But she knew full well that lies had a way of leading to more lies. So, she continued to keep it simple.

'No, sir. Not at all.'

'Are you familiar ...' He paused for quite a while at that moment, and quite efficiently alerted Jaya to the fact that the conversation was about to change. '... with a woman named Laksha?'

Jaya's pulse quickened and she took a calming breath before she spoke. 'Of course. She sleeps among us, downstairs. She's friendly, we've spoken a few times.'

'Are you aware of any conflict between Laksha and Sayida?'

'No. I'd heard nothing of the sort, and Sayida would have told me.'

'Are you aware, Jaya, that Laksha believes Sayida was murdered?'

'No. Really?' Laksha was more courageous than Jaya. Once again she felt guilty about betraying Sayida. 'That's awful if it is true.'

Jaya could not hide her tears. Lester got up and went to the side table. He poured her a glass of water. 'Here. Drink this. I know this must be a shock. You were close to the victim.'

'Yes ... I ... it's just ... it is awful to think Sayida suffered in any way. She was my friend. A kind woman who did not deserve anything like this.'

Lester sat back behind the desk and picked up his pen again. 'You sound as if you believe what Laksha is saying.'

'I have no reason not to. She must have her reasons.'

'Reasons such as?'

Jaya had said too much. She felt backed into a corner now. She began to cry again.

'Please, you must calm yourself,' Lester said. This upset Jaya even more.

Lester seemed lost. 'What can I do to calm you down?'

'Please,' Jaya said. 'I must speak to Colonel Edmundson.' Lester looked confused. 'He is my employer. I must go to see him.'

'Miss, this is a legal investigation, under the jurisdiction of the British Crown. Now, you must cooperate.'

'I will cooperate, I will cooperate. I just need to speak with the Colonel first. Please.'

Lester put his pen down and looked at her. 'Are you aware of something I need to know? Maybe something about a certain poison that was found on her body?'

Jaya froze, her breath catching in her throat. How did he know that?

Lester gave her a small nod. 'The surgeon examined the body and took samples. I'm certain he will determine a cause of death. Laksha mentioned some sort of poison, and we will know soon enough if she is correct.'

'Please ... I will help you. I just need to speak to the Colonel. I am very scared.'

'Does he know something about this matter?'

'No, he knows nothing. We are his employees, nothing more.'

Lester took a moment to consider the request. 'Alright. I will give you thirty minutes. Go and return in that time. I will wait for you.'

***

Jaya rushed down the passageways to William's room. Luckily, he was there alone.

'Please, William, I must speak to you. It is very urgent,' Jaya said.

He took her hand and led her into the room. 'Sit,' he said.

Jaya began to relate her meeting with the officer as he poured her a cup of tea, adding four spoons of sugar. He held it out to her.

'Drink this. Sayida's death is a shock; it is taking a toll on you. I think that investigator's questions have upset you unduly. I will make a complaint to the captain. It is wrong to bully you so.'

Jaya drank the tea down and held up her hand. 'No, I'm not

finished with him. I begged to come to you. I need to know what to do. I am in a terrible situation, a deadly one. I need help, William.'

William sat next to her and listened to what she had to say. She told him the whole story, from Komali's initial conflict with Laksha, to Laksha's plan to stop Komali, to her own outburst in the investigator's cabin.

'And where is the poison now?' William asked.

'I've hidden it.'

She explained her dilemma. Should she admit that she suspected Komali was guilty of murdering Sayida? If she did, what would happen if the investigators couldn't prove Komali's guilt? Then she would live in terror of being murdered too. But supposing she said nothing, and Komali remained furious with her for stealing the poison, and she forced her to return it. If she'd killed Sayida, then why wouldn't she kill Jaya, Laksha and the others?

William listened to all of her questions and fears and took only a minute to see the answer clearly. 'We must tell the investigators the truth.'

Jaya closed her eyes, thinking of the implications. 'You're right,' she said, looking at William. But she was not sure she could do it.

'And we must add,' he went on, 'that you are frightened of

Komali. Not only for your own well-being, but for everyone else's.'

'Yes,' she said, feeling more love for him than ever before.

'I will go with you,' he said.

'You will?'

He nodded and took her hand in his. 'Let's go.'

He held her hand all the way back to Lester's office. Amidst it all, Jaya noticed that he seemed unconcerned about who saw them.

***

Inside the office, William explained Jaya's complete story to Lester, emphasising that Jaya was now terrified of Komali. At the end of William's account, Lester read every word of it back to Jaya to receive her formal confirmation that the account was accurate. William sat by patiently, watching and listening carefully.

'Where is the poison now?' Lester asked.

'I've hidden it,' Jaya said.

'Can we go and fetch it now?' Lester said.

Jaya nodded and the three went to the ayahs' quarters. Luckily the room was empty. It was mid-day and all the ayahs were with their families. Jaya lifted the board and was relieved to find the cloth bag was still where she'd left it. She gave it to Lester.

Looking at Jaya he said, 'I believe you. Especially when I compare your statement with Laksha's.'

'We must imprison this woman, Komali,' William said to Lester. 'Do you understand?'

'I am still gathering evidence, sir,' Lester replied.

'I understand, sir. But you have the testimony of two excellent ayahs, who both swear to Komali's guilt, and you have another ayah, who helped to raise my children and my wife, who is now dead. The results of the tests will be confirmation that this was murder. All of this is very distressing so, if it's not too much to ask, I'd like this investigation to conclude in a manner that is favourable to both ayahs. But speaking for Jaya, she cannot have her life in danger on this ship. That is simply not acceptable. Do you see?'

A powerful silence engulfed the air. But when it finally broke, it did so in the best possible way …

Lester said, 'Not to worry, Colonel. Komali will be put under lock and key. When you leave, I will arrest her myself. When we reach the coast of Spain, she'll be handed over to the authorities for security purposes and then transported to Britain for sentencing.'

Jaya felt faint with relief.

***

It was four days before the ship docked in Spain. During that time, gossip was rife. News leaked that Jaya had been the one to give the investigator information about the poison and Komali's plan. On the second day, Lester called for Jaya to come to his office.

'Thank you for coming, Jaya,' he said. 'We have the results of the tests from the ship's doctor.' He held a paper in his hand. 'I'm sorry to tell you that, unfortunately, your friend was murdered by asphyxiation – in other words she was suffocated to death. I'm surprised that none of the women saw or heard anything.'

Jaya knew this must have happened when she had gone on deck to get some air. If she had stayed in her bunk that night, Sayida would still be alive. She felt sick with guilt, her mind plagued with 'if only' and 'what if'. Jaya felt partly responsible, knowing that she left her friend alone and in a vulnerable position.

'Do you think Sayida suffered?'

Lester started to answer and then hesitated. 'No … no, I don't think she did.'

Jaya suspected he was lying to her as a kindness.

'In Spain, the police will continue the investigation. But I'm certain Komali will not be a free woman again. She may even hang for this.'

Jaya was surprised that the information didn't make her feel much better. At least justice would be done, and herself and others would be protected from Komali's evilness but, in the end, a good woman was dead.

'Oh, and another thing, that white powder. It was not poison. I'm not sure what Komali was playing at. Maybe she wanted to make people think it was poison, or maybe it had already been swapped out before you stole it. It was bicarbonate of soda.'

Jaya wasn't sure what to think about that last bit of information. Maybe her earlier thought about the powder being a red herring was correct. That seemed a more straightforward explanation than the idea that someone had swapped it.

As she left the office, Jaya found Laksha waiting in the passageway. 'So? What did he tell you?'

As they walked to the end of the passageway, Jaya answered the question. 'He said Sayida was murdered, suffocated.'

'I knew it! You've been very brave, Jaya. You saved us all from Komali.'

Jaya stopped and looked at Laksha. 'What I know is that I didn't save Sayida.' A wave of exhaustion hit Jaya, leaving her cold and empty.

Laksha's eyes tightened and when she spoke her tone was softer than Jaya had ever heard it.

'I'm not a nasty person, and my heart and soul knows that murder is wrong, but I have seen what someone like Komali can do. When I was a child, my father was threatened. He owed a merchant some money, but didn't have the means to repay it. They threatened him and said that they would murder his wife and children if he didn't pay. He asked for more time. One night, four men arrived at our home. When my father heard the banging on the door, he told my mother, my brothers and me to hide. My older brother refused to hide and wanted to defend my father, so they went to confront the men together.' Laksha's voice was shaking and her eyes held a faraway look. Jaya put her arm around her and told her that she didn't need to explain, but Laksha continued. 'They had no chance. The men didn't even ask for the money. With four men against two with no weapons, they could not defend themselves. My father and my brother were murdered.'

Jaya was shocked. She cried with Laksha and told her that she understood.

***

All of the ayahs stood on deck to watch Komali being

escorted off the ship by the Spanish police. Jaya stood near the front with Laksha. It was a bittersweet moment for Jaya. The culprit had been caught, but it did not abate Jaya's grief over the loss of one of the best friends she had ever had.

As soon as Komali was brought out into the sun, her head turned, and she looked directly at Jaya. 'I will get my revenge!' Komali shouted at her, her red-rimmed eyes glowing with rage and her mouth frothing at the corners like a rabid animal.

'I'll never forget your face and what you did to me.'

Komali's words felt like a vicious slap. Jaya even stepped backwards in response. Laksha consoled her, 'Ignore her. She can't do anything to anyone again.'

'Yes, you're right. I know that.' But Jaya did not believe the words she spoke. Komali's sort of evil would be with her for the rest of her life.

CHAPTER 15

England, 1902

The ship docked in England in February. Jaya and the family
travelled in two carriages from the port to North London,
where William had organised a house for them. Their luggage
was piled at the back and on top of both carriages. Jaya was
shocked at the cold of the place, a cold that went through all
her layers of clothing, including the blankets the carriage driver
had provided. She'd heard about snow, seen drawings of it in
books, but she could never have imagined that something that
looked so beautiful could be so cold and awful. She hated it
from the first touch, and her feelings would never change.

She wondered what Krishnan would think of this place. She
missed him desperately, and thought of him constantly. Now

that they had arrived safely, she wondered if he would reply if she sent him a letter. Probably not. She wanted to hear about the wedding, about Loki, about their home together.

The transition to this new place where everything was so strange, where all the people were white and they stared at her shamelessly as if she were a monkey on a leash: it was difficult, and she was lonely. When she left India, she thought she could survive here and, even if she struggled, she would have Sayida by her side. But now she was absolutely alone with no one to talk to.

She also thought about Rafik. How was he doing? Had he found someone to marry? She didn't like to be regretful, but sometimes she was sad when she thought of him. Had she made the wrong decision? Increasingly, it felt that way.

The new house in North London, in Hampstead, was handsome, though smaller than the one the Edmundsons had had in Banka. Though it was respectable, with heavy velvet curtains and elegant oak and walnut furniture, the rooms were dark, and either smoky and too hot from the fires in the fireplaces, or bone-achingly cold. There was a housekeeper, a middle-aged Irish woman called Molly. Sara had also hired a young girl, Kate, to be her personal maid. Sara was halfway through her pregnancy when they arrived, and needed near constant help. Kate was like a scared little mouse and Jaya feared for her at first. But, in England, Sara did not beat her servants, though she still shouted. Her frequent criticisms were more than enough to set Kate to crying in a corner downstairs, where Molly rubbed her back and told her she must be tougher or she'll never last.

Jaya found it strange to see white people as servants, though Molly assured her it was common. Molly was from a large poor farm family in the north of Ireland, and all her sisters except one worked in houses as domestics of various sorts. One of her sisters had married well, so she didn't need to work, except on the farm her husband had inherited. Molly saw from her own parents what marriage was all about and ran away to London before anyone could get any ideas. She'd been working as a maid since she was fourteen and she was now thirty-five. There was a lot of work for Molly, and Jaya sometimes helped her. In a way they'd become friends, and that helped to alleviate some of Jaya's loneliness. She tried to help Kate too, but Sara kept Kate fully occupied, so she and Molly rarely saw her.

William secured a position on the Council of India that advised the Secretary of State for India on matters pertaining to policies for the colony. His eleven years in Banka qualified him for the position. It put him in the elite ranks of London society, but it also meant he was often away.

Upon their arrival in London, the first person to visit the new house was Sara's sister, Victoria. That first day Jaya could tell Victoria was very different from her sister.

Jaya answered the knock at the door that day.

'Oh, you must be the nanny,' Victoria said, holding out her hand to Jaya. 'I heard that Sara wanted someone to help with the boys.'

'Good afternoon, madam. I'm Jaya.'

Jaya stared at Victoria. Her hazel eyes glistened from within a friendly face. She could see some similarities between the sisters. Victoria and Sara shared the same shade of brown hair and both were tall and pretty, but Victoria seemed more approachable, with a natural warmth. Victoria's voice and manner made Jaya feel shy, but she was no Sara.

'Sorry, my manners are awful. I've had one of those days. I'm Victoria, Sara's older sister.' She indicated behind her. 'Jaya, that's my husband Richard and our little girl Anna.'

'I'm very happy to meet you, sir,' Jaya said, holding out her hand.

'No sir here, Jaya. I'm just Richard. Now let us in – it's as cold as a witch's bum out here,' he said.

Once inside, all three of them looked around the house. 'Is this where my aunty lives?' the girl Anna asked, obviously impressed. She was about ten with an open face, and long dark hair plaited into two tails. 'Is she the Queen?'

Both Victoria and Richard laughed loudly.

'Sorry, Jaya,' laughed Victoria. 'Neither Anna nor Richard have met my sister. I came to England to get away from that stifling British community over there in India. Even looking at this house is making me uncomfortable. You must hate it here. I know I suffered with the weather first I came. But there is a freedom here, less separation in society. You might come to enjoy that.'

Just then, William and Sara came down the grand staircase. Sara smiled as Jaya had never seen her smile before. At the bottom, the two sisters fell into each other's arms.

'Oh, how I've missed you,' Sara cried into her sister's shoulder.

Jaya was witnessing a softer side to Sara that hadn't been evident before. She had only ever seen emotions of rage, frustration and dissatisfaction, but never tears of joy. Jaya's spirits lifted. Victoria was a beacon of hope. Perhaps now that Sara was on home territory and closer to her sister, her mood would improve.

Everyone was introduced and then Sara, exhausted already, begged Victoria to come and sit with her in her bedroom, and they disappeared up the stairs.

***

Jaya knew the boys would be awake from their nap, and went into their room to collect them so that they could meet their cousin, and aunt and uncle.

'I've heard voices. Is everything alright?' Edward asked. If he had been full of worry in India, it was double here. Like Jaya, he disliked the cold. The many carriages that raced up and down the streets frightened him. The death of Sayida had affected both boys. Jaya did her best to try and explain it to them without mentioning murder and Komali.

'Everything's fine. You have visitors. Your Aunt Victoria is here. And there is a surprise, your cousin Anna is visiting too!'

Christopher jumped from his bed enthusiastically and rushed over to Jaya. 'Is he a boy like me?'

Christopher had been told many times that Anna was a girl, but he still hoped that somehow the situation had changed.

'She's a girl. A bit older than you two, but I'm sure she will be fun.'

'Let's go then,' Christopher said, pulling back his brother's blankets and grabbing both his hand and Jaya's. 'Maybe she'll agree to play in the snow with me.'

Unlike Edward, Christopher loved the snow. The only person who indulged him was his father. Jaya also hoped Anna liked snow.

Downstairs they found Richard and William sitting by the fire in the study. Anna, obviously bored, was moving chess pieces back and forth on the board in the corner by the window.

Christopher ran to her straight away. 'Hello, Anna. I'm Christopher. Do you like snow?'

Anna smiled. 'I do, Cousin Christopher.'

'Good. Then it's fine that you're a girl.'

Edward was old enough to be embarrassed on his brother's behalf. He held out his hand like the quiet gentleman he was.

'I'm Edward. I'm happy to finally meet you, Anna. Please excuse my brother's bad manners.'

Anna laughed. 'We don't mind his manners.'

Victoria entered the room. 'Oh my, are you two not the dearest?' She grabbed up her nephews and gave them uncountable kisses. 'You must be so excited that you will soon have a baby in the house.'

Jaya looked at William. No one had explicitly told the boys about the baby and because Sara was so unwell, she hadn't gained much weight. Unless people were told, no one would have guessed that she was pregnant. William had thought it would be better to wait since Sara was so sick and a miscarriage could not be ruled out.

'Are you giving us a baby?' Christopher asked. 'Please make it a boy my age who knows how to build a snowman.'

Victoria laughed loudly. Jaya could not help but smile. She

was used to British women who laughed softly, with their hand covering their mouth. Victoria was free about all things, and Jaya liked her immediately.

William stepped in. 'We wanted to be sure that all was well before we began preparing for the baby.'

William looked at Jaya for help.

'Come, boys! Let's get dressed in our warm clothes and show Anna the garden,' Jaya said. She quickly herded the children out of the study, leaving the adults to their conversation.

***

Without question, William continued to be the bright spot in Jaya's life. In fact, now that he was back in his homeland he revealed an ease and an optimism that she had never witnessed before. His sense of humour reached new heights. He seemed to become happier each day. And Jaya, accordingly, loved him more than ever.

The first week they arrived in England, William called her to his office in the new house. They'd not had a chance to meet what with all of the moving and sorting out of things, so Jaya was excited as she walked along the hallway to the room at the end on the second floor. Even though it was late, and she was exhausted from a busy day, she was looking forward to seeing him alone. She knocked on the door, heard his voice and her heart began to beat faster, the exhaustion she felt minutes before evaporated.

'Jaya, come sit.'

William stood when she entered. He took her hand and led her to the long chaise longue near the bay window where they sat next to each other. He reached for a small, brown leather case at the side of the chair.

William kissed her cheek. 'I bought you something.'

He handed her the case. Opening it, inside she found a set of exquisitely crafted horsehair paintbrushes of various sizes, and a complete set of watercolour paints. She ran her fingers over the tubes, with their colours indicated by a spot on the outside. She'd never felt so rich in her life.

'Oh … and this.' William handed her two pads of foolscap paper, thick and of good quality.

'William, if nothing else,' Jaya started, 'if you should no longer need my services, if you fall out of love with me and we part forever, I shall never forget this kindness. Except for my brother, you are the only one in this world who has seen me as special, who has seen me as talented and my art worthy of praise. Thank you. You don't know what this means to me.'

She kept her tears of joy at bay. She stood, locked the door and went back to William. William held her closely until their bodies remembered each other again. On the chaise longue, he and Jaya would have so many nights of passion, but this particular night was like one they would never experience again. Jaya would remember it forever.

***

Victoria visited the house often, and it soon became clear that she and Sara were close when they were growing up, but a lot had happened in their lives that had caused them to grow apart.

Sara was soon confined to bed as the pregnancy was making her sick and, worryingly, mentally unsound. She often became confused about where she was, sometimes calling out for Sayida.

On most visits, after seeing her sister, Victoria would join Jaya and the boys in the nursery or, if they were sleeping, Jaya, Molly and Victoria would take tea in the kitchen.

'I feel for the young girl,' Victoria said. 'Your Kate has a handful there.'

'Don't you worry, it's good Kate got in at the deep end with our mistress. It will make her next house much easier,' Molly said, always practical.

'I hardly know my little sister anymore. You won't believe it, but when I look at Edward and Christopher and see their

temperaments, I see me and Sara. And you'll not believe
this either – Sara was just like Christopher. She was fearless,
running into all sorts of dangers without a care. I was Edward
following behind, picking up the pieces. Now, Sara is afraid of
things that are not even there. It makes me so sad.'

It sounded like a fairy story to Jaya. To think Sara had been
anything like Christopher was unimaginable. Could marriage
and children change a woman so much? What had happened
to Sara to make her so bitter and mean? So *frightened*? Had
William told Victoria that Sara took daily medication in her
tea? Jaya doubted it. Who could really know the person who
lived under the spell of laudanum? Perhaps that was where the
problem had started. Jaya tried not to think that William was
the one who had destroyed the brave courageous Sara who
had once flourished. Perhaps Victoria was remembering things
incorrectly.

***

In the middle of March, Molly and Jaya were in the scullery
folding the washing they'd just brought in from the line when
they heard shouting upstairs.

'Now what is that?' Molly said. Then they heard Kate
scream. 'We'd better go!'

Normally Jaya and Molly did not get involved in Sara's screaming tantrums, leaving Kate to deal with them, but this sounded more serious.

They rushed upstairs. Kate was standing in the hallway looking in the room, her hands over her mouth, her face white, tears streaming down her face. Was that blood on her hands?

'Look what you've done now, you stupid, stupid girl!' Sara shouted from inside the room. Kate was slowly stepping backwards, away from whatever was going on inside.

'Kate, my girl, what's the matter?' Molly said, coming up to Kate.

When she saw Molly, Kate turned to her, throwing her arms around the other woman, bursting into a flood of tears. Jaya rushed into the room, her heart pounding.

Kate was crying and mumbling into Molly's neck. 'I didn't do it. I didn't do it. It wasn't me!'

Inside, Sara was lying on the bed. The blankets were thrown back and she sat in a pool of blood. When she saw Jaya, her face, which had been looking confused, changed to rage.

'What do you want here, you black witch? Get out!'

'Memsahib, let me help you.'

Jaya stepped forward despite the insults. Sara was five months' pregnant. Jaya needed to help her. When she pulled the blanket completely back, she could see it was too late. The tiny, quiet baby lay to the side of Sara's leg. Something cold brushed against her neck. Who had moved it? It was bluish purple, but besides that it had everything a baby needed, except life. It was clear that it was dead. When Jaya looked closer, it looked as if the cord had been wrapped around the tiny neck, twice. How could that happen? The placenta was also on the bed, as if a complete delivery had taken place.

Jaya could hear Molly taking a near frantic Kate down the hallway. It was left to Jaya for now.

'Let me help you.'

Sara reached for her cup of tea and swallowed it all in one gulp. She'd been drinking her drugged tea more, not less, since arriving in England. She sat a moment and then made to stand up. Jaya reached to help her and Sara slapped her away.

'I can do it myself. You take care of that … thing,' Sara said.

She went to the bowl and pitcher on the side table. She took off the bloody nightgown and threw it on the floor near Jaya. Then she began to wash herself.

Jaya took all the bedding off and cleaned the mattress as best she could. She left the baby wrapped in the blankets. She would sort everything downstairs.

'I'll take this down … and come back with new bedding,' Jaya said.

'No. I want the mattress burnt. Bring one from the guest

room for now.' Apart from the mess, Sara seemed unconcerned about what had just happened.

As Sara returned to washing herself, Jaya carefully picked up the blankets with the tiny, perfect girl inside. As she left the room, she heard Sara humming a tuneless song.

***

Jaya carried everything to the scullery, grateful that no one was there. She set the blanket on a table and removed the tiny baby, unwrapping the cord from her fragile neck. Jaya didn't know enough about pregnancy and delivery to know if this was something that could happen, but she suspected not.

She carefully wrapped the little girl in a clean towel, as though she were a delicate piece of valuable china. She was afraid of hurting her even though she knew this perfectly formed little human could no longer feel pain. Jaya instinctively held the lifeless body close to her own, her vision blinded by tears.

'So now, what's this?' Molly said, coming in alone.

'She's dead,' sobbed Jaya.

Molly came closer.

'Oh blessed Jesus!' She moved the towel away to see the little face. 'Kate is too upset to speak properly. I gave her some of the madam's tea and she went out like a light, but I didn't know this had happened. Oh the wee bairn is gone! It's no wonder that little Kate is upset.'

'I think Sara might have murdered her. The cord was wrapped around the baby's neck.'

'Oh, that can happen, and nothing can be done about it; the cord can twist around the baby in the womb. It's not time to jump to conclusions. It's a sad day.'

'No, Molly, you don't understand. The baby was lying next to her, not between her legs, and the chord was wrapped around the baby's neck twice.' The more she thought about what she'd seen in that room, the more she believed that something wicked had taken place.

Molly sat on the high stool where she normally sat to peel potatoes. She thought for a moment and then, being a practical-minded woman she said, 'No matter, the bairn came too soon in any case. It would not have survived. Maybe it was a blessing, a mercy.'

'We must tell William.' As soon as she said it, she heard her mistake. In her heightened emotional state, overwhelmed with sadness, suspicion, and anger towards Sara, she did not consider her words before she spoke them. Jaya knew that Molly suspected something was going on between William and her, but she had never referred to the Colonel in that way before. The look of realisation on Molly's face showed that her assumption was true.

'I meant … the Colonel …' Jaya tried, but it was too late.

Molly shook her head, clearly not wanting to know what she now did.

'What good will telling him do? The baby was not going to live; it was God's will. Leave the other things. We both know those drugs she puts in her tea don't keep her right. And she doesn't buy those herself; it's your William that does that.'

Jaya exhaled loudly and responded with a small nod. 'Better to keep it to ourselves. I'll stay with the baby,' Jaya whispered. 'Sara wants Frederick to take that mattress out and burn it. She wants the one in the guest room put in her room. Maybe you can go and fetch the Colonel and give Frederick the message on the way out.'

With a blank expression, and without replying, Molly turned to leave, but then stopped and spun round to face Jaya. 'I'll only say this now, once, and never again. But I must say it, Jaya. Watch yourself. I've seen these things. They never end well. You're a young girl, and you don't want to find yourself in a foreign country all alone with a fatherless child just because you were thinking you might take the madam's place. I've seen it many a time. It will never happen.'

Despite the blunt warning, Jaya knew Molly was speaking

from a place of kindness. 'Thank you for caring, Molly. I'm not expecting anything from anybody. But I'll watch my step.'

Before she left, Molly asked Jaya to check Kate and make sure she was alright. She said she'd collect the boys from school as well.

Jaya took the wicker basket for collecting clothes from the line and laid the dead baby inside, a cloth napkin placed carefully over her tiny body. Jaya attempted to dissociate herself from the distressing scene; a life had ended before it had had a chance to begin. Her eyes were sore and tears blurred her vision, but her heart felt as if it had been ripped to shreds. She reluctantly put the baby in the pantry so that no one would accidentally stumble across her while she was absent. Then she left the scullery to check on Kate.

Jaya opened the door to Kate's room, and she looked up, her face still pale with shock, and her eyes red and swollen. 'Oh, you're awake,' Jaya said softly. 'I thought perhaps you'd still be resting after such an ordeal.'

'Yes.' She spoke slowly with a slight slur, the drug still affecting her.

Jaya sat on the side of the bed and took the young girl's hand. She was only fifteen and had just witnessed a horror that no young person of her age should ever have to see.

'Maybe when the Colonel comes, he'll agree that you should

take a few days off, Kate. Should I ask him for you?'

'I won't go back up there.'

'You'll have to at some point. I'm sure in a few days you'll feel better. You've had a terrible shock.'

'No. I'll never be able to go up there. I saw her do it,' Kate said, as her tears fell and a look of shock covered her face.

'Saw her do what?' Jaya was alarmed and afraid of what Kate would say.

'That baby was alive. She was mewing like a cat. The madam took her out from between her legs and wrapped that cord around and around the tiny neck. I tried to stop her and she bit me.' Kate held out her hand. There it was – bite marks straight through the skin. 'Satan was in that room, *inside her*. I'll be gone as soon as the master arrives. I'll not sleep another night here.'

***

Later that day William arrived home and called the doctor. He arrived quickly and examined Sara. After a long, private conversation with the Colonel, he took the baby away. William decided no funeral was required; it was best just to forget all about it. That night Molly and Jaya walked Kate to the carriage that would take her back to her family's farm in Yorkshire. She'd not try another house, she told Molly. This work was not for her.

Jaya swallowed what she knew. Molly was right in that it would only cause harm. William carried on as if he had not just lost a little daughter, and Jaya thought maybe that was how he convinced himself that it had never happened. But still, she found it odd, almost inhuman. In the coming days, Jaya and Molly were more careful around Sara.

No one thought it appropriate to tell Christopher and Edward what had happened. Not only did they deem it inappropria¬te, but thought it might be too traumatising for them to process. However, the boys soon noticed that people stopped talking about the forthcoming baby. They were too afraid to ask about it. On the few visits to their mother's room, they couldn't understand why their mother was always crying. They had also heard her shouting, but never asked any questions that might result in them being scolded. Eventually, they realised that there would be no baby.

Jaya kept the boys away from Sara as much as she could. Her job was to protect her charges, even from their mother if necessary.

After the death of the little girl, everything began to unravel for Sara and, in many ways, for Jaya too.

CHAPTER 16

Life went on. Molly organised a woman she knew, Clara, to take over for Kate. She was near Molly's age, and they all hoped she would be able to manage the increasingly unhinged Sara better than a young girl might.

Jaya's days were filled with Edward and Christopher. She got them ready for school in the morning, made sure they ate breakfast and then walked them through the neighbourhood to their day school, Belsize School, a boys' school where they quickly made friends. Sometimes after dropping them at school, Jaya would wander through the neighbourhood looking at the houses and learn her way around. The people in England, she found, seemed to keep to themselves. She wondered if they were lonely. In Khesar, and even in Banka, people greeted her, some stopped to ask her about her family, about her health. It was sometimes annoying that everyone seemed to be involved in her life, and had opinions about it. But here people did not want to know anything about each other, and somehow that seemed worse to her.

After dropping the boys at school, if the weather was not too cold or too rainy, she would walk to a park not far from Belsize and take out her sketching materials, spending time drawing and painting until it was time to collect the boys and walk them home.

Jaya found it difficult to adjust to her new home, but as spring took over from winter, and the situation with Sara seemed to calm down, things improved and she thought maybe she could find a way to be happy here. It would simply take time.

***

When William returned home from work early one day, it was clear he was in a good mood. Smiling broadly, he breezed into the nursery to find Jaya sitting with Christopher and Edward, reading them a story. He scooped both of them into his arms and asked them whether they wanted to play outside before the last rays of sunlight disappeared.

'Yes, Father,' Edward replied. Then, looking at Jaya he said, 'Is it fine that we go, Jaya?'

Jaya smiled to see her lessons in good manners were finally bearing fruit.

'Yes, go. We'll finish the story at bedtime.'

As he followed his sons, William brushed his hand down Jaya's upper arm and said, 'Thank you.'

They ran out and Jaya sat at the window watching William with his sons. They had the cricket bat out and he was tossing the ball to them, each boy taking a turn at the bat. It was nice to see William in such a buoyant mood. The reason became clear at dinner.

'I've purchased us a new house,' he announced with excitement. 'It's bigger, with an exceptionally large garden where the boys will have lots of room to play. There is a stable nearby, I want the boys to learn to ride,' he told Sara and the boys.

'Father, can I have a white horse?' Christopher asked. He'd become enamoured with the knights in the stories Jaya read them, and he knew that knights rode white horses.

'Yes, I'll make sure you have a white horse,' William said, smiling at his younger son.

As Jaya stood waiting for the boys to finish their dinners, she could see the storm brewing on Sara's face.

Spittle forming at the corners of her mouth, she jabbed her finger at William and spat, 'Moving us around again? Like a piece of furniture, are we? You could not even take a moment to consult your wife? What was so urgent? We only just settled into this house,' she said. 'Have I not suffered enough, William?' The muscles in Sara's jaw twitched as she gritted her teeth, and the skin on her chest became red and blotchy.

Most people would think a wife would be happy to be moved to a larger house, but those who knew Sara would understand she was not like other wives. Jaya had some sympathy for Sara's position. William saw nothing wrong in what he'd done. If he wanted to do something, he did it, and saw no reason to consult his wife.

Jaya remembered when she first began to work in the Edmundson household. William had taken one of Sara's most prized possessions and sold it without her knowledge or consent. It was a necklace – a family heirloom; a gold chain with a large emerald pendant surrounded by tiny diamonds. Her father had left it to Sara in his will. Jaya had been shocked by the callousness of this act.

Sayida had told Jaya that Sara's parents had not been warm and loving. Her father was a cold harsh man, even feared by his subordinates at the colonial administration where he'd worked. Her mother spent her days at tea parties with other English wives and, on the rare occasion that she was home, showed no interest in the little girls. Victoria seemed largely unaffected by the lack of love, but Sara suffered greatly.

Perhaps because they were girls, their parents didn't value them. That was what Sayida had thought. Both of them were ignored and even deprived, despite the fact that the family was well-off. So, when her father died and left Sara the necklace, she viewed it as the love she'd been lacking. The loss of the necklace, and the reason behind it, caused a deep wound inside of her.

Jaya learned later that William required an impressive new suit for dinner with the viceroy, and there was no spare money to purchase one. There was, however, the old-fashioned necklace Sara never wore, kept in a box in the bureau. William's view was that they were married, and what was his wife's, was his. This was a tacit understanding between husband and wife. The necklace was sold to the local jeweller. William got more than enough for his new suit, and purchased a silver ring for Sara as well, something more suitable that she could wear and look at every day.

The same thing was happening again. He would move his family where he wanted, without asking her opinion. He was her husband and, in his eyes, she was only slightly above Edward and Christopher. It would seem preposterous to consult his sons about a new house, just as there was no need to consult Sara. He was the master of this family, and he knew what was best.

Jaya's head pounded. Was she any different than Sara? Were they not both William's property to do with as he liked? Indeed, they both depended on him. These traits in William were making Jaya cautious. He could be so kind, and then so callous and cruel. She found herself even questioning whether he could be trusted. Because of that, she held back from giving him all of herself.

And too, his seemingly callous regard of Sara was not something she could ignore. She knew her relationship with William, albeit secretive, only added to Sara's burden. There were times when she was sure she hated Sara, but she also had empathy for her situation and her emotional state. Even though Sara had been unkind to her, Jaya did not want to add to her troubles.

'You're horrible,' Sara said, as she picked up a glass. 'I am little more than this glass of water to you; an object to move about, a possession to use, and then forget until it is required again.'

'Now, Sara, calm down,' William said. 'And you know that's *not* true ...'

He did not finish his words because she threw the glass and it crashed on the wall behind his head. Sara laughed at first when William dodged the glass and it shattered into pieces. The boys froze on their chairs and became silent. They looked at Jaya. Christopher held out his hand to her and she took it. Edward raced over to her side.

William continued as if the glass had never been thrown.

'The fact that we can move,' he continued, 'is a measure of my increasing success. It is cause to celebrate.'

Sara, however, was not interested in a celebration. She stayed only a few minutes longer, silently glaring at William across the table, and then called for Clara to bring some of her special tea to her bedroom. She had a headache and wanted to retire for the night.

Sara had not even looked in the direction of her sons. She'd lost interest in the scant mothering skills she'd had back in India. They died with that baby. In a way, Jaya could not blame her. She would not let the boys blame themselves either. If Sara was like this because of her unfeeling parents, did she want the same for her boys because of her own inability to love them? No, Jaya would protect them from that.

She took their hands and bent down to them. 'Don't worry. Everything will be fine. Your mother has a headache is all. Let's go up to your room and finish that book.'

They both smiled up at her hesitantly.

As they passed William, he let his hand pass lightly across her thigh.

'When you're finished, Jaya, could I see you in my study? I want to discuss the move,' William said.

Jaya was angry with herself for the surge of excitement that spiked in her body.

***

In the study, Jaya found William waiting for her. He pushed the door closed and took her in his arms.

'The new house has a wonderful study located in the farthest wing. No one will hear us,' William said, nibbling at her neck.

Jaya pushed away from him. 'Those outbursts between you and Sara are not good for the boys to witness.'

William went to refresh his drink. 'I know, Sara is becoming more and more unstable.'

'But you provoke her,' Jaya said candidly.

When William turned, Jaya could see he did not like her going against him.

'Let's not speak of such things. I will try harder to keep Sara and her moods away from the boys. You are right. I can see they are moving away from her. It's not good. No matter what, she is their mother.'

He went to Jaya and she weakened against him.

'I wanted to celebrate my promotion and the new house, with

you, the woman I love,' William said into her neck.

Despite herself, that declaration made her happy. He'd sought her out, and wanted the celebration to be for both of them. He loved her.

William, in his enthusiasm, had neglected to lock the door. It was only when the door flew open that he realised his error. But by then it was too late. The consequences of his carelessness came crashing down.

Sara stood before them. Her jaw gaping. Her eyes wide and glossed. Jaya's heart hammered against her chest as she hurried to recover herself. Her hands shook as she brushed at her hair and clothes. She felt exposed and weighted all at the same time. It was dizzying. William stared at Sara, who stood motionless in the doorway, before something seemed to snap within him.

'Sara!' he gasped, holding out his hands.

Sara stood in her nightgown saying nothing, which was much against her character. Jaya wished that Sara would scream or shout in her normal way. The silence was worse. Anything – *anything* – would have been better than the sight of Sara standing there in the doorway, pointing a finger and moving her lips without forming a sound. Clearly, whatever words she needed were eluding her as a result of the trauma of what she'd just seen.

Jaya could not believe what happened next.

William went to Sara and held her, and then spoke to her in a quiet soothing voice, 'You're having a nightmare, my darling!' And with that he turned her away from the room.

Sara shook her head, saying in a knowing voice, 'No! No! I know what I saw. This is no nightmare.' Jaya's stomach churned. She wanted more than anything to look away and yet she found that she could not.

'It is ...' How skilful William was at maintaining a calm demeanour in the middle of such bold lies. 'Sweetheart, you must go back to sleep. Let me help you up to bed.'

Jaya stood there, wide-eyed, wishing she could disappear, and wondering whether Sara would fall for the deception. Or would she accept it, as many wives did, choosing to ignore their husbands' affairs and act as if nothing had happened?

William, purple-faced and his muscles straining, lifted Sara off the floor as she fought against him, and carried her back to her bedroom. Jaya felt sick at heart as she heard Sara's piercing screams and the violent thumping of her fists against her husband's chest.

Jaya closed the study door, placed her hands over her ears and shut her eyes. *What now?* Her legs were trembling and she felt dizzy. Images of what could ensue flashed through her mind. She wanted to flee – to hide – but instead was rooted to the spot. *Why had she not heeded Molly's warning?*

If Sara did not believe that what she saw was a nightmare – an unlikely proposition – then the only way Jaya could remain in the house would be if Sara chose to ignore what she had witnessed. And that was even more unlikely. The only solution to this situation would be for Jaya to leave. Would William pay for her to return to India? Or would she have to find alternative employment in England?

None of the choices were ideal. She would have to wait and see what would happen. She sat down on the chaise longue, wrapped her arms around herself, and rocked to and fro.

CHAPTER 17

As she waited for William to return, she heard the click-click of Clara's quick steps in the hallway. Later, heavier steps indicated that Molly was passing by. She hoped they weren't required to help in Sara's room. Perhaps they were just investigating what the noise was all about. Their rooms were on the ground floor, and Sara's screams could easily have been heard down there.

Then the house was silent again and still William did not return.

It seemed an eternity before William returned to the study. Then, finally, she heard the doorknob turn, and he was there. She waited to see his reaction. He appeared composed, but serious, and she found it difficult to read his expression. He moved quickly towards her and held her tightly. Jaya could feel his heart pounding.

She pulled her head away from his chest and looked up into his eyes, waiting for an update on Sara, or an explanation, a reassurance, or a solution to their dilemma. Although he seemed outwardly calm, Jaya was shaking.

'It was awful. I'm sorry, Jaya. Let's go outside. I can't be in here,' he said. 'I need air.'

It was a cool spring night and, when they were outside, Jaya felt the weight of the house lift from her shoulders, and the fresh air clear her confused mind.

William held her close and they walked to the back of the garden where a clump of young willows hid a small stone bench. They sat down and he clung to her as if letting her go would set them both adrift.

'How did you get her to sleep?' Jaya asked.

'I gave her some of her tea,' he replied. 'She went to sleep quickly after that.'

'What shall we do?'

He looked away from her. His eyes, such beautiful eyes, soaked up the crisp light of the moon, and even now he was so handsome her breath caught in her throat.

He said, 'I've given it some thought. I think the only choice is to send her away. She's been unwell for a while. The loss of the baby sent her over the edge. I've known it, but I've tried to ignore it. She needs help, and you and I need each other.'

He'd been forced to choose between his wife and his lover, and he chose her. Jaya was happy, of course, but Sara's situation stopped her from letting the joy take over.

Jaya smiled as she moved closer to William. She asked, 'Are you sure about this?'

'Entirely.'

'When? When will you take her to the hospital?' Jaya asked. Hospital was a kinder word than the real one – asylum.

'Now. As soon as possible,' William said.

'Now? In the night?'

'No. In the morning after she's had some rest. I will send a message to work to say that I'm not coming in. As soon as the light arrives, I shall summon the doctor. He'll sign the paperwork to have her committed. He wanted me to do it after she lost the baby. He'll be relieved that I've finally made the decision.'

'You must contact Victoria. She needs to be here too. She will help Sara.'

William thought about it. 'Yes, yes, you're right. I will make sure Victoria is here when the doctor arrives.'

***

In the morning, Jaya took the boys to school as usual and

returned home directly. She got to the house just as Victoria was arriving.

'Oh Jaya, I'm so glad to see you first,' she said, taking Jaya in her arms. 'What has happened to cause this? My poor Sara.'

'You know she has not been well for a long time. Losing the baby was very difficult for her,' Jaya said.

'Yes. But an asylum?' The distress and fear on Victoria's face were evident as she added, 'Jaya, you must know how horrible those places are.'

'You must speak to William. He says the doctor thinks it is the right thing to do. Maybe it will only be for a short while.' Jaya could hear her own culpability building. She took Victoria's arm to lead her into the house.

Inside, William was waiting, his face sombre and drawn. He hugged his sister-in-law. 'Victoria, I'm so happy you are here before the doctor arrives. I fear Sara is completely lost to us.'

Victoria began to weep silently, tears pouring down her face. 'May I see her?'

'Of course. Jaya, go with Victoria, please,' William said.

Upstairs, Sara laid facing away from the door. When they went in she turned, hearing Victoria's voice. Then spotting Jaya she shook her head violently, clearly distressed.

'I'll not have that black whore in my room! Take her out! Take her out!'

Victoria turned to Jaya, her face pained by her sister's words. 'Jaya, it is the drugs talking. We both know that. Please, I am sorry for the things she says.'

'I'll wait outside.' She patted Victoria's hand. 'Do not be concerned. I know that she is not in her right mind. I do not take it to heart.'

***

An hour later the doctor arrived with two assistants to help him. Sara screamed and fought them. Jaya was astonished by the sheer, brute strength that Sara possessed as the men attempted to carry her from the room. But they were prepared. The doctor gave her an injection as the men held her down, and then she collapsed like a doll. Jaya should have felt relief that Sara would be gone – that the brutality would end, and that there would be no barrier to her relationship with William. Instead, she felt wretched. The guilt crushed her, knowing she was partly responsible for Sara being committed to a place she didn't belong.

***

William walked to the carriage with the doctor, and they

stood on the gravel drive together in conversation. Jaya could not hear everything, but she knew the doctor was talking about her.

'We'll ensure she has a comfortable home,' the doctor said. Then he leaned towards William and said, 'But if I were you, I'd have a new white woman around quickly. You do not want people getting the wrong idea. Such things have been known to cost a man a good position.'

Once the carriage drove away, William came inside and found Victoria and Jaya waiting for him.

In obvious pain and confusion, Victoria declared, 'I don't even know her anymore, I really don't. You know, she was telling me about seeing both of you in the study, in a … compromised way … and she claimed that was why she was being taken away. I tried to tell her it was just the drugs, and that neither of you would ever do such a thing. She would not listen. I only hope that they can help her at that place.'

'Do not worry on that account, Victoria. Everything that can be done, will be done. The doctor assured me that she is going to a very good hospital. She will be back soon, and back to the Sara we all know and love,' William said, doing his best to ease his sister-in-law's pain.

Watching the deception she was part of was terrible for Jaya. She left Victoria and William to continue their conversation and went to sit by the pond in the park, and think about all she had heard. She still had an hour before it was time to collect the boys, and she needed to settle her confused thoughts. The doctor's words came back to her. Would William quickly replace Sara with another white woman? William had said that they could now be free, and implied that they would be together. But no matter what he said, Jaya knew William would not stand up for her against the pressures of society. She wanted to think otherwise, but in many ways William was a weak man. In her heart of hearts, she knew their life in the study would never leave those four walls, even with Sara gone. She looked out at the ducks on the pond, skimming along as if by magic. Molly had warned her. She would not be taking Sara's place, now or ever. But despite everything her rational mind told her, Jaya tried to think otherwise.

CHAPTER 18

Her name was Rebecca. Red hair. Green eyes. White porcelain skin. She looked like a princess out of the children's storybooks. Jaya loathed her from the moment William brought her to the house in Hampstead, only a month after Sara had been taken to the asylum. First she came for short daytime visits, then dinner. Jaya knew the next step was not far away – a quick divorce from Sara, and a new wife at William's side.

'Rebecca,' said William, that first day she came to the house for a visit, 'this is Jaya. Jaya, this is Rebecca.'

Jaya reached down deep and managed to wrench up a small smile. 'A pleasure to meet you,' she said. Rebecca nodded and said nothing. To her, Jaya was a servant, one among the others, nothing more.

The boys hid behind Jaya.

'Are those your boys, William?' Rebecca asked.

'Yes. They're being shy. Edward, Christopher, come and meet Rebecca,' William ordered.

Jaya moved to the side and pushed the boys forward. They held her hands tightly.

'Oh, they are adorable!' Rebecca said, smiling in a way that felt perfunctory. Jaya could see that Rebecca was not the mothering type.

'Where is Mother?' Edward asked.

'We've spoken about this, Edward,' William said, embarrassed.

The day after Sara was taken away, William sat the boys down to explain that their mother was sick and had to go to a special hospital. He'd told them they might visit her one day, but after his first visit he told Jaya it could never happen. The place was not something children should ever see.

'Why is this lady here? You said Mother was coming home soon.' Edward was now old enough to partially understand what was going on, and had begun to ask specific questions.

Rebecca reached in her purse and pulled out two small bags of toffee. She held one out to Christopher who snatched it up greedily. When she held the other one out to Edward, he ignored it.

'Do you not like toffee, Edward?' Rebecca said, annoyance

creeping into her voice. 'I bought it especially for you.'

'No. I like toffee. I just do not like you.'

He turned and ran up the stairs. Christopher was confused for a moment. Then he gripped his bag of toffee and ran after his brother. Jaya made no apologies for either one of her charges. They'd both taken a stand. Edward would not accept Rebecca as a replacement mother; Christopher would take what Rebecca offered, but would live by his own rules.

***

For a month, Jaya and William had spent long nights together, no longer on the chaise in the study but between the luxurious sheets on the bed he'd shared with Sara. There William had whispered his desires and made promises that were forgotten with the arrival of Rebecca.

After that first visit from Rebecca, Jaya did not go to William's bedroom that night, and instead headed to her room on the ground floor. She had pride, and would not be, yet again, second in William's eyes. She was just falling asleep when there was a soft knock at the door. She got up and opened it and, as expected, there was William.

'I've been waiting for you,' he whispered. 'Come now, it's late.'

'No, I'll sleep here.' Jaya turned to close the door on him, but he grabbed it before it shut.

'Why? Jaya, don't be silly. Come now.'

She feared Molly who had the room next to hers might hear, so she followed William upstairs to his room. She planned to explain her feelings, and then return to her room.

He closed the door and took Jaya in his arms. She broke free and stepped away from him.

'William, I'm not sure what you think I am,' she said.

'I don't understand. What have I done to upset you?'

'The fact that you don't understand is already a problem. William, who is Rebecca to you? What plans do you have for her?'

William laughed. 'Are you angry about her? Oh, Jaya, you're very silly. Come now, let's get in the bed. I missed you today.'

'You intend to make her your wife.'

William sat down on the bed, but Jaya remained standing by the door. The next words were spoken sombrely.

'Jaya, already there have been rumours, rumours about Sara, my insane wife. And there have been rumours about me living in this house with the beautiful nanny I brought from India. You don't know this country, or the people I work with. These rumours can be enough to have me removed from the Council, even ostracised. Rebecca is nothing to me. She is a cover, nothing more. I've started the paperwork to divorce Sara and, yes, I'll need to marry Rebecca. It's a good move for my career because she is a niece of Lord Darlington, one of the senior members on the Council. But none of that affects us. I love you, *only you*. You know this.'

Jaya breathed slowly. She would not let him see her tears. To him there was nothing cruel in what he was saying. It was about practicalities, about protecting himself and his position. As always, William only viewed the world through his own eyes. Jaya, like the furniture, could be moved – or replaced – whenever or however he liked.

'William, I'm not feeling well tonight. Let me sleep in my room,' Jaya said.

He stood and took her into his arms. 'But you've understood what I've said, I know it. You're a practical, intelligent girl. Rebecca will not trouble us at all.'

Jaya said nothing. When he released her, he gave her a goodnight kiss and she returned to her room.

***

A few days later, William and Jaya had just put the boys to bed, a new habit he'd begun following Sara's departure. In part, it stemmed from his guilt over the absence of their mother, but also because he liked to give Jaya a hand. She liked the new arrangement because she liked watching William with his sons. He was a loving and playful father, and that was endearing. The boys were still fragile with their mother gone, and they enjoyed their father taking a more active role in their lives.

They were in the living room and he'd been setting out logs to build a fire.

'I must leave, I cannot stay here anymore.' Jaya surprised herself when she said aloud the thing she'd been repeating in her head for weeks, since that first time Rebecca visited the house. When Jaya spoke those words, William stood and brushed a smudge of soot from his trouser legs.

'I'm officially divorced from Sara now,' he said, his tone not unlike that of a wounded little boy. 'Why would you leave?'

'You'll be free to marry Rebecca now. That is your life, not mine.'

'Rebecca?' he said. He sat down next to Jaya on the sofa and took her hand in his. 'I've told you, my dear, Rebecca is for show. You know that. I can hardly bear her presence.'

Jaya looked at him. She did not believe him. She'd had a front-row seat to their little 'show,' and it was clear there was more to it than pretence.

'Please, Jaya, don't speak of silly things. We have so little time together; let's not waste it being unpleasant. None of that concerns us.' He leaned forward and kissed her.

Jaya, in many ways, had no defence against William; she loved him. Until she could harden her heart to him – and she wondered if that would ever happen – she was at his mercy.

***

In the end, William never moved the family to the new house. Jaya advised him that the trauma of Sara leaving was already too much for Edward and Christopher to deal with. It was better to stay where they were, in a house that they knew, and be able to remain at their school and with the friends they were familiar with. William agreed, though Jaya suspected it had more to do with the added cost of the asylum, the divorce and the many needs of Rebecca and her busy social schedule.

Summers in Hampstead were a welcome change, and almost made winter tolerable. The air was filled with the scent of lilacs, the birds filled the air with song and finally the sun stayed up and warmed the world, the sun Jaya had been aching for. In this season, could anyone be unhappy, she wondered. And yet, with each passing day, her life seemed be leaking its colour.

The warmth and the sun made her long for home. She'd not received any letters from Krishnan even though she'd sent him so many letters herself. How long would he punish her? She wondered if she left William, would she return to India? Could she? And to do what? To live where? Would her mother even have her back?

Though she still loved William, her situation was becoming untenable and she knew she needed to leave the house. Guilt flooded over her when she thought of leaving Edward and Christopher, even though they would still have Molly and Clara who both loved them as Jaya did. She knew the boys would be devastated if she left them. But what could she do?

Despite William's assurances otherwise, he and Rebecca spent more time together. There were parties to attend, and picnics with the boys, who were slowly warming to her, if only because their father insisted they should.

William's protests that he could not bear to spend time with her were false. They laughed together at dinner, and held hands on their way out the door. Actions spoke louder than words.

Slowly, she and William began spending less and less time together. She often told him she was tired, or he was often working late or out with Rebecca.

When they did spend time together, they found themselves arguing a great deal, which was something they had not experienced before. Their arguments often centred on the topic of India's independence. William's intransigence on the issue showed Jaya, once again, that William was a selfish man. He wanted only what would benefit him, and he would never take a moment to walk in another person's shoes, or acknowledge that other people had differing wants and needs. Some of their fights were more cutting than others.

'Have you ever thought about converting to Christianity?' William asked Jaya one night, after the boys had gone to bed.

'Why would I?'

'You're in England now.'

Jaya found William's statement patronising. She shot him a venomous glance. 'I'm aware of that. I'm also aware of the many things your country has taken from mine, and I will not have my religion snatched away as well.'

William pulled his shoulders back and folded his arms. 'Please don't act as if we're the villains. Your people have benefited from the British. Education has improved tremendously since we got there.'

Even the term 'your people' irritated Jaya. With eyes of fire, and without pausing to consider her words, she sputtered, 'Great Britain has no care for the education of India's people. I can assure you of that. All they're after are profits.' She was sick of holding her tongue on these topics. William needed to take some responsibility for what his people had done, and continued to do, in her country. He should not plead ignorance.

'Profits?' William scoffed. 'That's the least of our concerns.

We're working to civilise an entire culture of people.'

'Civilise? It sounds as if you think we're animals. Is that how you look at me?' Jaya formed her hand into a claw and curled her lip into a snarl.

'No. Not at all. Why would you say that?' He laughed it off as if she were speaking nonsense. 'Although you are starting to sound rather mad with these odd ideas of yours.'

Inwardly Jaya was furious. She could not hear the word 'mad' without thinking of Sara. Is this what William did? Dismiss opinions and desires that were not his own and then silence them with drugs, using insanity as an excuse?

Nevertheless, such comments from William were useful. Slowly, incrementally, they cut away her connection to him. Soon would come the insensitive comment, the cruel act, the final straw that would set her free from him once and for all. In many ways she welcomed it.

Her thoughts of leaving were nearly constant. She had no plan though. What was a woman in her position to do? Her wages were hardly enough to create meaningful savings, as her basic needs absorbed almost every farthing of her earnings. Of course, she had the option of stealing, but that would land her in legal trouble, and once ensnared in the British system she'd have no hope of ever escaping.

So, the days wore on as she schemed and planned her escape.

CHAPTER 19

Jaya was nearly out the door so many times, but each time she stopped when she thought of the boys. Edward and Christopher were changing and growing up. Despite their initial reluctance to let Rebecca into their lives, they'd slowly come to accept her. Jaya tried her best to not get in the way of that, but it was difficult. A family was forming, a family that did not include her.

The boys were also adopting views that Jaya found objectionable. Perhaps the rich children they went to school with were changing their view on things. Some of their comments and observations seemed more like their mother's view on the world. Jaya tried to help them to see the world in a more charitable way, but she wondered if she was working against the tide.

One beautiful sunny Saturday, Jaya took the boys to the park. She sat with her sketchpad, basking in the warmth of the sun, as the boys tossed a ball back and forth.

'It's a lovely day, isn't it, boys?' she asked them.

Christopher said, 'Aren't you worried about the sun, Jaya?'

'Worried? Why?' she asked.

'Yes,' he answered. 'It will make your skin darker.'

Perhaps he'd asked out of innocent curiosity, but more likely he was repeating something he'd heard his mother say. Jaya could not pretend his words did not hurt.

'What's wrong with having darker skin?' she asked.

He hesitated for a moment, devoting some careful thought to his reply. 'Because isn't being dark a shameful thing?' he said. 'That's what the boys at school say. They make fun of dark people. I don't like dark people either.'

Before she could think, Jaya smacked his bottom. 'You should not say such things!'

Christopher looked at Jaya with hurt in his eyes. He'd never been smacked by Jaya. His lip quivered and he began to cry.

Jaya took his hand and kissed it. 'I'm sorry, Christopher. Your words were hurtful to me. I shouldn't have hit you. But you shouldn't say such things.'

Edward stood by. 'Stop crying, Christopher. All people's skin is created by God, and God would never give anyone bad skin.

You should ignore those boys at school. Jaya is beautiful, even Father knows that. I heard him say it.'

Christopher continued to cry. Jaya collected her pen and sketchpad. The day was ruined.

'Let's go home.'

***

Later, at dinner, when William asked the boys about their day, Christopher said, 'Jaya hit me.'

William looked in her direction. 'Is that true, Jaya?'

She thought it unfair of William to have this conversation in front of the boys and Rebecca, or to speak to her in that way.

Rebecca look surprised and asked, 'William, is your little boy a liar?'

William wiped his mouth with his napkin. Placing it on the table, he said, 'No, of course not. You know perfectly well that Christopher doesn't lie. Nor does Edward.'

'I'm sorry, dear, if I spoke out of turn,' Rebecca replied, smiling at her husband and her stepsons.

Jaya sighed, and then shrugged. She hadn't a particle of energy to discuss this.

'So?' he asked, directing his question to Jaya.

'So what?' she snapped back.

'Are you saying it's true?'

'Of course, it's true. He was rude and disrespectful.'

'Jaya,' he said, taking on a strict tone she hadn't heard since her early months of employment in the Edmundson household, 'we agreed at the outset that spanking was strictly prohibited.'

'Dismiss me if I have disobeyed your order, Colonel,' she said, her anger getting the best of her.

William did not reply, and Jaya left the dining room.

***

That night, she let William put the boys to bed himself. She went to her room hoping that he would leave her alone. Her mood was dark, and she was sure holding her tongue would not be an option. Was she to be disrespected by his son and disrespected by him as well? This was not the life she was meant to have. She knew she had made the wrong decisions in the past and, more than anything, she wished she could go back in time and choose differently and more wisely.

Molly tapped on her door after dinner was over. 'It's me. Are you alright? You left the dining room early tonight.'

Jaya remained on her bed and spoke through the closed door. 'I'm fine. Just a slight headache. I want to sleep.'

'Let me know if I can bring you anything, dear. Get a good

rest and I'll see you in the morning.'

Jaya liked Molly, but she kept her distance because of William. Molly was kind hearted, and perhaps she could help Jaya find another position in another house, but she wasn't sure she even wanted that. Also, she didn't want Molly's disapproval, which, no matter how much she tried to hide it, was always there. Jaya was hard enough on herself.

There was silence until a familiar knock at her door disturbed her thoughts. As she suspected, William had come to her door.

'What is wrong with you?' he asked her, clearly annoyed.

'Nothing,' she said. 'I'm just ... tired. Tired of all of this.'

Her deep, early love for William had blinded her to his true nature. Now she could see who he really was. He was a self-centred man, which made him unkind – to her, to Sara, to anyone who wanted to be considered an equal. Had he really sent Sara away to gain more intimate times with her? Or had he masterminded everything in order to create a pathway to Rebecca? Jaya would never know the truth. She certainly could not seek the truth from him. She suspected he did not understand his motivations for many things; the selfish find it hardest to know themselves.

Jaya, too, had cheated, but she had not been the one to betray her own spouse. This didn't make her morally superior to William, but none of it mattered anymore. She didn't care about being his equal. All she wanted was to be away from him; not only physically, but mentally and spiritually. She was finished.

'I will leave tomorrow,' she said, dispassionately. 'I ask only permission to stay the night.'

'You're hurting me,' William replied, in a tone that sounded more like that of a child.

Jaya continued, 'In the morning, I will take your children to school. Then I will return here for my things. And after that, I will leave.'

'And go where, Jaya?' William's voice began to shake, which was out of character.

He was suffering, but Jaya didn't know whether it was because he genuinely feared losing her, or whether he just didn't like it when a situation did not fall in his favour. He was, after all, a person used to control.

'Where I go is none of your concern.'

'It is, Jaya.' He touched her forearm and widened his blue eyes, giving her a forlorn look. 'I love you, and I thought you loved me.' William suddenly appeared vulnerable and, for the first time since she had known him, Jaya felt as if she held the power.

'I did love you, William, desperately. But not anymore,' Jaya said. He needed to hear the truth.

'Why? What changed?' he asked, appearing legitimately confused.

'You promised me a life that you never had any intention of giving me. I am yours on your terms only. My needs and concerns are irrelevant. In your eyes I am not a full person, deserving of a full and legitimate life. I am someone for back alleys and secrets.' Jaya spoke what was in her heart. If she didn't speak the truth now, when would she?

'Jaya, you know how people are. I could never marry you. You know that. It would be the end of my career.'

'I know nothing of the sort. Many British men marry Indian women in India. I thought the thing stopping you was your marriage to Sara. That is exactly what you told me. I left my home ... I lost my brother because of you! I left a kind man who wanted to marry me ... because of you! You made promises to me that you had no intention of keeping. I will no longer be a woman kept in the wardrobe and brought out only when you want to play. I want a complete life. I deserve one as much as any other person. I will not take the crumbs you offer. I am more than you think I am. I've always been more. I deserve a life of my own, not just a life prescribed by you, and your needs. I have needs too. I have desires and wishes, just like you.'

'I know that, Jaya. I do, truly. I want to help you in any way I can. That's why I purchased the paints and paper for you. You have talent I want you to nurture.' He looked at her and she could see he was hurt, near tears, but she would not waver from her decision. She'd given him everything, and now he wanted to act as if he had done the same for her. He'd done nothing. He'd given up nothing, sacrificed nothing. She'd given up everything.

Why she had been so stupid? Krishnan was right. William saw her as nothing more than a common prostitute. She had deluded herself.

'Please, Jaya, don't leave me. I don't know what I'll do if you leave me,' William begged.

'I'm leaving tomorrow. Of course, you are in a position to stop me; you have such power over me. I would be a fool to think otherwise. I'm your property for all intents and purposes. Only you can decide if that is the way you want to treat me.'

'No, Jaya, no … you know I would never treat you in such a manner. I only want you to be happy. I would never keep you here against your will.'

'Then goodnight and goodbye, William.' Jaya closed the door. She listened until she finally heard his footsteps as he walked away.

CHAPTER 20

Jaya didn't see William again before leaving. She carried out her plan just as promised. She made the boys breakfast and walked them to school. She suppressed tears as she turned away after Christopher waved one last time before running through the gate.

Edward hesitated. 'Are you alright, Jaya?'

'Yes … yes, I'm fine.'

He looked at her. 'Will you go draw in the park today?'

'No. I have something … to do.'

'I'll see you after school.'

She nodded silently, fearing the flood of emotion she felt would burst. She had so many things she wanted to tell Edward; play more and worry less. Do not carry his brother's burdens – Christopher was strong enough now to carry his own. She wanted to tell him to grow up, be good, find love and love in return, become the kind, caring man she knew he would be.

Instead, she watched him turn and walk away.

At the house, she avoided Molly and snuck into her room. Molly would try to convince Jaya to rethink her actions. She knew about life in London with no money, and she'd have advised Jaya to wait until she found a place to live and work. But Jaya could not wait another day.

As she was packing her belongings, Jaya picked up the iron kitten that Laksha had given her. She thought of her words to Laksha, 'I'll think only of you when I hold it in my hand.' That was true. The kitten wasn't just a memory of Laksha; it embodied everything that had happened since that time. She carefully wrapped the kitten in one of her dresses and placed it in the middle of her bag.

She'd saved a bit of money, but added to her resources by taking four place settings of silver. It was theft, though Jaya saw it as her due. She'd lost everything by coming to England with William. He owed her that much at least, likely much more, but she would not beg for money. She knew she deserved more, but she would settle for this. Perhaps Sayida's stubborn spirit was guiding her. She knew her dear friend would have approved.

She closed her door carefully and slipped out of the house. She was gone before anyone could talk her out of it.

***

When speaking to William about leaving she'd acted as if she had nowhere to go but, in fact, she had done her research. On the ship, she'd learned about The Ayahs' Home. A few of the ayahs on the ship had gone there, some a few times. They arrived in England with their British family thinking that it was only a two or three month home visit and then, for various reasons, their families decided to stay. The family, no longer needing their ayah, would turn her over to The Ayahs' Home. The ayah would wait there until a family, hired to the colonial service and requiring an ayah, was set to leave for India. The family would come to the home to recruit an ayah for the journey, and perhaps employ them once they settled in India. The home acted as a sort of ayah employment agency.

The home also took in abandoned and destitute ayahs. Many women were brought to England and, when no longer needed, they were cast aside in a foreign country with no employment and little money.

Jaya didn't think she was their ideal candidate based on her history with the Edmundson family, but they didn't need all the details about why she found herself in England, unemployed and with nowhere to live. She'd heard that Christian missionaries were active in the house, and they pushed the women to convert and to conduct themselves according to their moral and religious code. If they knew about her relationship with William they would judge her, so the less said the better.

The Ayahs' Home was in Hackney, along King Edward Road. Jaya approached a tall, light-coloured building and checked the address she'd written down: 4 King Edward Road. Yes, this was the place. She knocked on the door just as it was being opened. Coming out were two Indian women and a Chinese woman. Jaya greeted them.

'I'm looking to see if I might stay here for a bit, until I get on my feet,' Jaya said to the group.

One of the Indian women stepped forward and shook Jaya's hand. 'I'm Bhavna. We all stay here. But you need to talk to the matron. Her name is Matron Wilmington. Go inside and walk to the end of the hallway, her office is there.'

'Thank you. I'm Jaya by the way.'

'Good luck, Jaya.'

Jaya watched Bhavna and her two friends walk away, and then she went inside. The office door was open, and a large woman sat by the window embroidering.

'Excuse me,' Jaya said. 'I'm looking for Matron Wilmington.'

'I'm the very woman.' She stood up and set her embroidery work on the seat. 'Are you looking to stay with us?'

Jaya nodded. 'Yes. I've been abandoned. I was sent to the

shops and when I returned my family was gone. I waited two weeks for them, but then the landlady chased me away. I have no money.'

Jaya had prepared her story ahead of time. She'd even made up a fictitious name for the family, but it was never required. Matron Wilmington was not a suspicious woman, and she accepted Jaya's story with no more than a murmur of sympathy. In a large book she entered Jaya's name, age, caste and home village in India.

'Not many families travel to India at this time of year. Most British cannot bear your hot summers. You'll have to wait here for a while.'

With that, Matron Wilmington handed Jaya two keys: one to the house and one to her room. 'You'll be in by eight pm each night, and you will share a room with three other ayahs. There will be no fighting, and you will be expected to help with domestic and kitchen duties. We prefer you to attend the missionary sessions, but I hold it against none of the girls if they don't. You're entitled to keep your religion. I've learned a little bit about Hinduism and, personally, I find it fascinating. But don't let Reverend Milton know I said that!' She laughed as she walked Jaya to her room. She was a jolly woman and Jaya could see she was kind. She felt bad about lying to her, and wished she hadn't.

AN AYAH'S CHOICE

***

The next morning Jaya visited a pawnshop, by the name of Jameson, near the edge of town. In her bag were the solid silver place settings she'd taken from the Edmundson household.

Jameson examined the silver with impeccable care. He was a great bear-like creature, with a full head of grey hair, and his laboured breathing suggested a previous vocation involving no small amount of physical labour, perhaps in a deep mine somewhere. His hands told the same story, and using these hands he studied the silver from every angle.

'How does a woman like you,' he asked, 'come upon such silver as this?'

'Is it not good silver?' she asked.

'No, that is not what I am asking.'

'I'm here on behalf of my employer,' she said, her mind sprinting quickly to improvise the lie. 'He's in difficult times and doesn't want people to know, so he asked me to come.'

'Which employer?'

'I'm certain,' she said, without flinching, 'he would be ashamed to have you know.'

'I'd like to take these out back. Study them in the light.'

'That's fine,' she said.

Although she did not like to have the silver out of her sight, she knew that being left alone in his shop was a display of trust – countless expensive items surrounded her. Had he not believed her, he never would have dared to leave her alone. Unfortunately, Jaya's assessment soon proved incorrect. The man, Jameson, had not left her alone out of trust. He'd left her alone for another reason.

A policeman entered the shop before Jameson returned. Jaya saw his badge.

She'd only been alone in the world for little more than a day, and already her freedom was at risk. Jameson entered the shop and hooked his thumbs into his belt loops. Looking at Jaya, but speaking to the officer, he said, 'She tried to sell me stolen goods. No person of her shade ever comes in here.'

'Miss,' said the policeman, 'I must request that you come with me.'

Jaya had no option but to follow him.

***

Jaya woke up in a cage of some sort. The walls were white. The door and tiny window were encased by steel bars.

'Ah, you're awake. You must be fed.' The speaker was a woman dressed as a nurse. Jaya was struggling to get her mind in order to understand what was going on. Jaya realised then that she was hungry.

'Where are my things?' Jaya asked.

The nurse looked at her with impatient eyes. 'Miss?'

'I had some things with me. Where are they?'

'You won't be needing those in here.'

'*In here?* What is this place?' Jaya asked, but the nurse walked off without saying another word.

Jaya looked around the room and then became aware of background noise. People were crying. Someone shouted out: 'Let me go!' Far off she heard a scream, long and full of pain. She felt sick with worry as she looked at the white cinder block wall, and the bars on the window. Soon the nurse returned with a bowl of porridge.

'Eat up,' she said, setting the bowl on the small table.

'What is this place called?'

'The Winifred Lunatic Asylum. Now eat your food. We don't like dawdling here.'

Jaya fell back against the wall and tried to remember what had happened. She had been at the pawn shop, and had shown the silver to the proprietor. Then a police officer arrived and took her out to the paddy wagon.

'What are you doing here, a pretty girl like you?' he'd asked.

Jaya decided to tell him the truth. He had a kind face, and she thought he'd have mercy.

After explaining her situation he looked at her and said, 'But yous can't be comin' over here and stealing, even if he was lying and using you the wrong way. I'm sure your master will be looking for his property. Now if I take you to the gaol, you'll have all sorts of trouble. They might keep you for years. You've really set me a problem. Because I must do something, or else I'll be the one facing problems.'

The paddy wagon was dark and she bounced this way and that as they drove through the streets of London. It felt as if the journey took forever. She thought about the silver, which she no longer had. Jameson must have kept that for himself, the thief.

When the door opened at the back, two large men in white were waiting for her. The police officer stood to the side.

'Now don't be worried,' he said to her. 'I thought about it and this is for the best. This way I'll have an answer when people come looking for you. If you mind yourself, you'll only stay here a bit, and then you'll be free to go. Prison is far worse than this place.'

He smiled at Jaya as if he were doing her a favour. Then she felt the needle in her arm, and everything went black. The next thing she knew she woke up to the realisation that she was a prisoner in a place she never thought she'd find herself – an asylum.

She'd almost been free. She'd had a room and food at the

Ayahs' Home. Why had she been so quick to leave and attempt to sell the silver? She should have waited and asked around to find a trustworthy person to sell it to. Now she was in this awful place, and the value of the silver would fill the Jameson's pockets not hers. She was finally free of William but, through her own actions, she now found herself in an asylum like Sara.

CHAPTER 21

Two nurses appeared in her room twice a day to dose her, and each time she fought them although it was futile. One nurse held her arms back while the other one pried Jaya's teeth apart to push the hard spoon down her throat so that the medicine would reach its target.

Her days were long, and the drugs confused her mind. Still, she tried to get as much information as she could in order to find a way to get free of the place. She knew she was in a place called Winifred Lunatic Asylum, but she had no idea where it might be. It was not where Sara was; she had been placed in an asylum for the wealthy. This was a place for the poor, sick or not, a dumping ground to keep the unwanted. Out the barred windows was a patch of brown grass and a few struggling trees. A tall brick wall bordered the area. She could be anywhere in the vast city of London.

Jaya discovered that she had been deemed 'criminally insane', along with several other female patients. Jaya wasn't sure of the exact nature of their crimes. As she looked at them in the common rooms, none appeared to look the way she imagined criminals would look, but then again, neither did she. She suspected these women had committed petty crimes and had been caught.

There were also women who had been brought to the institution by family members, most often husbands, but sometimes by fathers or brothers. These women received different treatment from Jaya and other 'criminally insane' patients. They received less medicine and more quiet time, whereas patients with criminal backgrounds were made to take drugs and endure various other treatments.

Both groups of women were made to work daily doing laundry, cleaning and cooking. Though many of them were in a mental fog half the time, the work was always done.

One day Jaya found a small pad of paper and a piece of charcoal in the rubbish behind the kitchen. She snuck it to her room and during her quiet times she could get lost inside her pictures as she had when she was a girl. She drew pictures of the asylum, but also pictures of those she missed: Krishnan, William, Christopher, Edward, Sayida and even Rafik. She drew the river where she had found sanctuary as a girl, along with the trees and birds she remembered.

Sometimes she cried thinking of all she had lost. Krishnan especially. What would he think of her being here? Of her stealing from William? She knew her brother would be ashamed of her. Jaya knew, though, that he did not know of her life, and he never would. He did not know what a person was capable of when the choices were between life and death. Jaya was beginning to realise, especially when hearing the stories of her fellow inmates, that women are often faced with untenable choices, forced to choose one, and then castigated and called evil. Few men found themselves in that position, yet most women lived a life having to make terrible choices.

One day she came back from laundry duty and found Nurse Kelly with her drawing book.

'What is this now?' Nurse Kelly asked.

'It was in the rubbish. I didn't think anyone wanted it.' Jaya hoped somehow the nurse would show mercy and let her keep it.

'This is good. Who is it?' Nurse Kelly asked, looking down at one of Jaya's drawings of Krishnan.

'My brother,' Jaya said.

'You're incredibly talented.' Nurse Kelly paged through the book. 'Do you think you could draw me?'

Jaya hadn't expected that. 'Yes. The problem is supplies. My paper is nearly finished and the bit of charcoal I found is not very good.'

'I can find some supplies for you.' Nurse Kelly smiled.

'Yes, then,' Jaya said excitedly. 'I'd like to draw your portrait.'

***

The next day, when Jaya was meant to go to the kitchen and peel a mountain of potatoes, Nurse Kelly arrived. She unlocked Jaya's room and came in.

'Today, you won't go to the kitchen. Someone else is doing the job,' Nurse Kelly said. From her bag, she took a new pad of good paper, a fountain pen and a set of charcoals. 'Here. They're yours.'

Jaya look at the gifts and gasped. Her eyes lit up for the first time since she had been imprisoned. 'Thank you so much, Nurse Kelly. Shall I draw you now?'

'Yes, please.' Nurse Kelly answered and grinned at Jaya. Jaya felt as though she was viewing her as a normal person with real feelings and skills, and not just another troubled inmate.

Nurse Kelly sat in the thin light coming from the small window high on the wall. Jaya sat on the floor, her legs stretched out in front of her, and began to draw. Nurse Kelly was thin and tall, and in another life she might have been called handsome. But she was born to work, and that work had taken its toll on her looks. Jaya drew her as the person she was meant to be and, Jaya suspected, the person she was inside.

'I'm sorry about this place,' Nurse Kelly said, after a while. 'You seem a nice lady, I wish you didn't have to be here.'

'I stole from my employer. And I should have expected to be punished.' Jaya smudged the edge of Nurse Kelly's hair in the drawing, trying to show where the light hit it. 'My employer stole much more from me, but that theft will never be punished.'

Nurse Kelly looked at her and it was clear she didn't understand what Jaya was saying, so she changed the topic of conversation. 'Another one of yours is coming today.'

'Another one? I don't understand,' Jaya said.

'I mean another Indian woman. She was in prison somewhere in Europe. Now they're bringing her here. Says she's a British citizen and shouldn't be in Spain. I heard she's a bit violent.'

Jaya said nothing as she continued to draw. An Indian woman taken from her home, thrown in a European jail, and now she's violent. Her case must be one of hundreds.

She finished the drawing and handed it to Nurse Kelly. The older woman looked at it and covered her mouth with her hand. 'Is that me?'

'Yes. Do you like it?'

'It's beautiful. Thank you, Jaya. I'm going to frame it and give it to my husband. Maybe he'll remember how I used to be.'

'How you are.'

When Nurse Kelly left, Jaya realised that had been the first time anyone at the asylum had used her name.

She'd had a calm day, left alone in her cell. Drawing Nurse Kelly had been very relaxing. After Nurse Kelly left, she spent time improving some of her other drawings now that she had better supplies.

That evening Jaya went into the great hall where they ate their dinner. Normally dinner was a fraught business. Often fights broke out. Some of the women shouted out nonsensical things, others banged their head on the table. Violent patients were always threatening the others. Jaya tried her best to stay unnoticed. She often sat in the furthest corner, at a table in the shadows, and kept to herself.

She had her head down eating and, at first, didn't notice the commotion at the front of the dining hall. When she looked up, she saw a crowd had formed. Jaya suspected it was another fight. Nurses and male guards rushed to the group. There were shouts and screams. Then, after a few moments, the culprit was subdued. Two very big guards pulled the woman to her feet and put her in handcuffs. The person she'd fought lay on the floor, unconscious. Jaya tried not to look. It was not unknown for women to be killed in these fights, and she didn't want to see that.

Jaya watched and then the woman, now subdued, turned and looked directly at her.

Jaya gasped audibly, unable to contain her shock. Her heart pounded and she broke out in a cold sweat. Of all the asylums in the country, Komali, her enemy, was sent here. Then she remembered what Nurse Kelly had said about a violent Indian woman being transferred here from a Spanish prison.

Jaya quickly lowered her head, but it was too late. Komali had recognised her and smiled, a smile that assured Jaya her life was now in danger.

***

'I must get out of here,' Jaya said. Her words were directed at the head doctor, Dr Hills.

'Patience. You committed an impulsive crime. We must survey your mind for signs of impulse. Cure that affliction and I will certainly recommend your release.'

'No,' she said. 'You don't understand.'

He looked at her. His eyes dipped to her chest. She could hear his breath. The man was undoubtedly pleased to have achieved this station in life; surrounded by women over whom he had authority, including beautiful young women like Jaya.

'I think I understand just fine. You're unwell. As you know, you'll be in our care for eighteen months. That is if all goes well.'

'Eighteen months?'

'After which time, we shall reassess you to see whether or not you are fit to re-enter society.'

'Sir,' she said, her body leaning forward, 'I have an enemy here. Inside these walls. And I'm certain, if given the opportunity, she'll do me harm.'

He released a sigh. 'Symptoms of paranoia, as well.' He scribbled a note upon a sheet of paper. 'It's going to be a long eighteen months.'

The doctor stood up and Jaya was told to wait outside the office for the nurse. She stood alone in the main corridor. She looked around. She could leave, no one was watching her.

She told herself not to hurry; she didn't want to draw attention to herself.

She walked towards the end of the corridor, near the common room where women gathered to pass the time. Jaya could see two inmates inside; one flipped through the pages of a book, and the other sat staring at the wall.

Jaya entered the room and walked to the large window at the end of the room. It was one of the few windows in the asylum without bars. The room was on the second floor and was always well supervised with nurses and security guards, so any attempts to escape would be difficult. At night, or when there was a lockdown, a heavy steel gate was drawn closed, typical of many Victorian asylums.

Jaya touched the cool glass. The day was sunny, the sky so wide and blue. The grass, extending from the building to the high brick wall, shone with such emerald brilliance. So close, and yet so far. Jaya sighed in frustration.

Her palms stayed flat against the glass, and little by little her thoughts came together. Then she knocked upon the window, gently, to get a better feel for it. She turned around and eyed the room.

More people had arrived and a few of the women looked up at the sound on the glass. Two supervisors walked swiftly in her direction. She moved away quickly, not wishing to arouse suspicion. Without looking back at the window, she left to return to her room and the supervisors resumed their previous positions at the edge of the room.

***

A jump from the second floor was approximately twelve feet. Jaya thought she could survive such a fall if she had blankets and pillows packed tight beneath her. She would risk breaking or fracturing a bone, but such a risk was worth it. The big problem was to find a way to shatter the window and get free before the staff could stop her.

Her plan was entirely feasible; the room was filled with small wooden tables, square in shape, none of which were bolted to the floor. And she knew the window glass was not of any notable thickness. One good, hard whack with the use of a table, and the window would be shattered. Then she'd have to jump, scramble over the brick wall, and then be off as quickly as possible. The only way to get to the top of the brick wall would be by climbing up a tall bush that grew against the wall.

Then where would she go? She hadn't the faintest clue since she had no idea where she was. She knew for certain the police would be alerted, but she'd rather be pursued by the police than stay locked up and murdered by Komali.

It was a rash plan, yes, misguided even. Perhaps other women had attempted it in the past. Maybe they'd snapped their necks upon landing. Or maybe guards had appeared with rifles. But Jaya would not allow her mind to be ruled by such thoughts. She needed to get away from Komali, or she might very well die in this place, suffocated in her bed like her dear Sayida. Looking out at the world through the window, she'd felt an ache to be free. It was unfair that she was here. It was a matter of justice and survival.

Tomorrow, Jaya decided, she would either die or escape.

CHAPTER 22

The next morning, Jaya went into the great room for breakfast and spotted Komali. She crossed to her table and sat down opposite her.

'Good morning, Komali. What a coincidence that we should both be here,' Jaya said.

Komali looked up from her porridge as if she had been expecting this exact conversation.

'No, not a coincidence. It is Karma. You need to repay what you stole from me. I am here to make sure you do.'

'I'll not be bullied by you. You killed my friend,' Jaya said. 'If you want to fight me, then let's fight. If I die, I die. I want this settled once and for all.'

'Settled?' she asked.

'Yes. Meet me in the common room on the second floor,'

she said to Komali. 'Thirty minutes after breakfast. Make sure you're on time. It's when the guards take a break and only two nurses are on watch. There will be no one to stop us.'

'I will bring friends.'

Jaya shrugged. 'Bring whomever you like.'

Having said her piece, Jaya rose to go and eat elsewhere.

***

As the plan snapped into motion, Jaya's mind sharpened and her excitement at the possibility of success gave strength against the fear that threatened to immobilise her.

'Nurse Kelly,' Jaya said when her friend came to her room. 'May I take my blanket and pillows to the common room? I'd like to read in comfort.'

'I'm afraid not, Jaya. Those items must remain in your quarters.'

'But why?'

'We fear the inmates will harm themselves,' Nurse Kelly explained, compassion in her eyes.

'You mean we'd tear them? To hang ourselves?' Jaya inquired.

With a nod, Nurse Kelly said, 'Or use the pillows as weapons. Jaya, I'm afraid it's not a good idea. You can enjoy the books,

262

but you must leave those items behind.'

'What about just the blanket, then? I can't tear that. Nor smother someone with it.'

Jaya felt the impulse to smile, given the outright ludicrousness of their discussion, yet she knew full well that the nurses took the inmates' safety very seriously. But she'd learned from William that the human animal was naturally political, a natural negotiator. So now that the pillows were off the table, perhaps Jaya could get the rest of what she was after.

'Just the blanket,' Nurse Kelly finally said after considering the request.

Jaya smiled; things were going according to plan.

When Jaya showed up in the common room Komali was there already, just as they'd planned, along with a nameless friend whom Jaya sized up at once to be docile and cooperative. Good.

Jaya checked the nurse's station: only one nurse, not two, and no guards at all.

'How is it you wish to settle our business?' Komali asked, walking towards Jaya.

Jaya walked towards the window. Then she smiled and started screaming, 'Stay away from me, Komali! Stay away!'

The woman with Komali looked shocked. 'What is she doing?'

Moving fast, as she screamed in protest, Jaya picked up a table and hurled it at the window with all of her might. The window shattered, as expected. Komali stood frozen and confused, trying to work out what was happening, but everything was moving so quickly.

Then Jaya, keeping her blanket bunched up between them, grabbed hold of Komali. They looked like a pair of crazed dancers as Jaya led them towards the open window. Komali was confused and had no chance to react.

As they reached the shattered window, a nurse and two guards entered the room. Jaya's calls for help must have travelled further than she'd expected. The guards had heard her, too.

She called out once again. 'Help! She's trying to kill me!'

Jaya looked Komali in the eyes, pushed her away, then turned and jumped out of the window.

The blanket only partially broke her fall, her knee taking the full impact on the ground below. She wasn't sure if it was broken or simply twisted, but she couldn't bother about that now – she needed to go! Immediately, she got up and ran to the wall, the pain in her knee disappearing as the adrenaline surged through her body, acting as an anaesthetic.

As planned, she quickly climbed the bush, got to the top of the wall and rolled off the other side. Luck was on her side. Her fall was broken by a hedge. She fell lightly onto the ground, incredulous that she had made it over the wall.

She stood and ran as fast as her injured knee allowed. She would attend to her injury when she was far from the asylum. At one point, she considered leaving the bulky blanket behind, but knew that would be foolish. She might need it.

She ran for some time before stopping to see if anyone was following her. She saw no one. But in the far distance she heard gunshots. Maybe, if her luck held, she wouldn't be found. Even though she didn't know where she was, she knew she had covered a considerable distance.

Outside the wall of the asylum, there'd been a stretch of pasture and a wooded area, and she was now deep inside the woods, tall trees all around. She wondered again where this asylum was. What would she find once she left the trees? London? Or some other place? For now, she needed to keep moving.

Jaya ran and ran through the forest, breathing in the humid scents of the leaves and the rich mustiness of litter beneath her feet. Freedom at last! So precious and valuable. Jaya vowed never to lose it again.

PART III: A CHOICE

CHAPTER 23

Night descended and Jaya had been walking all day. She knew she must be near the edge of the forest because she could hear noises in the distance – she could hear people's voices. She decided to wait until morning and walk towards those sounds. She would spend the night amongst the trees where she would be well hidden. She wasn't sure if the authorities were looking for her. She wore the uniform of the asylum, which would identify her quickly. She would venture out of the forest at sunrise, and her priority would be to find something to wear.

She wasn't sure how much time would be spent looking for a poor Indian woman who had escaped from the asylum. Surely, they had more important things to attend to.

Without a friend in the world, without a plan in her mind,

without a single notion of what might happen, Jaya dropped to the ground and prayed. As she pulled her blanket around her, she prayed with all her heart that a path to real freedom would be shown to her.

Why should such a right not belong to her? If the universe did not deem it fit to grant her such freedom, then she at least prayed for the will and wisdom to find it on her own.

All she needed was a chance – a single chance. She fell asleep beneath a million stars and hoped that her prayers would be answered.

***

She dreamt that night, and she dreamed of Rafik. In her dream, she had married him. It was a simple, honest life that they shared together. They lived happily, and Jaya's belly soon blossomed with child. They laughed together with their children, dancing under the hot glorious sun. Her days were filled with her art, her children and Rafik. It was a good life, a happy life. And Krishnan was there. He was smiling, and he was happy and proud of Jaya. All was well. Perfection. As it should have been.

In the early morning, well before dawn, Jaya opened her eyes and something sharp snagged on her throat when she realised it had all been a dream. Her eyes pricked as she thought of the mistakes that had brought her to this. The pain in her knee drew her back to reality. She reached down and touched her knee. It was swollen and felt hot. Placing her cool hand there, she fell back into a fitful sleep.

After what seemed minutes, but later Jaya realised were a few hours, someone was shouting at her. 'Wake up! Wake up!'

Jaya opened her eyes and saw a woman she didn't know. Whoever she was, she was not a person of authority. Wide at the hips and sagging at the jaw line, this was a modest lady of about forty-five, with fair hair in a messy bun and wearing battered boots.

Jaya sat upright. She knew this woman was not from the asylum, and then wondered if she was perhaps some sort of bounty hunter, sent out to find escapees like Jaya. If that were the case she had nothing to protect herself with except her hands, fingernails and teeth.

Sensing Jaya's fear, she held out her hands and said, 'Be still. Relax, my dear. I am a friend.'

'Who are you?' Jaya asked, her throat clenched and dry, despite feeling some relief.

'I'm Ruth.'

The woman extended a hand and, after shaking hands, Ruth lifted Jaya up from the forest floor. Jaya's blanket fell to the ground revealing the asylum uniform, but Ruth said nothing about it.

'We must get you warm, dear,' she said instead.

'Who are you?'

'A friend, as I said. Come now. We must go quickly and get you to a safe place.'

Jaya stood and then nearly stumbled when she tried to put weight on the leg with the injured knee. Ruth broke a branch from a nearby tree. She took a folded knife from her satchel and whittled off the leaves and small branches. She handed the branch to Jaya. There was a perfect Y that fit snuggly under her arm and even a spot to hold on to, so that it could work as a crutch.

Impressed she said, 'Do you fashion such things often?'

Ruth smiled, a wide accepting smile that went all the way to her eyes. 'I do many things, some often, some not.'

They began again, walking slowly through the trees. Though the sun had not yet risen, the sky was a dark grey. Eventually the trees gave way to cultivated fields.

The more they walked, the less suspicious Jaya felt. Ruth seemed comfortable walking ahead in silence. It was this very silence that built Jaya's trust. Ruth's origins and objectives remained unknown, yet Jaya didn't want to start launching inquiries until more time had passed.

Just as dawn began to break, the pair edged their way towards a city street. It was then Jaya realised that the woods ran parallel to a city. Ruth remained two or three steps ahead of Jaya and wasn't in the habit of turning to make sure the younger woman was keeping pace. It was only when they finally reached the road lined with neat, terraced homes that they stood beside one another.

'You must be hungry,' Ruth said. Jaya gave a nod. 'At the house, I have soup. Bread. Would that suffice?'

'Of course. Thank you very much, madam,' Jaya said respectfully, bowing her head towards the woman.

'Oh, you mustn't worry about formalities with me, dear. I'm just Ruth.'

They stopped under a tree and Jaya rested her aching leg.

After a few minutes Ruth said, 'Ready?'

Jaya nodded and the woman smiled and proceeded to move again. Rather than cross the thoroughfare, she kept them walking along the pavement's outermost perimeter, which meant that Jaya followed in Ruth's footsteps once again.

Occasionally a horse and carriage passed. Window curtains and doors opened as people began their days. As this occurred, more faces came into view on the streets. Jaya pulled her blanket around her to hide the asylum uniform as best she could. Jaya found her eyes looking all about, studying faces and wondering if any of them were studying hers. Were any of them looking for a woman who had escaped from the asylum? She had no idea where she might be. She could be close to the asylum, or far away.

Jaya was weak with hunger and thirst. Ruth looked back at her and must have seen something in her face.

'It's not much further,' Ruth said. 'Can you manage another fifteen minutes?'

Despite herself, Jaya began to cry, and her tears turned into full-blown sobs. Ruth gently touched Jaya's back. 'You mustn't do this,' she explained to Jaya. 'Too many nosy people about. You mustn't be noticed, at least until we get you some different clothes.'

Jaya realised then that Ruth was aware of her fugitive nature. 'I must know who you are. I can't just follow you.'

'Not much time to explain. I'll do so at breakfast.'

'Where are we going, though?'

'My home.'

Jaya looked around. 'Where are we?'

Ruth looked at her. 'We are on the edge of London. You don't recognise it?'

Jaya shook her head, very surprised to hear that. She hadn't travelled around the city much before being caught, and thought it strange that the asylum had been so near to London.

'Is it your home, this place we're going? Or yours and someone else's?' Jaya wasn't quite certain what her own words meant. She just knew the presence of more people might prove threatening.

'There are many of us. Come now. It's urgent you hurry this last little way before the streets are filled with people, and you look as you do.'

They walked on and, as before, Ruth didn't turn back to check on her.

Jaya's thoughts raced ahead as she looked at her surroundings. The forest where Ruth found her was adjacent to the road that they were walking on. Which meant Ruth, a perfect stranger, had entered the woods on purpose. Had Ruth appeared specifically for the sake of finding someone like Jaya? She thought again that she might be working for the asylum though, in her heart, she knew that was unlikely. So who was she then?

As it turned out, the home to which Ruth led Jaya was an abandoned factory. In contrast to what Ruth had said, there were not many people present. In fact, the only people present were Ruth and Jaya, until Ruth led Jaya up a staircase.

When they reached the top, Ruth stepped towards a large oak door, thick and heavy, indicating something of importance existed beyond it. When the door opened, Jaya saw women.

Dozens of them. All of them living together in a large open room that extended the length and breadth of the building. Bunk beds were visible at one end, and thin mattresses covered a great deal of the floor. Clothes dried upon washing lines that were extended from wall to wall, droplets of moisture dripping onto the floor.

Upon entering, Jaya felt many eyes on her. But unlike the eyes on the street, these bore warm, calm gazes. They all had grubby hands and worn boots. These were not homeless women, rough sleepers; Jaya could tell that much. It went far deeper than that. Though Jaya did not know where she was, she knew this place was safe.

***

Jaya didn't see much more of Ruth that day. It appeared that Ruth had acted in the manner of a kind of soldier, sent out into the forest to conduct a rescue. Ruth spent the rest of the day resting on a mattress and then, well after sundown, she disappeared.

A woman named Elizabeth found clothing for Jaya, gave her some food and helped her take a bath.

'I'm British, mixed with Persian,' Elizabeth explained. Jaya nodded, noticing that the combination made for a beautiful and unique appearance.

They sat together on chairs near the massive windows and ate their lunch later that day. More soup, but Jaya was thankful for it. Elizabeth shared a stale loaf of bread, occasionally breaking off a piece to hand to Jaya.

'We learned of you last night,' Elizabeth explained.

'How?'

'We have a loyal friend at the asylum. I think you know her as Nurse Kelly. She asked us to find you, to help you.'

'Did she?' Jaya was stunned by this news.

'Yes, she said you had no business being there. She also said that she would do what she could to stop them looking for you,' Elizabeth said.

Filled with emotion and barely able to speak Jaya managed, 'She's very kind.'

'It's rare to learn of escapees; you're very lucky you made it out of there. It's a terrible place. Most women are being held without cause, all of them victims of massive injustice.'

Jaya pulled up the skirt of the dress Elizabeth had given her and looked at her knee. It was red and swollen, although not broken, according to Ruth.

'I didn't escape injury free. I'm surprised I was able to run with my sore knee,' Jaya said.

'When we want freedom, it's amazing how our bodies will

help us get it,' Elizabeth said.

Jaya heard an unspoken story behind those words. She suspected Elizabeth had had similar experiences to her own, and perhaps one day Elizabeth would share her story.

Elizabeth went on, 'We assumed you were in the forest. Nurse Kelly suggested it too. I suspect the people looking for you did, too, but it takes them longer to organise than us. Plus, we move quietly.'

'Forgive me,' Jaya said, unable to bear her own lack of information any longer, 'but who are you? Who are all of these women, and why are they here?'

A brief glimmer lit up Elizabeth's eyes. 'Did Ruth not tell you?'

Jaya shook her head. 'No, Ruth said she'd tell me later.'

'That's Ruth. She's all business. Not much for chatting. We're a branch of the suffragist movement. We exist together in support of women's rights. Along the way we've been able to provide a refuge for women in need. We heard a woman needed help, and we came to offer you some.'

'I'm so grateful you did,' Jaya said. And she really was. This abandoned factory and these women committed to freedom already felt like family.

The day Ruth found her in the forest, Jaya found her faith to be perfect and whole. Had she been possessed of a different perspective, Jaya may have come to view her existence until then in less favourable terms. After all, she had struggled, and known heartbreak, and known an appallingly limited form of freedom – both in India and in England. Yet her good fortune on that day was immense. Not only had she been rescued from the forest, and from starvation, but she'd escaped from the asylum where she'd been trapped. These women, who supported other women, had ensured her survival, and they had done so without questioning her innocence or sanity. Her escape had signalled to them her sense of endurance and determination, which was enough for them to align themselves with her.

That afternoon, one of the women took Jaya's hands in her own and told her all about the work she had done as a missionary in India, only a few years before. She recalled the towns she'd visited with such clarity, it was as if she had just returned from India the night before. She asked Jaya about her home village, and she even knew of Khesar. That made Jaya homesick, but happy, too.

Warm exchanges like these made Jaya feel safe and secure, as if she was exactly where she needed to be. Jaya couldn't remember ever meeting a group of women more welcoming.

Jaya remembered Sara and her occasional visitors talking about the women in England who were fighting men for the right to cast their vote, and of their leader called Emmeline Pankhurst. They called it a suffragist movement, but Jaya had assumed it had nothing to do with her. Perhaps this group was connected to them.

After speaking with other women, she soon understood that the suffragist group was a movement that was about suffrage for all. Since India was under British rule, Indian men and women did not have the opportunity to vote. White British men were the only ones represented in government. Groups of Indians living in Britain protested against this, and wanted Indians to have the right to vote since they were British citizens themselves. Jaya had no idea that women in England were also struggling to enact the same vision for themselves. She learned that all women, no matter colour, religion or creed, were denied the right to vote.

Their mission included ending racial discrimination of any kind. It was a pressing issue, one that instilled a deep sense of purpose in each of them. Securing the vote for the women of England occupied most of their time, but they knew that if women were given the right to vote, it would be an opportunity for women to finally start being heard and respected in all areas of society. It would mean that women would have a chance at becoming the social equals of men, and would mean that their opinions on a myriad of issues would finally matter. Hopefully everything would improve, including the many problems that led the women to come to this abandoned factory.

Jaya would have to contribute in some essential way to the group if she was to stay, either cooking or cleaning, and offering whatever special skills or talents she possessed. The women in these quarters lived quite well and did not seem to be lacking in terms of food or comfort, but Elizabeth made it clear that was because they maintained a strong commitment to organisation and productivity.

Many of the women held steady jobs outside the factory, such as factory inspectors or welfare workers. Those who didn't were expected to contribute even more to life inside. Some children lived there, along with the women, but for the most part this group of women did not seek marriage or any normal sort of family life. Elizabeth was quick to explain that many of those in the suffragist movement did not live in conventional ways, complete with husbands and traditional homes. Their numbers were many, and this community was only part of a far greater whole.

'If it's permissible,' Jaya said to Elizabeth following their conversation, 'I wish to take a nap. I haven't slept very well in a long time.'

Elizabeth ushered Jaya to a spare bed in the far corner. It was quiet there and in minutes she was sound asleep.

***

When Jaya woke, Elizabeth told her that she must consider changing her appearance so that the authorities would have trouble finding her. Jaya agreed and the women got straight to work.

Two of the women set about cutting off Jaya's long black hair. She'd been proud of it for so much of her life yet, if it threatened her freedom, she was more than happy to watch it fall to the floor. Her eyebrows were shaped into a thin arch.

While one woman applied an herbal whitening potion to Jaya's face, another massaged her scalp. For a moment, Jaya perceived the motion to be friendly and soothing until she realised that a reddish hue was being added to her hair. Jaya questioned why it was urgent to move so quickly on her appearance, especially since she wasn't planning on leaving anytime soon. But the woman explained matter-of-factly that they never knew when the police might arrive.

'Have they come here before?' Jaya asked.

'Never,' said another woman.

'But we can never be too cautious,' said a third. 'We don't need more problems.'

By the time they were through, Jaya not only looked different, but she also felt different, younger somehow and lighter too.

She could easily pass for Persian now.

A yawn escaped from Jaya's mouth. The past months and the escape from the asylum had taken a toll on her, and she was suddenly exhausted.

Knowing she needed to rest, a woman named Grace motioned to the mattress that Jaya had slept on earlier.

'Thank you, I am so tired. When shall I wake?' Jaya asked.

'When you wish,' Grace explained. 'You are free here, my dear.'

CHAPTER 24

For the first time in a very long time, life progressed in a state of relative peace. Autumn was arriving and a chill filled the air while leaves fell in every direction. Jaya's knee had healed completely by the time she had been at the factory for eight months. The authorities never came after her, and she was thankful, but she knew she needed to remain vigilant. She loved her freedom far too much to risk being caught and returned to the asylum.

She loved living at the factory. It was a happy productive group of women who supported each other in their work and in their lives. Jaya could not remember a time when she had been so happy and content.

Jaya became more interested in the suffragist movement, and the women involved in it. In her culture, it was never questioned that women existed as second-class citizens; it was just how it was. Throughout her life, Jaya always felt that she had to fight to do anything in a different way from the norm.

Even in England she saw that Sara, for example, had to follow whatever William decided for her, and as his wife she was completely at his mercy. Sara had as little to say about the path her life took as Jaya did. This had astounded Jaya when she first witnessed it. She and Sara were so very different, but in other ways they were the same. The suffragists understood this. They explained things in a simple but profound way that opened the world for Jaya. She now understood that her battles in life were actually the same battles most women everywhere were fighting.

Jaya wished that she could write a letter to Krishnan about what she was learning. Maybe if he knew about the suffragists, he might understand that the mistakes she had made were the same things that mattered to all women. She'd been trying to find a way to live her life in the way that she wanted in a world that had already decided who she could be.

Listening to Elizabeth and the other women speak, Jaya respected these women and understood the problems that they spoke of, but she wasn't sure she was made of the stuff of politics and protest. Her affiliation with these ladies was a matter of necessity, but she envisaged a future where she had a respectable job that paid well enough for her to move out of the factory and survive on her own. Then, beyond that, the inevitable would occur. She would go back to India. She didn't speak of these plans to Elizabeth and the other women; she didn't want to disappoint them. They had helped her so much, and in return she would do her best to help them, too.

She thought of the dream she'd had in the forest and, after everything that had happened to her, it seemed like a calm, beautiful life had she said yes to Rafik. But at that time she'd been a different person, and that woman had been unable to say yes to his proposal. That woman hadn't seen such a life as valuable. It had taken sadness, strife, time and even imprisonment to see that such a life, even if small and simple and contained, was also a good one.

Sometimes, despite everything, she lay in bed and thought of William too. There was a part of her that still loved him and maybe always would. He was flawed, but who wasn't? She and William had so much passion and excitement together. She wondered if she could ever find that with someone else. She doubted she would find that with Rafik. But that sort of passion came at a cost. Jaya knew that now.

She wondered if all lives progressed as hers had done, learning important lessons too late to use them. She tried to alleviate her regrets by telling herself that, at least, she knew better now, and she would make better decisions in the future.

While growing accustomed to her new, liberated life amongst her fellow sisters, and due in no small part to her newfound commitment to helping other women in need, one day Jaya returned to the Ayahs' Home and knocked on the door. Matron Wilmington herself answered.

The matron looked her up and down. It was clear she didn't recognise Jaya. 'You look well-cared for to be searching for our help.'

'I'm not looking for a place to stay. I'm here to lend a hand. I was an ayah, I know how important this place can be for a woman abandoned far from home,' Jaya said.

Matron Wilmington stepped back to let Jaya pass. 'Well then, we can always use the help. Come in.'

They walked toward the kitchen with the matron chattering away, and it was clear she'd forgotten completely about Jaya. Though perhaps reckless, Jaya asked, 'Do you ever get police coming around looking for ayahs who've run away from their houses or who have run into problems?'

The matron stopped and turned to look at Jaya. 'They might well pass here time and again. But I don't abide them. A policeman has never been a friend to a woman in trouble, most often the opposite. I owe them nothing.'

In the kitchen, the cook gave Jaya a massive pile of potatoes to peel. Though not her favourite job, Jaya smiled. She was happy to be helping a woman like Matron Wilmington and the Ayahs' Home that had offered her a room when she needed it most.

***

Jaya began volunteering at the Ayahs' Home once a week, doing many things from washing dishes, to running errands, to sitting with a baby who was the daughter of an ayah and her employer. She had been dismissed when his wife discovered she was pregnant.

'Let me help you, Jaya!' offered Deepa, an enthusiastic young ayah. She was about Jaya's own age, but Jaya felt older than her.

The copper cauldron was massive, so big and heavy that it took both of them to lift it.

'Thank you, Deepa,' Jaya said, smiling at the young woman.

The pair lifted the huge tub of boiling water and placed it on the kitchen table, where they had more space to work.

'Well, you always need a partner on wash day, don't you?' said Deepa. It made Jaya think about the days at the river with Sayida. Washing the clothes in the warm sun and hanging them in the surrounding trees and bushes to dry. Those had been lovely days. Oh, how she missed her friend!

'How have things been since I was here last?' asked Jaya as they bent down together to lift a large pile of clothes into the enormous tub of hot water.

'Everything is as usual,' Deepa said. 'There is talk of the Ayahs' Home moving again to bigger premises when the time comes, when the numbers call for it. I don't expect I'll still be here by then though.'

Jaya scooped some soap and soda into the tub and began to stir them around with wooden tongs. The steam rose and filled her nostrils, warm and aromatic.

'Have you found work then? Someone to journey with back to India?' asked Jaya.

'Not quite,' Deepa said.

'What is it?' Jaya asked, emerging from the steam. She looked into the frail girl's face.

'I've decided not to return. I'm not going home.'

Silence hung in the air. Jaya was confused.

'I've found other work, Jaya.' Deepa looked down into the swirling tub. 'I have two or three hours of work per day, and then I am free. Soon I will increase my hours. Then I will have enough wages for my own lodgings.' She smiled at Jaya. 'Can you imagine it? A place all of my own.'

'That's wonderful,' Jaya said. It was exactly what Jaya wished for herself.

'How are the staff treating you … the sisters?' Jaya asked as she looked at the pile of laundry. There were thirty rooms in the home, and over one hundred ayahs boarding at any one time, so the washing of linen alone was a near constant activity.

Deepa handed her the washboard and Jaya slipped the base of it into a tub she had prepared.

'They're fine,' Deepa replied.

'I know they're trying to save souls as well as people, but I've heard they can be a little bit preachy, even pushy. Is that so?'

'A little bit,' Deepa said, laughing.

The Christian Sisters of the Ayahs' Home were wonderful people, but Jaya and many of the other former ayahs couldn't help feeling a little patronised by them. The constant bullying to convert to Christianity was tiring. The sisters made Hinduism look backward and uncivilised, and Jaya didn't like that. The nuns thought their evangelism was a gift, but for the women staying at the Home, it was more of a nuisance than any form of enlightenment.

The women at the home were mostly Indian and Chinese. People with culture. People with religion. People with an identity established long before they arrived in England. They came from cultures that went back centuries. To be told they were living wrongly, or in sin, often drove the women away from the books these Christian nuns worshipped, further from the Christian god that was ever righteous and judgemental.

The nuns gave everything they had to help those with nothing, and Jaya noted that all of the women here held a reverent respect for these charitable and good-willed women of God.

'Anyway, I don't mind listening to some hymns and Bible verses,' Deepa said. 'At least I had this house when I needed it.'

'Yes, you're right.' Jaya looked at Deepa. 'Before you leave, make sure you say goodbye. Do you promise?'

'Yes, I promise, Jaya.'

***

The following week Deepa rushed over to Jaya when she arrived. 'A British man stopped by yesterday and mentioned your name. I tried to hear what he wanted but that is all I know. Matron Wilmington will want to speak with you. I hope it's nothing bad, Jaya.'

'Thank you,' responded Jaya. 'I'm sure it is nothing.'

Wondering who could be looking for her, she went to matron's office. Could it be someone from the asylum?

'Come in,' said Matron Wilmington when Jaya rapped on the door.

Jaya closed the door firmly behind her before continuing the conversation. 'Good morning, Matron Wilmington. Deepa told me I had a caller yesterday?'

'Yes, indeed. A gentleman by the name of William Edmundson stopped in to see if we had anyone with your name lodging here.'

Jaya stared blankly at the woman, while her heart raced. William? What did William want with her now?

'So,' continued the matron, slotting her fingers together in her lap, 'I thought it best to tell the truth. I said no, there was nobody lodging here by that name. I took his address, should you choose to contact him.'

From her desk drawer she removed a small piece of folded paper. She handed it to Jaya who smiled in gratitude. Matron Wilmington was indeed an ally. She didn't even ask a single question. She stood her guard and protected the women under her care. Jaya thanked her.

Sadly, she knew she must leave immediately and not return. She could not allow William to find her. Who knew what his intentions were? He might be angry and decide to take her to the police or back to the asylum. She could not risk seeing him again even if her heart ached as she tore the paper into shreds and tossed it on a pile of rubbish.

AN AYAH'S CHOICE

***

It was mid-afternoon some weeks later and Jaya had just returned to the factory having spent the morning handing out flyers to spread the word of the cause. Sunlight flooded through the windows. It had been a rather bleak month, so the unexpected rays of sunshine were welcome. She was surprised to see Ruth sitting at an old wooden table. Jaya had hardly spoken to Ruth since the woman had rescued her and brought her to this haven. There was always work that needed doing and Ruth was always busy, nearly always out.

'Good afternoon, Ruth, how is your day going?' Jaya said.

'Quite fine, dear, are you just back from the flyer run?' Ruth smiled, her eyes warm and kind, just as Jaya had seen them that early morning in the forest.

Thanks to discussions with women at the factory, Jaya had begun to understand people in a deeper way. In part this came from meeting the factory women, and in part from her own experiences. She became aware of the differences between women themselves, knowing things like race and wealth influenced women's lives, and often separated women. Jaya mentioned this observation as she sat down near Ruth.

'I agree with you and you're right to say that,' Ruth said.

Jaya told Ruth about Sara, and how she saw no connection

between herself and the Indian women all around her. Sara had not viewed Jaya, or even Sayida who she claimed to love like a mother, as worthy of the same rights as her and her friends. She knew Sara and her friends were unhappy about not being able to vote. In her way, Sara was a suffragist just like Ruth and the other women in the factory, but she wanted the vote for white women only. Sara wanted the vote but, at the same time, she could not see that she was oppressing Jaya and Sayida.

Ruth agreed that even women had blind spots.

'Looking back,' said Jaya, 'privately I thought Sara and her friends were nothing more than gossiping spoiled wives with too much free time on their hands.'

'You have such a way with telling stories,' Ruth said. 'Go on.'

'I believe that was one of the many reasons Sara had been so awful to me and my friend was that she was generally unhappy. Her husband controlled her, and even I saw it. She didn't like it, but she had no power to change anything.'

'Maybe,' Ruth said.

'She was addicted to laudanum too. I'm not sure if all her cruelty was Sara's nature, or if it was the drugs. I think about that often,' Jaya said.

'Unfortunately, some women claim to support our cause, but they are often more interested in the social connections it can bring, or perhaps the image it conveys. It may even become popular to be a suffragette,' sighed Ruth.

The women in the factory called themselves a 'branch' of the suffragist movement. It made sense that they would be reluctant to affiliate with all branches of the movement. Some corrupt and self-serving female aristocrats labelled themselves as the default suffragist movement. It was more complicated than it seemed.

Their conversation was interrupted when a woman arrived at the door and Ruth excused herself to speak to her.

Jaya watched as Ruth walked over to a beautiful woman in a white silk dress. Who could she be? It was clear she respected Ruth because she was listening to her with rapt attention. Though, anyone who could get past Ruth's scruffy exterior would respect her. She was a strong, admirable woman.

Jaya waited for Ruth at the table in the corner, looking out one of the windows at the beautiful clouds. She was exhausted. This work was emotional, and she was becoming passionate about it too, making it even more tiring.

Ruth returned and asked if Jaya wanted tea and then disappeared again to fetch it. When she returned, Ruth said to Jaya, 'I was thinking about your old employer, Sara, while brewing the tea. Have you heard of the plans circulating about a new organisation starting up to combat the things Sara struggled with?'

'No, I haven't,' Jaya said as she sipped her tea.

'Well,' Ruth said, 'I have heard rumours about a new type of organisation that proposes to call itself the Women's Social and Political Union. It seems women over in Manchester have started a new unified suffragist group.' Ruth looked up from her mug. 'They work for the rights of all women, regardless of their nationality. Their goal is to bring freedom from all sorts of oppression to all women.'

Ruth had an exceptional way of sourcing information, and this new Women's Social Political Union sounded like the bridge between Jaya's biggest desire to support all women: women back home, and women here in England.

Later, as she got ready for bed, a thought hit her. Could such a thing exist – a dual regard for all women? Could the many different races coexist in a single suffragist movement? Jaya held hope in her heart, but the rational side of her held little faith in the proposed joining of these opposing branches. Still, Jaya was more than happy to be under the suffragists' umbrella at all.

Rain began to trickle onto the factory's metal roof. Jaya pulled the blankets over her and stared up at the ceiling, thinking about her path forward. Her life had changed so much in little over a year! She wondered what her life would be like after another year passed. It was hard to even imagine.

CHAPTER 25

'I want to do more.' Jaya spoke these words to Elizabeth as the two of them attended to an intimidating pile of laundry.

'You mean chores? Duties?' Elizabeth asked.

'Not chores. Not duties,' Jaya said. 'I want to be involved more. As a campaigner.'

Elizabeth smiled. 'I'm pleased to hear you say this, Jaya. I think you have many talents and experiences that will help us be successful.'

'What shall I do? Beyond handing out pamphlets?'

Elizabeth nodded. 'Well, it depends, Jaya.'

'On what?'

'On you.'

'I am willing to do whatever it is you ask of me.'

'I understand. Yet the nature of every movement is

dependent upon the talents of its supporters. You must bring your own strengths, your own personality. What is it that you can do that no one else can?'

'I've given up on my best talent, which is art. It was a dream I had when I first came to England, and one I thought my employer might help me to achieve. I soon learned it would never happen, so I gave it up,' Jaya said. She felt sad admitting that she'd given up on her dream to be an artist, but it was true.

Elizabeth took Jaya's hand and led her to a bench away from the washing area. 'Tell me about your dream.'

Jaya thought how kind it was of Elizabeth to be interested in her in this way. At the factory, Elizabeth and Ruth were the leaders and they had many responsibilities. Still, Elizabeth wanted to use her time to hear Jaya's dreams. That meant a lot.

'Wait here,' Jaya said.

She rushed to the corner where she slept and kept her few meagre possessions. Among them was a pad of paper. In her free moments, she sketched the factory, the women who lived here and the streets of the city.

She went back to Elizabeth and handed her the sketchpad. At first Elizabeth looked confused, but as she began turning the pages she began to smile, and even giggle, at some of the drawings.

'You really captured Ruth's impatience here,' she said,

lingering on a drawing of Ruth carrying a spade and bucket, dirt smeared on her cheek, trying to get away when one of the women wanted to talk to her.

She looked at the drawings of women: holding babies, cooking food, carrying water up to the factory living place, handing out pamphlets, being shouted at by angry passers-by, women sitting and drinking tea and laughing. Rich and poor women, brown skinned, white skinned and black skinned. There were drawings of Chinese and Indian women at the Ayahs' Home, as well as Missionary women and women wearing complicated feathered hats driving past in ornate carriages.

When Elizabeth looked up her eyes were full of tears. 'Jaya, you have a beautiful gift. Thank you for letting me see.'

'Do you think it could be useful to the movement?' Jaya asked.

Elizabeth nodded. 'Definitely.'

***

Elizabeth suggested that Jaya try to make one drawing that somehow symbolised the movement. She didn't say what it might be used for. Jaya thought it would be used on one of their many pamphlets.

She decided to draw a woman, a single woman, strong and determined, casting her ballot. In the background were shadows of all sorts of women standing in a queue waiting to vote too. On top she wrote: *Votes for Women*. She looked at her work when she was finished and she was proud of it.

The women living in the factory had regular meetings after dinner to discuss the many issues that might arise. Usually, it involved household duties. Occasionally, business was discussed. Other times, when there was nothing to talk about, a few women might stand and sing a song for the group. Lena, one of the older women, wrote poetry, which she shared with the group. And Ruth had a battered violin that she played so beautifully Jaya thought she could have worked in an orchestra if it wasn't for the fact that most refused to hire women.

On that night, Elizabeth stood saying she had something she wanted to discuss with everyone. Earlier that day Jaya had given her the drawing. Jaya thought it might be taken to the printer to be used in the future. She was happy that she'd found a way to use her art to help the movement.

'I have something to show you,' Elizabeth began. Then she reached down and held up Jaya's drawing. The group came closer to look at it.

'That's wonderful,' Tillie said. 'Who did that?'

Jaya suddenly felt shy. Elizabeth looked at her. 'We have an artist living with us. This was done by Jaya.'

Everyone was impressed. Ruth looked at Jaya. 'I knew there was something special about you.'

Such a comment from Ruth was a gift to Jaya.

'I was thinking,' Elizabeth said, 'that we should have Jaya help us make this into a big mural. Twenty-feet tall, at least. It must be seen so it can teach people about the cause. What would you need to do that, Jaya?'

'A mural?' Jaya said. 'I'll need many assorted colours of paints. Reds, yellows, purples, greens. And it will depend on the size to know how much paint will be needed.'

'But where would the mural go?' Lena asked.

'A public building, a government building,' Ruth suggested.

'But that will take time. And you're talking about public property. It would have to be done in secret, likely finished in a single night,' Elizabeth said, thinking for a moment. 'How long would it take to paint this, Jaya?'

'It won't take long if I have help,' Jaya said. 'If we plan it well beforehand.'

'How long, then?' Elizabeth asked.

'I need two days to dissect the drawing. I must break it down into parts. Then I think if we have the paint, ladders and many brushes, we could all paint it. I'd have everything planned out, and we could do it in a night if we needed to,' Jaya said. She was surprised at how quickly the plan materialised in her mind.

The building Ruth had in mind belonged to the government. It was the working men's college, The Mechanics Institute on Crimea Road, in North London; a building where adults could learn useful skills to engage in new trades: barbering, cookery, woodturning. Jaya knew the building. She often saw it when it was her turn to go out and buy groceries. She liked Ruth's choice since it had a western wall that was wide and tall, facing the busy Brougham Road where many people and carriages passed by regularly.

'If we're caught, it could mean prosecution and even prison,' Elizabeth counselled. 'Only women who know the consequences and are willing to accept them should offer to help.'

Five women volunteered, among them Ruth and Elizabeth. Jaya couldn't ignore the gnaw at the pit of her stomach. Was she doing the right thing? She had vowed to protect her freedom at all costs, but now she was willing to risk everything. After her time in the asylum, she knew what being in prison was like. Also, if she was arrested, they could easily discover that she had escaped from the asylum and return her there. She was willing to take the risk, though. This was important to her. She wanted to make a significant contribution, and this would be it. Warmth spread across her chest. She felt like a true artist now.

CHAPTER 26

Forty-three. That's how many chalk strokes Jaya would have to make to recreate her drawing of the female voter on a large scale. In three weeks' time, she would complete the drawing very quickly.

She was surprised that, as she planned how to create the large drawing, and how to do it fast, her nerves disappeared. She was excited to get out and do it. She had always wanted to be a useful person, and now she had at last discovered the path to being one. To be sure, she yearned to take this process to greater heights but, for now, this would suffice.

On the day of the event, the group prepared themselves, practicing what they must do that night. Ruth was among them, and when the occasion called for strength and instinct, Ruth was always everyone's first choice. For the first thirteen strokes, the ladder would not be needed. For the remaining thirty strokes, however, it was an absolute necessity, and Jaya would be required to run up and down the rungs several times.

They decided to leave at two hours past midnight. At that time, lone Bobbies were known to roam the streets. The women had no secure way of learning their routes and schedules ahead of time, but they reckoned that the building itself was not a high-priority for law enforcement. The building and the assets within it were modest, and the place was most active during the day. Just the same, this was most certainly a risk.

Ruth helped Jaya come up with a new identity in case they were arrested. She would ask questions, and Jaya had all the right answers ready in case she actually had to take on the identity of this alias. She said nothing of her past with William, or her experience at the asylum. Instead they created an entire narrative that involved a fictitious employer hiring her to watch their children on the voyage to England. Upon arrival, they had abandoned her on the streets. After wandering for days without food, Jaya's story was that she came upon a few women's rights campaigners in the street, passing out pamphlets, and they offered her food and a place to stay.

If she was arrested, it would be for vandalism. They would be locked up for a few weeks, and pay a fine. They were certainly strong enough to handle that. Perhaps they could even form new alliances inside the walls of their jail cells. Jaya had had her freedom tampered with and her life endangered so many times before that the present risk almost seemed non-existent to her.

***

'Stop!' Deborah, their lookout, whispered in an excited hiss. Jaya looked down. Deborah was looking at three men who were approaching, none of whom were officers of the law.

Jaya stepped down off the ladder, initially feeling unfazed by the advancing men. The good news was the mural was nearly done, except for a couple of minor background details. If they were forced to flee at this moment, their message would remain intact. Things had gone as planned. Jaya had mapped out the drawing in less than an hour and then everyone got to work painting. It had gone perfectly – until this moment.

Ruth stepped towards the men. Elizabeth and the others hung back.

The men stood under the nearby a streetlamp some twenty yards away. Two of them were older, with hats and bushy moustaches, but with them was an individual who was much younger. Jaya thought he looked about sixteen.

'That's public property, is it not?' the eldest asked. Jaya noted that his moustache was greying and decided they were three generations of the same family: grandfather, father and son.

'Are you Bobbies?' Ruth asked.

'We are concerned citizens,' the other man replied, smiling at the young boy.

'Well I suggest you take your concerns to law enforcement,' Ruth replied. 'We've no obligation to explain ourselves to you.'

Jaya nodded, approving and admiring Ruth's steadfast attitude. Any sense of positivity was rapidly cut short when the eldest of the trio came forward and slapped Ruth across the face. The boy laughed.

Jaya ran forward. Her fists were in motion. Sideways, front-ways, backwards, they landed like stones upon the oldest man's head. His son swept in and tried to peel Jaya off, but he met with Ruth, who locked him up in a chokehold. The youngest of the men stood back, yelling for everyone to stop, not willing to enter the fray.

From the corner of her eye, as Jaya pummelled the older man, she saw the ladder moving. Deborah held it high, heading towards the younger man. She swung it and it landed on target. The youngest man fell to the ground, blood spraying from his nose. He groaned in pain.

Jaya's eyes met Ruth's. They didn't have to say anything. Although no one had been killed, they'd be in serious trouble for this. It was time to run. Ruth called out and the women scattered in all directions, carrying the equipment they'd brought. Ruth grabbed Jaya's hand and they headed down a narrow alley. They hadn't got far before a huge figure with a baton in one hand and a torch in the other, cut them off.

CHAPTER 27

India, 1902

Rafik woke well after dawn, once again. He heard the cold rush of wind outside his window and some chatter from people walking down the road. He'd always reliably sprung out of bed as soon as the sun rose, but for the past year he didn't see the point of it. Rising before the sun just made his long, lonely days even longer. Since Jaya left, a great grey melancholy had seized his soul. He felt no will to get up and greet the new day.

Somehow, the few hours they'd had together had managed to bind his heart to hers. It seemed inexplicable, but he knew love and rationality often didn't work together. He thought of her all the time. He'd asked her brother about the situation with her employer. He'd thought Jaya had made up the story that day by the river, claiming her British employer was her lover. He'd believed she'd said it so that Rafik would forget about her. An odd sort of kindness. But Krishnan had confirmed that it was correct.

It could have put him off her, but instead it drew her even closer. He knew such things happened, and knew women were cruelly judged when often they had no choice or, at least, limited choices. Even Jaya's brother Krishnan had passed judgment on his sister. Rafik felt terrible about that.

Rafik now lived in Khesar. He'd joined his brother, Sanjay, running their family's bakery. The heart that had motivated Rafik's work when he first came to the bakery was beginning to fail him completely. Despite Jaya's refusal to marry him, and the unkind things she'd said that day by the river, he'd hoped that she would see him as a suitable husband and return. But every day that seemed more unlikely.

He remembered the day Krishnan told him that she'd left for England with her employer. He'd advised Rafik to forget about her, and find someone else to marry, someone more suitable. That was when he'd lost all excitement about his retirement from the bank and his new life at the bakery. For him, the dream had included Jaya, without her it did not exist.

'Have you heard from Jaya since she left for England?' Rafik asked Krishnan one day.

'We parted on bad terms,' Krishnan said.

He went on to describe how ashamed he'd been to learn that his sister was involved in an adulterous relationship with her employer. How he had shouted at her that day of the engagement party. Rafik could see that the anger still simmered in the younger man.

Rafik had sympathy for both of them. 'Have you no room for any grace for your only sister? She was very young when she took that position.'

Rafik remembered the time he saw the wife of her British employer slap Jaya. He'd wanted to turn around and save her even then. He stopped because she had looked away in embarrassment, and he did not want to make it worse for her. Thinking of that day, he wondered if Krishnan knew the full story. Even if he did, he was still her older brother and that must account for something.

At Rafik's words, Krishnan had hesitated. 'Do you think I've been too harsh?'

'Yes. I do. You know your sister. I think I know her, too. She is a good person. People make mistakes. But for those we love, surely we can find forgiveness.'

Krishnan nodded his head in consideration. 'Your words are wise. Thank you, my friend.'

Rafik hoped he had given Krishnan an alternate perspective,

and that he would consider his sister in a different light.

***

The customers hadn't yet started to complain about Rafik's lack of enthusiasm about the business, but he knew that his work was not as good as it used to be. He paid less attention to detail. He felt rushed and less motivated to take his time and put in the care that gave their bread its competitive edge. None of it seemed important anymore.

One Tuesday Sanjay confronted his brother. Although two years younger than Rafik, Sanjay generally acted as his equal, particularly when it came to matters involving their business.

Rafik walked into the shop and was surprised to find it dark. Sanjay had not yet bothered to open the blinds, even though they were supposed to have opened two hours prior. Moreover, the smell of fresh bread was not in the air.

Inside there were no customers and even Kendra, the girl who often assisted them, was nowhere in sight. He was just about to call out Sanjay's name when his younger brother emerged from the curtain separating the main area from the kitchen.

'Is something wrong?' Rafik asked, surprised to find his brother with an odd look on his face.

'Yes.'

'What is it?' Rafik asked.

'Please, sit.'

Sanjay gestured to a small wood table, surrounded by stout stools, intended for the customers. Never before had Rafik taken a seat there himself. He felt clumsy and his hands grew restless.

'Is it bad news?' Rafik asked.

Sanjay shook his head. 'I don't know. You tell me.'

'I don't understand.'

Sanjay said, 'You've been late every day now for a month.'

'Ah,' said Rafik, suddenly relieved that nothing grave was occurring. 'It hasn't been a month. I don't think it's been that long. Two weeks perhaps.'

'A month, Rafik.'

Rafik shrugged. 'I always make it, don't I?'

'That's not the point.'

'What is the point then, brother?'

Frowning, Sanjay went on to say, 'I feel my trust in you slipping. We need to respect what we have inherited. We each need to do our share to maintain the business.'

'I know this, Sanjay.'

'I know you do, but you don't act like it. Your mind is in other places. You seem so unhappy.'

Rafik looked at his brother. 'I'm lonely, Sanjay. I didn't tell you, but there's a young woman, a woman I love. I thought she was to be part of my life here. I thought eventually I would convince her to love me as I love her. I've failed and she has gone off to England. Sometimes I find it pointless to get up, to continue.'

Now the sharpness left Sanjay's eyes. In its place was a note of brotherly tenderness. 'I understand. Heartbreaks can happen. I have felt the same in the past, too. But sometimes we must accept that our journey is headed elsewhere. What is her name?'

'Jaya ...' Rafik said the name the way a bird sings towards the setting sun.

'Jaya. I'm sorry, Rafik, but she is gone now. There will be others. You will find another woman to care for you. Your wife died and you found Jaya. Now you will find someone else again. There is no need for hopelessness. You need only a bit of time to heal.'

Rafik ignored his brother's words. 'I was thinking,' he said, 'of making a journey. To go to England ... to try to bring Jaya back.'

'Really? With all this work to do?' his brother replied with surprise in his voice.

Rafik waved his hand, and then looked at his bother again. 'That's the difference between us, Sanjay, you think life is all work.'

'This bakery is our livelihood, it's our life now,' Sanjay said.

'You don't realise how small this is in comparison to the rest of our existence.'

'You are wrong, brother. I think life is a blessing. And I think this business is very much a part of that blessing. So, I don't wish to see it falter,' Sanjay said.

'Nor do I,' Rafik said. 'But I need to go and find her and tell her what I need to tell her.'

Sanjay said, 'So, England, then? When do you wish to leave?'

'I'm not sure yet,' Rafik said. 'I haven't thought about it.' But the truth was, he'd thought about it each and every day since he'd learned of Jaya's departure.

She had been ideal for him, such a gentle and kind-spirited woman. Even her drawings made him love her more, with the way she drew attention to the tiniest detail of a bird or flower, of a face, and brought beauty to it. Only a person full of love could capture such things.

The idea of leaving his country scared him, particularly as it involved several weeks on a boat. Never before had he experienced such a thing. Yet he knew that if he managed to get there, the effort that he'd made to do so would appear to Jaya as a gift, and as a representation of his true love for her. For that alone, to say nothing of seeing her again and perhaps saving her from a terrible situation, this would most certainly be a journey worth undertaking.

The problem was, even if he poured the whole of his being into his work duties, which he intended to do in any case, he was not confident he would accumulate ample savings for the journey. The last thing he needed was to get there and then be unable to make his way – and hopefully Jaya's – back home.

'How do you plan to travel all the way to England and back on your earnings from the bakery?' Sanjay asked, confirming Rafik's own doubts. 'It's not possible and you know it'.

'Then tell me what I should do? Tell me how to find peace.'

Sanjay paused and then said, 'Go see father. You should speak to him. Get his advice.'

***

'A letter?' Rafik asked.

The older man nodded. His father had retired and these days he spent most of his time drinking mango lassi in his garden and retiring to bed before the sun went down.

After explaining everything to his father, Rafik feared that he was fated to remain single and never make his way to Jaya. He and his father sat upon matching white chairs beneath the shade of an apricot tree. He had spent nearly half an hour explaining to his father how much he loved Jaya and how he yearned to pay her a visit. And then, after finally giving his voice a rest, his father suggested that he write a letter to the woman first.

'It is not realistic for you to travel to England. Please think about it and understand, beta. Perhaps you should write a letter to Jaya.'

Rafik was not keen on the idea of writing a letter. First, how could he be sure that it would reach Jaya? Anything might happen to it on the way. If she were still employed by the man who took her as his lover, who was to say that man would give her his letter?

Also, any man could write her a letter. But to take a ship to her so that he might plead his case, was an action that would be respected by a woman. Jaya deserved such a grand gesture, Rafik was sure of that.

'You don't make such a journey so rashly. It's too fast. Too romantic,' his father said. 'You've been married once. You're old enough to stop with such things.'

'*Too romantic?* Is there truly such a thing?'

'Indeed there is, my son.'

'I doubt Mother would be thrilled to hear that.'

'Your mother and I have lasted partially due to romance, yes, but also due to practicality. We function well together. We run a home together. Chasing after a woman across the globe is impractical. You are too old for such things.'

'Well, thank you, Pita,' Rafik said, frowning. 'I pour my heart out to you, and you tell me to write a letter.'

The older man laughed, impervious to his son's sarcasm. 'Make it an impassioned letter. I'll even buy the paper.' His father then proceeded to howl with laughter, clapping his knees and enjoying the many shades of fury upon Rafik's face.

It would take Rafik the rest of the afternoon to re-establish a state of calm. Once he did, he had to admit something to himself – writing a letter wasn't such a bad idea after all. In many ways, writing a letter would allow him to express his thoughts in an orderly manner. He was sure that in person his emotion would cause him to act and speak rashly.

He began to organise his thoughts, and then made many attempts until he had the letter finished. He explained his position well, and his only hope was that Jaya would receive the letter into her beautiful hands and feel the love in his heart. He would send it off and wait, though he knew the waiting would not be easy. He hoped she would be kind enough to respond quickly, even if it was to say no.

CHAPTER 28

London, 1903

William's hands were shaking by the time he finished reading the letter. It was from a man in India, professing his love for Jaya, asking if he might come to her and bring her back to his home so that she could be his wife. The language conveyed such caring love, such passion and pure adoration for Jaya. William felt sad for both of them but something lay beneath that sadness. A burning sensation that hardened his stomach: jealousy. Of course he felt jealous, why wouldn't he when his heart still ached for this same woman.

Never before had a letter for Jaya arrived at his home, not here in England nor back in India. At first, his instincts prevented him from reading it. Then, two days later, he thought to throw it away. What if Rebecca had seen it? She had long ago made her disapproval of Jaya known and was happy when she left. The last thing he needed was to grant her a sudden reminder of the young, gorgeous Indian woman whom she suspected he loved.

But no, he could not simply toss it away. It seemed to William as though God himself, in the course of placing this letter in his possession, was issuing a test of some kind. And not necessarily a test as to whether he could resist opening it and reading it. More of a test as to whether he had truly stopped feeling so intensely for Jaya. He had failed the test.

Although William had never heard of this man, Rafik, he bore no hatred towards him. It seemed that Jaya had been courted by him back in India. After reading those three crinkled pages, it was clear that what had begun in India between Jaya and Rafik had been left incomplete. William determined from his careful and precise language that this man was of fine intellect. Whether Jaya's heart would lift upon reading the letter, William did not know.

William shifted his body towards the crackling fire, and prepared to throw the letter into the flames. The moment before he pitched the letter into the hearth, a voice came from behind him.

'What is that?'

William dropped the letter in the fireplace. The flames slowly enveloped the paper, beginning to create a charred pile from what used to be Rafik's letter.

He spun around to face his wife. In the low-lit room, with only the orange flames to illuminate Rebecca's face, she looked threatening and nearly demonic. Indeed, her elegant cheekbones took on supernatural proportions.

'Why are you behaving like this, William? What are you playing with there at the fire?'

'Behaving like what?' he asked, this despite the beads of perspiration blooming upon his forehead. With each new day William grew less fond of his wife, and if her words and actions were anything to go by he suspected the feeling was mutual.

She sneered at him; such had been her custom as of late. He wasn't tidy enough for her liking. He tended to run a bit late, which was cause for criticism. Often, the way he addressed the children bothered her: he was too abrupt, too aloof and too casual with his buffoonish humour.

'It's her, isn't it?' Rebecca asked.

'Mmm?'

'Mmm?' she mimicked, mocking him. 'Mmm? Where did she write to you from? The gutter? The poor house? A whorehouse?'

'Rebecca, stop it! It wasn't from her, from Jaya.'

320

'And yet you tossed the paper in the fire.'

'Correct. It concerned official business that is not fit for our home. Sensitive information. I will not wilt my spirit by discussing it. Come now.' He held out his hand for hers. 'Are we leaving for this dance tonight or not?'

They had plans to attend a social gathering at the home of her uncle who was also his boss. Rebecca, resplendent in a green satin gown, looked especially beautiful with her pale skin and red hair. William could not deny that Rebecca was stunning, and he enjoyed being seen with her. He was vain in that way.

Despite the mood the letter had caused him, William was looking forward to drinks, music, dancing, and socialising with others from the Council. He hoped it would distract him from the man in India, and the fact that he had destroyed his heartfelt letter. What he'd done was wrong. He should never have opened it at all. He had no willpower when it came to Jaya. He thought about her more now that she was gone than when she had been with him. Back then he had been nearly obsessed with her.

It was unfair. Jaya was not his property; her life was not his to decide. But he had, and he knew it hadn't been the first time he'd committed that sin.

And now, here was Rebecca talking on and on about it. He

felt a headache forming behind his brow and wished he could skip the party all together. It was clear Rebecca had spent much time preparing, and cancelling would cause yet another argument he didn't want.

'I'll ask my uncle then,' Rebecca said, petulantly.

'Ask him what?' William said, confused about what they'd been discussing.

'If there was any sensitive information sent here to the house.'

'Even if he knew about that letter, he certainly could not tell you. Sensitive business is sensitive business.'

She stepped towards him. 'You're a liar, William. I know you. I can see right through you.'

William hated every moment of this. She wasn't nearly the burden that Sara had been but, in her own way, she was proving terribly overwhelming at times. At least Sara could be depended on to hibernate in the bedroom for long periods of time, or be too confused to follow events closely. Rebecca was the opposite. She was always around, forever attentive, and critical to boot. He was beginning to loathe the way he felt around her, too. She undermined him and criticised him constantly until his manhood was nearly decimated.

But what could he do? Cut her loose? Doing so would cost him his job. So, instead, he smiled and touched her stiff, cold arms.

'Rebecca,' he said, 'let's go and enjoy ourselves. Jaya was uneducated. She could barely write a single word, let alone write a letter. So stop being silly. Your jealousy is endearing in a way, but sometimes you do go too far.'

'She was awfully fond of drawing, wasn't she?'

'Is that what you suspect, dear? Really? You think she'd drawn me a picture and managed to have it stuffed in the mail?'

At last Rebecca smiled. Her arms relaxed and she melted into his. He held her, allowing her to press her soft cheek against his chest as he stroked her hair.

'I love only you, dearest,' he assured her.

'And I you,' she said in reply.

Yet he didn't care about her. In his heart of hearts, he would have liked nothing more than to find out Rebecca had taken a lover. Such a finding, albeit far from probable, would go a long way towards untangling his problems.

He did, however, soon seize upon another way to untangle their relationship. As he and Rebecca held hands in the rear of the carriage on the way to the party, breathing in the crisp, cool autumn air, William made a private decision to attain some freedom for himself – if only freedom of mind. He would go looking for Jaya. He needed to know where she was. At least if Jaya was in his life again, he would have some happiness. Did he not deserve a little bit of happiness too?

***

William and Rebecca stayed too long at the party. The following day was Monday, a workday, and when he awoke, William regretted the amount of wine he'd drunk. He wondered why his boss had chosen to throw a party on a Sunday evening. Sunday tended to be a time for winding down, for gathering one's spirits in preparation for the week ahead. Why the man had seized upon this day to encourage drink and dance was beyond William's comprehension.

'You'll be late to work,' Rebecca said, rolling over in bed to look at him.

'I'm not going in today,' William replied as he got out of bed and walked into his dressing room.

'Why ever not?'

'I feel dreadful. My head and my stomach feel sick.'

'You drank too much last night. Uncle Aaron won't be pleased.'

William was in no mood for this conversation. Yes, her uncle could make things difficult for him, but he was tired of Rebecca holding it over him. 'Uncle Aaron,' William said, forcing out a bitter laugh, 'has no choice. He might be my boss, but the

Council employed me. I'm tired of him lording over me as if he might kick me from the Indian Council at any moment. He is merely a civil servant, nothing more.'

'William, that's enough. He is my family.'

'I'm your family now, Rebecca. You should learn to show loyalty.'

'Don't mock me. I love my uncle.'

'I'll do as I want in my own house. Rebecca, it's time you learned that. I'm growing tired of your behaviour. I am the master of this house, and I would expect you to recognise that.'

He'd never snapped at her before. She became quiet and William thought he might have made some inroads in terms of dealing with her. He would be pleased if he had. He needed Rebecca around for many purposes, and it would work better if she kept her opinions to herself. Maybe he had finally taught her a lesson.

Rebecca was crying. He suspected it wasn't the substance of his words that upset her, but the fact that he'd spoken them at all. He didn't care. He finished dressing and left the room. He had somewhere he needed to go.

***

He arrived at the Ayahs' Home late morning. He stood a

moment outside and wondered if this was the right place. It was quiet and didn't seem like a place full of ayahs. He hoped Jaya would be inside and then, in equal measure, he hoped she was not. He still felt much guilt about destroying her letter. He knew now he'd done a terrible injustice both to her and the man who loved her. Nevertheless, he wanted Jaya back, and he would get her no matter what he had to do.

He climbed the stairs and found the front door unlocked, so he stepped inside.

The first thing he saw was a middle-aged woman sitting by a sunny window working on some sewing. She looked up from her work. 'Can I help you?'

'I hope so. I'm William Edmundson. I work at the Indian Council. I'm looking for a young woman who used to work for us. Her name is Jaya Devani. Does she live here?'

The woman stood and held out her hand to William in a direct way. 'I'm the matron here. Why are you looking for this woman, sir?'

William was not sure it was this woman's business, though he sensed she wouldn't help him if he didn't answer her questions. 'Jaya used to work for my family as an ayah. The boys miss her desperately. I … we … hoped that she might want to return to our employ.'

'Why did this Miss Devani leave in the first place?'

William tried not to lose his patience with the woman. 'She … I … mostly I think there was a misunderstanding.'

'I've found that few women choose to leave employment to walk the streets in a country they do not know unless there is a very strong reason to do so.'

William had had enough of this woman. 'Does Jaya stay here or not?'

The matron shook her head. 'No. She does not stay here.'

William wrote his name and address on a piece of paper and handed it to the stubborn woman. 'If she comes here, can you at least give her this?'

The matron took the paper. 'Certainly, sir.'

William left, feeling frustrated, and got in his waiting carriage. Now what could he do? He could not take more days off to go prowling the streets of London looking for Jaya. He reconciled his mind to the fact that she was gone. Maybe she had returned to India, back to her Rafik.

William vowed to forget her.

***

Some days William succeeded in forgetting all about Jaya, but some days she was constantly on his mind. Months, then years passed. He and the boys rarely spoke of Jaya, and never in front of Rebecca. She'd changed too. They'd both retreated from their hearts and lived as far from them as possible.

The day that he'd gone looking for Jaya, Edward found a drawing Jaya had done of him when he was small, and they were still living in India. By chance William entered his room just as he was looking at it.

'What's that you've got?' William asked.

When Edward looked up his eyes were filled with tears. When Jaya left, it had hurt Edward most of all. He remembered arriving home from school that day, and he'd looked for her all through the house, even though William assured he and Christopher that Jaya was not there. After that day, and for a long time afterwards, Edward retreated inside himself. He was a sensitive boy. He'd been affected when his mother was taken away, but losing Jaya cut much deeper. They'd been closer than if she had been his mother. It was a loss, but also a terrible betrayal. Why had she not even said goodbye when she left them at the school gate? Why had she not, at least, told him?

He handed his father the drawing. 'Do you think Jaya is happy where she is, Father?'

William looked down at the drawing and thought carefully before replying. He was silent for a bit while he looked at his son in the drawing, smiling, so happy to be with his ayah, and to be in that beautiful country.

'Yes, of course. Jaya is happy where she is.'

He handed the drawing back to Edward and left, saying he'd be late for work.

In the carriage on the way to his office, his mind and his heart was full and overflowing with memories of Jaya. Where was she? Was she in good health? Just then he spotted a signboard: 'J.K Davis, Private Detective'. William called for the driver to stop, and he stepped down to the street.

'Wait here,' he said to the driver. 'I'll be right back.'

Inside the offices he found a scruffy man with a furrowed brow. 'Can I help you, sir?' J.K. Davis asked.

William explained that he needed to find a woman, an Indian woman, who used to work for him. He gave Mr Davis all the details.

'When did you see her last?' Mr Davis asked.

'Nearly four years ago now.'

Mr Davis shook his head. 'That's a long time. She could be anywhere. It will be expensive.'

William gave him the money he required. 'Contact me when you find her, and only at my office, never at home. It's a private matter.'

'Understood.'

William left. He wouldn't hear from Mr Davis for more than

a year. In fact, he'd accepted the fact that he'd been swindled. Then, both happy and surprised, one morning his secretary handed him a cryptic message asking William to meet his 'friend' at a café two streets over.

William found Davis waiting for him. 'Sir, unfortunately a difficulty has arisen,' the detective said.

'Where have you been all of this time, Davis?'

'Looking for your Indian woman, sir. But, like I said, there's a problem.'

'What sort of a problem?'

'I found her,' Mr Davis said.

'Good. That's good. Where is she?' William asked, trying to keep his emotions in check.

'The Northern District Jail.'

'In prison? For what?'

'It's not the first time, I'll have you know. She stole from you. Some silver. Did the police not get in contact with you?'

'No. I never heard anything about it. It doesn't matter. But why is she in jail now?'

'Typical. The police nowadays,' Davis said, annoyed. 'They likely took the silver from her and kept it for themselves. Then they took her to the government asylum. She escaped from there and became involved with the wrong crowd – those suffragettes – living in an abandoned factory in the northern part of the city.'

'Is she there now?' William asked, finding it hard to take in everything at once. It seemed so unlike the Jaya that he knew.

'No. She was found committing a crime. Defacing public property. Mr. Edmundson, she's one of those vote-seekers. Big in the movement from all I could discover. She was arrested after painting a big mural on a government building. A protest painting pushing for the women's rights and all.'

'Jaya?' William said. 'You must be mistaken.'

Again, the man shook his head. 'Nope. It's her. You can go and see her yourself if you like. She's not going anywhere. The trial is scheduled for the fourth of December. In light of her escape from the asylum, it's reasonable to expect she'll receive a four-month sentence at least. The asylum might want her back after that, as well.'

It all seemed unbelievable; the fact that Jaya had been found and that he need only take a carriage ride and he might see her again. And too, he was astounded to learn she was one of the suffragettes and likely headed for prison. His Jaya in prison? He could not bear it.

Davis began to move away. 'That concludes our business, then, Mr. Edmundson. I'd advise you to steer clear of that one. She sounds like bad news.'

He slipped a note to William that had the amount of his final payment written on it. William paid him and Davis left. Still stunned by what he'd learned, he watched the detective stride away.

CHAPTER 29

William decided to attend Jaya's trial, but to keep himself hidden. He just wanted to see her, he wanted to see if this woman who now fought for the women's right to vote and who painted on government buildings instead of drawing portraits of his sons in charcoal, could still be the Jaya that he remembered and loved. He sat at the back of the courtroom, hidden in a corner. The room was full of women there to support the cause, all noisy and simmering with anger.

There was a sudden commotion and a door opened. The room erupted in shouting. At the front of the room, William saw Sylvia Pankhurst, the most famous of the suffragettes, standing away from the fray. He'd seen Sylvia's face in the newspapers many times alongside her mother, Emmeline.

Had Jaya risen so high up in the organisation that she was a friend to Sylvia? It seemed unbelievable to William. For him, Jaya was still that young girl from the village who had appeared in the long queue of women hoping to be the ayah for his sons. Her beauty and innocence had captured him with the first look and had never let him go.

The crowd parted, pushed by the police, and there was Jaya.

She was in handcuffs and leg irons like a criminal, but still she was his Jaya. If anything, the passing years had made her more beautiful, not less. Someone had cut and dyed her long luxurious hair, the same hair that had covered them, like a safe tent, in their lovemaking. It was now shoulder length, making her appear more modern. It had been over five years since he'd last seen her, and his yearning was the same. He wanted to run to her and take her into his arms. His heart beat wildly in his chest and more than once he wanted to shout out to her. He wanted to rush to her and free her from her chains and her captors.

Davis had told him she'd been put in an asylum for pawning some of his silver. William wished he had known that. He wished the police had done their job and come to him. He would have insisted that she keep the pieces. What did some pieces of silver mean compared to Jaya? He couldn't think what the asylum must have been like for her. Sara's asylum was a private institution, which had little in common with the government places, and still it was awful. He'd heard the stories about them just like everyone. Any sane person would try to escape. Jaya had chosen the only option she had. The mural painting would not normally require her to serve prison time, he would have thought, but unfortunately the escape from the asylum combined with that was more serious.

Jaya sat at the front, her back to him. His chest seemed to tighten as the trial progressed. Perhaps he should have never hired her, not when he had known how attracted he had been to her. He was married and it had been a selfish act. He'd destroyed the life she might have had with Rafik. Then he tore her away from her country. He brought her here and then never kept his promises to her because he was not courageous enough to stand up to societal pressure.

When he knew he could not marry her and give her the life she deserved, he should have paid for her passage back to India at least. He hadn't believed she was really going to leave that day. He'd often wondered where she had gone. He knew she must have suffered greatly in the ensuing years.

Looking at her sitting there, so small and vulnerable, facing the might of British law, he felt even more guilty about destroying Rafik's letter. He'd had no right to read it, let alone burn it in the fire. William wondered what he expected to find here. Did he think that Jaya would be happy to see him after everything he had done? Probably not.

William realised then that there was only one way forward. He'd been selfish with no excuse to justify any of his behaviour. He'd not given Jaya's life more than cursory attention, and the best thing he could do now would be to leave her alone.

He left the courtroom, got in his carriage and headed home to Edward, Christopher, Rebecca and their baby girl, Jane. He needed to find a way to be happy with that life, and forget Jaya forever.

CHAPTER 30

'We don't approve of hunger strikes, Jaya. You must eat,' Mr. Hynes, the governor of the prison, said firmly. He stood in Jaya's cell, exuding kindness in his warm facial expressions, but there was something under the surface that Jaya didn't trust.

'I will not eat.'

'You will eat or die. And if you die, it will be for nothing. The newspapers will report it as a suicide, which it will be. We'll see to that, I assure you. So, be wise now. You starving to death will solve nothing and will not further any cause you think you are fighting for.'

Mr. Hynes gave her one last look and then closed the cell door. The metallic sound was followed by the sound of a food tray sliding across the floor. The tray had an apple, a banana, a bowl of rice pudding, and another bowl of boiled potatoes. On the side was a bottle of milk.

The temptation to eat overwhelmed her. She'd begun refusing food two days before to make a point to the owners of the jail. The point was that the jail was more suited to wild animals than human beings. Meals were erratic and the shower and toilet areas were cleaned only once every two or three days. Jaya had long been accustomed to physical discomfort, but the current circumstances had stretched her to breaking point. She had heard that the men's jail was kept in a much better condition, and knowing this made her newfound quest for equal rights run that much deeper. All her requests had fallen on deaf ears. The guards who didn't ignore her, tended to scream and beat her.

So, a hunger strike appeared to be the only solution. Such an act had a high chance of attracting outside attention, ideally by way of the newspapers. Prisoners routinely met with visitors and updated those visitors on what was happening within the jail. If enough people spoke up about Jaya's strike, word would spread; at least that was what she hoped. The governor's appearance was a strong sign of progress.

She wondered about her friends who had also been arrested. What would Elizabeth have done? Would she have ignored the governor's evil threat and simply continue with the hunger strike until her demands were met, or her life concluded? Was this truly a cause worth dying for? Would Elizabeth give in? Would Ruth?

Jaya's hands flew out and she snatched the apple and the banana. She cried out and hurled them against the cell wall. The apple bounced off and rolled through the bars, well beyond her reach. The banana lay on the floor of her cell and it took everything in her not to grab it and shove it in her mouth. But she would not.

***

The following day, everything took a turn.

'Get up!' the morning guard shouted.

She opened her eyes and felt the weakness of lack of food flood through her. She sat up with difficulty, her headache much worse, and her vision swirling.

She knew this guard. It was best to get up, she wasn't sure she could take a beating this morning. The guard opened her cell and came towards her, pulling her arms behind her back.

'You're gathering a lot of attention,' he said.

'Newspapers?' she asked, her throat dry.

'Let's go,' he said, pushing her out of the cell. 'You're wanted before the judge.'

As Jaya was pushed along by the first guard, two others

joined them, women, walking behind. She hadn't been in this part of the prison before. It was much cleaner. The guard stopped at a door, unlocked it and pushed her inside. It was a shower room.

'Wash yourself,' he said. 'Quick.' He closed the door and left her alone with the two female guards waiting outside the shower stall.

Jaya stepped into the shower. She stripped and turned it on. The cold water gave her a deep, harsh fright. Unable to help herself, she let the water hit her tongue. Then she let the water flow all over her body. She was surprised to see there was even soap. Despite the cold water, she felt so much better afterwards.

One of the guards handed her a fresh, white towel. She was used to stiff, grey huckaback rags. What was going on here? Why was she being treated so well?

After drying herself, Jaya put on her prison uniform and followed the guards. They stopped in front of a room walled in with glass. Jaya could see a table and some chairs inside. At the table, hands folded before her, sat Sylvia Parkhurst.

'Inside,' one guard said.

Jaya entered the room and the woman rose, holding out a hand.

'Hello, Jaya.'

'Hello.'

'My name is Sylvia Pankhurst.'

The guards shut the door behind Jaya.

'Hello,' Jaya repeated, dizzy with confusion and general fatigue.

'Sit. You are tired.'

Jaya sat facing the woman. She was struggling to concentrate. 'I need food. I can't think clearly.'

Miss Pankhurst nodded and then fished into her purse and withdrew some chocolates. Jaya plucked the four chunks from her hand and popped them into her mouth. In seconds, she felt better. Sylvia Pankhurst's mother, Emmeline, was the founder of the suffragist movement. It was important that she was here.

'I'm so grateful,' Jaya said, 'to see you. To meet you both.'

'Our gratitude is mutual,' Sylvia said. 'You know I saw your mural. It was beautiful. It was a crime they painted over it so quickly. But for two days it was the talk of the city. You did important work.'

'Thank you,' Jaya said. She'd not heard what happened to her mural, or if it was still there. When the police caught her and Ruth and Elizabeth, the others managed to escape. Ruth got off with a fine. Despite her disguise, Jaya was recognised by an officer who had been looking for the asylum escapee. When he saw her, he took a chance. The officer brought in one of the asylum's nurses who identified her as the patient who had jumped out of the window. Because of that, Jaya was given a prison sentence and the threat that she would be returned to the asylum as well. At least, if a few people saw the mural, then everything she had done was not in vain.

'You've also drummed up quite a bit of publicity with your hunger strike. The people are calling for reform in the prison. For such a young, Indian woman, who only arrived in this country a few years ago, you certainly know how to make big waves. The Movement has had lots of publicity.'

'Good or bad?' Jaya asked.

'There's no difference,' Sylvia said, smiling.

'The guard said I'm to see the judge.'

'You are. In less than thirty minutes. They're expecting you.'

'And you will accompany me?'

'I shall. But we have a moment now to discuss your future. The staff here knows me, through my mother, we exchange favours sometimes.' Sylvia continued, 'I've struck a deal with the state on your behalf.'

'What do you mean?'

Nodding, Sylvia said, 'We have the help of legal resources in the movement. Very costly sometimes, but they keep us going. We're trying to remain inside the law, although at times I must admit that force, or protests such as the one you staged, are more effective.'

'Was my protest helpful? Did I do any good?'

'Much good, Jaya. Much, much good.' The lady's voice was low and loving. She reached out and placed her palm atop the back of Jaya's hand. 'You have helped us enormously. The story caught on. They ran your photograph and you're very beautiful, as you know. The public sympathises, and that is good for the movement.'

Jaya had never felt so important, so special, so appreciated. Suddenly all those moments when she'd forbidden herself to take a bite of food, were proving helpful.

'Can I go home then?' Jaya asked.

'Well ... not exactly. You shall leave here today. I think that must be good news for you. We've come to an agreement, but you won't be able to go home.'

'What agreement?'

'You are to join the Voluntary Aid Detachment.'

'The army? But I've no experience in fighting. I'd be useless. I'd be better off in here.'

A gentle smile graced the older woman's face. 'You won't have to fight, my dear. In light of your experience as an ayah, they will find the right job for you.'

Jaya wondered how the woman knew that, and then determined it could only have been by way of her friends at the factory.

'I imagine they'll put you on medical duty,' she said. 'Caring for patients, wounded soldiers coming home. You'll train to become a nurse.'

Jaya considered that. It didn't sound too bad at all. In fact, it sounded rather welcome. Employment. The chance to show compassion. And she would be employed by Great Britain's government, which gave her some solid status in the country. Jaya's spirits, so low just a moment prior, began to soar.

'Thank you so much. Really, thank you.'

Jaya was thankful on so many levels. For her freedom, for the chance to meet this amazing woman, for the new direction her life was about to take – and for this moment of sisterhood. She and Sylvia Pankhurst were, at that instant, total sisters, shoulder-to-shoulder, no matter their station in society. It was precisely what the suffragette movement stood for; Jaya thought again how grateful she was for being found in the forest by Ruth.

'So, I'll have to leave the movement, then?' Jaya asked.

Now Sylvia's face betrayed a hint of concern. 'But why?'

'I don't know.' Jaya shrugged. 'Because of being in the VAD?'

Sylvia smiled. 'Not at all. Our movement is full of women serving in the government and the army, in all sorts of organisations in fact. You can do whatever you wish, Jaya. England is a free country, or so it presents itself. We're getting there. So, use your freedom. I'll hope to see more of you. But first – you must see the judge. Then you need a proper meal.'

***

Her suffragette-appointed barrister, a middle-aged woman, whose name Jaya had trouble retaining, stood by her side, occasionally leaning in to explain something. The trouble was the barrister spoke so quietly that Jaya was often confused about what was going on.

After several long minutes of confusion, the judge's gavel came thundering down, and he looked Jaya dead in the eye.

'You are to report for duty two mornings from now, on Thursday the eleventh, at seven am near the Grayson Docks. Is that understood?'

'Say yes,' her attorney muttered.

'Yes,' said Jaya. And then, unable to help herself, she added, 'Thank you, thank you so much.'

Smiling, her barrister cupped her elbow and led her away. 'Don't thank them, my dear,' the lady whispered. 'They released you because they fear you, not because they are kind.'

***

Leaving prison began the best time in Jaya's life since her arrival in England. The best time she'd had in years, she realised. Because of Sylvia's intervention, she was now in possession of actual freedom. Free from William. Free from the asylum. Free from being a fugitive. Free from incarceration. She had a shiny new life ahead of her.

Sylvia met Jaya as she left prison, and she took her directly to a café for lunch.

Jaya looked forward to being part of the army. It scared her a little but, on the other hand, an organised environment was welcome. It was not yet confirmed that medical detail would be her specialty, but Sylvia seemed confident that such was the most appropriate fit.

As they ate, Jaya became fully aware of the extent of Sylvia's material comfort. The barrister, Jean Fisk, joined them for lunch. Jaya found herself nearly squealing with delight each time a new dish was brought to their table. Poultry. Potatoes. Lobster. Rolls. Butter. Jaya felt as though she were a queen. It was extravagant.

Jaya leaned in towards Sylvia and whispered, 'Are we being watched?'

'Come again, dear?' Sylvia asked.

'Is this a show? It's as if they are all watching us. As if they've never seen people eat like this before.'

Sylvia laughed uproariously and then looked at Jean, who was smiling for the first time since Jaya had met her.

'She's clever,' Sylvia remarked, cocking a thumb in Jaya's direction. 'You're right. I don't always eat like this. It is a bit of a show for the public.'

Jaya took a bite of bread and, after swallowing, she asked Sylvia, 'Who's the show for?'

Sylvia let her gaze trace their general surroundings. 'Society people, dear. Important people. The eyes and ears of the world; the mayor of London's wife, the owners of three newspapers. This is their lunch hour. I won't point them out, but trust me they are here, and watching your every move, mine too.'

'So, they'll report on my release?'

'They already are, Jaya,' Jean remarked.

'Our lunch will certainly make the headlines,' Sylvia added. 'You see, Jaya, legitimacy is an important concept. We're a scrappy movement, there's no denying that. We don't bask in luxury. But we urge our culture to take us seriously. Let them watch us eating lobster and enjoying your freedom, legally gotten. Let them write about it. Let the world understand that we are serious, and we will be successful.'

Sylvia again looked about the room. Jaya followed her gaze. To be sure, people were taking note. She felt powerful. Then Jaya noticed, she was the only person in the restaurant whose skin was not white. Jaya thought to mention this to Sylvia but didn't. Sylvia explained that, naturally, the lead 'story' in the papers would be about Jaya's release. That alone was a credit to the suffragette movement's power. Any racial undertones were surely secondary.

'Plus, you're Indian,' Sylvia noted, nonchalantly.

'I'm sorry?' she asked, shocked that Sylvia seemed to have read her mind.

Sylvia said, 'You didn't think I'd missed that, did you?'

'No, of course not.'

Leaning in towards Jaya, Sylvia said, 'It's a perfect scandal. You brought that prison to their knees.'

Jaya smiled.

'A woman of dark skin,' Sylvia went on, 'took the wind right out of the system. Isn't that wonderful, Jean?'

'It certainly is,' Jean agreed.

'So, I say we should have a toast.' Sylvia took up her glass of wine. Jaya and Jean followed.

'To what then?' Jean asked.

'Oh,' said Sylvia, 'the usual things. Freedom. Women. Jaya!'

She'd spoken loudly. Heads turned. Some smiled. Most of them were grave. But not Sylvia Pankhurst; Sylvia Pankhurst laughed as the trio toasted Jaya.

CHAPTER 31

London, 1909

'Do you understand what I am saying to you?' Hilary
Stark asked. Miss Stark was in charge of nurse training.
The Voluntary Aid Detachment (VAD) had only just been
established and Jaya was in the first group of trainees. After
being released, Jaya had spent a single day gathering her
belongings from the factory, during which she traded tearful
goodbyes with her fellow suffragettes, especially Elizabeth and
Ruth. Afterwards, though Jaya thought of them often, they
would only see each other rarely, even though they were still in
the same city.

Jaya was stationed on a ship docked on the Thames.
Unlike the last ship she had been on, this one was not going

anywhere. It was permanently docked, a floating hospital, one that received the wounded soldiers who were coming in from battles and other endeavours at sea. Some of the men were permanently disabled and were to be kept at the ship hospital for constant care. Many had been wounded in the Boer War, even though it had ended seven years before, but they still needed care and rehabilitation. But Jaya did not see such men right away.

First, she underwent an intensive first aid and nursing course that lasted for sixty days, weekends often included, during which time she became thoroughly versed in matters of human physiology, common diseases and about the care of wounds and broken bones. To her great fascination, Jaya realised that much of what she was now learning were things she had picked up intuitively during her time as an ayah looking after William's boys and from her time at the factory.

Now that her life had settled down, she spent a lot of time thinking about her days back in India. She thought about the cuts and scrapes she and Krishnan used to get as children. They had many local plants that were known to be used to heal wounds. She wondered what her brother would think of her working in a hospital such as this one, soon becoming a nurse.

At those times she desperately missed her brother. She was surprised that she missed Khesar, a place she had been so keen to leave. She'd written two letters to Krishnan since she'd left prison, but he never wrote back. Jaya supposed that she was dead to him. She wondered what would happen if she somehow raised the money to return to India. Would he let her see him? See his wife? She wondered if she would go and see her mother.

She wondered too about Rafik. She wondered how Rafik's life had changed over these years. Was he married? Was he happy?

In some ways she was happy in England now. She felt her life had real purpose, and that mattered. But she could not deny that she was lonely. She even wondered sometimes what had happened to William. It had been six years now since she'd left him. What had become of him? She wondered if he had ever read the stories in the newspapers about her mural, or her hunger strike in the prison.

She had her own life now, she had freedom and interesting work, but she had paid a price for it. Sometimes, even now, she got so homesick that she thought of going to the Ayahs' Home and asking for a new ayah job that would take her back to India.

In the end, it was Hilary Stark who inspired Jaya to stay the course in England.

The group of nurses-in-training were all white except for

Jaya. From the first day, Sister Stark noticed that too. She liked to single out Jaya, especially when she was certain Jaya would not know the answer.

'When you set a break, you must do your best to align the skeletal structures so as to give the bones a chance to resume their natural form. Do you understand this, Miss Devani?'

'Yes, madam,' Jaya said.

'Are you certain?'

'Yes. I'm certain.'

'Please repeat back to me what I've just told you.'

'I'm sorry?'

'Did you not understand what I just said?' Sister Stark looked around at the other students. To their credit her classmates either looked down or away from their teacher's eyes. They did not want her to think they were her allies in bulling Jaya.

'Of course, I did.'

'Then, please, go ahead.'

'I just don't understand.'

'So, you don't understand?'

'No, Sister Stark, I just don't understand why.'

The classroom fell silent. Everyone had been witnessing these exchanges for weeks. Jaya had always complied with Sister Stark's requests, but today she was tired of the abuse. If a confrontation was to happen, she was ready for it.

As for Sister Stark, she put her hand on her hip. 'Miss Devani, your role in this classroom is to learn. Not to question me. Do you understand?'

'Yes, of course.'

'Well, good. Then if you understand so well, repeat back to me what I just said!'

'You said,' said Jaya, 'to set the bone so that it grows back naturally.'

'No, Miss Devani, that's not what I said.'

'Not what you said? Really?' Jaya asked.

'A bone, Miss Devani, will never grow back perfectly, the way it was in nature.'

'I don't think that was your point, though,' Jaya corrected her.

'Oh! So tell me what the point is?' The teacher's face was growing red.

'I only wanted us to keep on point.' Jaya remained calm, which made Sister Stark even angrier.

'Ten-minute tea break,' Nurse Stark said, and stormed off. Jaya smiled. A few of her classmates patted her shoulder as they left for the dining hall.

***

Despite winning a point that day, the bullying continued. Jaya wanted to finish the course. In fact, she had to complete the course if she was to remain outside prison. But Nurse Stark was making her life difficult, finding ways to contradict and ridicule her. The situation was becoming untenable.

One afternoon, following a particularly gruelling debate, Jaya sat at a desk in the students' quarters. She pulled out a fresh jar of ink and a sheet of paper, dipped a pen into the ink and began to write. Her letter was addressed to Sylvia Pankhurst.

Jaya presumed that since Sylvia had been resourceful enough to get her out of prison and into a job in the army, she would certainly be able to handle a prejudiced instructor. Jaya wrote with feverish passion. She summarised the cruelty to which she was being subjected. She emphasised its prejudiced nature. She apologised for troubling Sylvia with such concerns, but expressed a legitimate fear that her freedom was being threatened, and that Sister Stark would push her to resign, no matter the cost.

Jaya truly didn't care about the woman not liking her. What bothered her was that Miss Stark held Jaya's future in her hands. That was unacceptable. Jaya was too close to genuine freedom now for it to be undone because of one woman's foolish ideas.

'Don't do it,' a voice said from behind Jaya's back. She looked behind her and saw that it was Edith, one of Jaya's fellow VAD students.

Jaya and Edith lived together in the same quarters with two other women. Jaya and Edith weren't actually friends, but they managed to live together in harmony.

'I didn't mean to spy,' Edith said.

'It's alright,' Jaya said.

'I wish to offer my opinion if you don't mind.'

On instinct, Jaya gathered up her pen and paper, stacking them neatly upon her lap, concealing the words on the paper with her hand.

'Go ahead,' Jaya said, realising that she and Edith had never spoken at any length. Perhaps she had something helpful to say. She had witnessed the altercation between Jaya and Sister Stark from a distance. Perhaps she had an insight that Jaya didn't have.

'You're writing to that woman, yes? The suffragette leader, Emmeline?'

'Sylvia Pankhurst. Yes, I am.'

'Asking for help?'

'Yes …' Jaya said, slightly annoyed to have been spied on.

'I wouldn't do that,' Edith said.

'Why? She got me out of prison. She helped me before; I thought she might help me again. Miss Stark is being unfair.'

'Yes, I read about you in the newspapers. But you must understand that Sister Stark intends no harm.'

'It doesn't matter to me what she intends,' Jaya said. 'If I don't pass this course and get a place, I'll be living on the streets or worse.'

'I understand. I have my own situation that keeps me worried as well. But still, I think this is not the right path for you. There may be an easier and more effective way.'

Jaya had heard that Edith's husband had been killed at sea due to a simple slip that sent him falling to the water undetected until he'd already drowned. After his death, the army had awarded some meagre funds to Edith and her two children, a paltry pension, hardly enough for them to live on. Now she was here for training, her two children living with her mother in Ireland. It was also imperative that she pass the course and get working, so that she could have her children back.

'So, what do you propose I do?' asked Jaya.

'You have to understand the way she thinks.'

'Does she even think at all?'

Edith smiled. 'What she's doing is something my father always talked about. He called it "casting a shadow".'

'I don't understand.'

Edith went on. 'Casting a shadow is what people do when the light hits them, they cast shadows. You look at your own shadow, and you know it's you, but part of you thinks it's someone else. That's what I've seen Sister Stark do with you. She doubts her own mind, so instead of dealing with it she puts it outside. She casts a shadow. She makes it into a trait that you possess, not her.'

'I think it makes sense,' Jaya said. 'You're saying she doubts herself and sees her doubts reflected in me.'

'It's what we all do, Jaya,' Edith explained. 'Unless we catch ourselves.'

'But how do I deal with such a thing? I can't surgically remove her brain.'

'You needn't remove her brain. Nor write to Sylvia Pankhurst.'

'What then?' Jaya said.

'What I suggest is that the next time we are in the classroom, when she starts having a go at you, and we know she will, don't fall into the trap of pride. Just think about getting a passing score. Don't think about what she's doing as coming from a place of hatred. Think about it as an expression of her own fear and insecurity.'

Edith's words played on Jaya's mind. She couldn't deny that they were good insights. She would try to think in this new way. She wanted to pass this course, and if it meant seeing Miss Stark's attacks in a different light, she would do it.

***

The following day, upon entering the classroom, Jaya felt tense. They were continuing the lesson on managing skeletal breaks and fractures. Jaya easily understood what was being taught. Jaya loved the things that she was learning. She felt that being an orderly or a nurse was an admirable position, where a person could truly make a difference. She loved learning about the wonderful way the human body worked, and the way it could be repaired and healed when things went wrong.

On this day, they were to focus on the human skull. They had an actual skeleton on hand for reference. When Sister Stark finally got around to harassing Jaya, it was while referring to the front of the skull, which was thicker than the rest.

'When injuries occur here,' Sister Stark said, 'the injured party is often fortunate, as the brain is quite protected by this region of the skull. The top, sides, and rear are thinner, but the forehead bone is quite protective. Are you following me, Miss Devani?'

Jaya remembered what Edith had said; she was merely a prop in Miss Stark's ongoing internal drama. Whatever the woman was sending out represented what was unfolding inside of her, and had little to do with Jaya herself.

'No,' said Jaya, 'I don't understand. Could you please explain it one more time?'

Jaya did not look at Edith, but she sensed that her classmate was smiling.

'Yes, certainly,' Sister Stark said to Jaya.

She then proceeded to repeat the information about varying skull thickness, using the skeleton as a reference. Jaya nodded along with her words, and when at the end the nurse again asked if she understood, Jaya not only answered in the affirmative, but also took the liberty of echoing the lesson back to the woman, assuring her that her answer was sincere, and the teaching had been a success.

From that day on, the two women were mostly at peace. It wasn't a perfect relationship, but it had improved significantly. Edith had been right. It was a valuable lesson in compassion, and one that Jaya would take with her for the rest of her life.

In the end, Jaya graduated the course at the top of her class, and along the way she made a good friend in Edith.

CHAPTER 32

England, September 1914

Jaya was working as a nurse on the hospital boat. Almost immediately after Prime Minister Asquith declared allegiance to the Allied Powers, especially France, in their war against the Central Powers led by Germany and the Ottoman Empire, the wounded began to arrive from The Front. It would be a long, sad and busy war for Jaya.

Still, in her quiet moments, Jaya wondered about William. How were Christopher and Edward? What were they doing during this terrible time? Edward was now eighteen, and she hoped he had not done something so foolish as to enter the army. She occasionally looked through articles about the Indian Council, in case William's name was mentioned, but it never was. She supposed that he was still on the Council. It was a good paying job, which required little effort from him; he'd be foolish to leave it.

Jaya had a small life now. She never thought of love and romance, though she was still quite young, only thirty-three. She had a few friends, especially Edith, among the nurses she worked with. They'd grown even closer in the years after passing their course.

Work with the suffragettes had become busy before the assassination of the Archduke. The movement had been close to outright success, but patriotism and the need to consolidate everyone's efforts toward the coming war meant even the suffragettes decided to postpone everything until after the war. Elizabeth took a job in an ammunition factory in Manchester, and Ruth, who Jaya had grown close to since she left the factory, was now an ambulance driver at The Front.

She'd received a letter from Ruth three weeks before:

Dearest Jaya,

Your letters always raise my spirits. This job, like yours, can take its toll on my mind. So many young men losing their lives for things we are not even sure about. Patriotism is the easy way to get through this war, but as soon as you move even a slight distance it falls apart. Like so many things those

in power try to get us to accept. Giving your one life for a cause you don't
completely understand, in the name of a country that has not always been
fair, seems the definition of injustice. The men fight under a flag and the
women clean up the wreckage. Women like you.

The poor patients you spoke of in your last letter saddened me deeply.
These young, working-class men think the world will be different for them
on the other side. I wish it were so, but I know it will not, at least not
without a fight. We know this.

You keep up the good work and I will try to stay alive.
Love from your friend and ally in the struggle,
Ruth

Jaya feared for Ruth. It was dangerous where she was. She
often asked the men who came in from The Front if they'd ever
come across her, but there had been no one yet.

Perhaps loneliness was what occasionally drove Jaya's
thoughts to William and even, occasionally, to Rafik. Would she
spend the rest of her life making the decision between the two
men over and over again in her mind? Following each to the
end in her imagination, as if she'd made the choices that she
hadn't. It was a common mental occupation for her. In the end,
she'd chosen herself, and that had put an end to those parallel
lives she might have lived, at least in reality, though not in her
constant fantasies and questioning regrets.

She continued to draw and paint regularly when she had the time. Just as when she'd been a girl, drawing was her place of relief and happiness. There she was in control. She could decide where she wanted to go and what it would look like once she got there. She could decide what would happen and how it would end.

She'd been sitting on a bench in the park along the Thames, where the hospital boat was docked, and was sketching a scene from her memory. It was one of the few times that she and Krishnan had had a bit of money. They'd bought a half-pound of sweets and had gone to the centre of the village where a travelling juggler was putting on a show. Jaya had never seen a juggler before and, at first, thought it was some sort of magic.

Later she and Krishnan practiced and practiced using small stones. Soon Krishnan was juggling four stones at a time. Jaya thought her brother would always be the best, the best at everything he ever put his mind to. She'd idolised him.

While she drew the picture of Krishnan juggling, she tried to ignore the aching wound in her heart that never healed. She would think of only good things about her brother. Never about their last time together, which was the saddest day of her life.

She was engrossed in her drawing and didn't hear Edith until she sat on the bench next to her. 'That's good. Is it Krishnan?'

'Yes,' Jaya said, smiling at her friend.

Edith knew much about Jaya, just as Jaya knew much about Edith and her two girls: Ruby and Madeline. Jaya sometimes went to Edith's house for dinners or birthday parties. She enjoyed being included, since she missed not having a family in England. Edith made her feel like she was part of her family.

One night, after the girls were in bed, Jaya told Edith about William.

'I felt he loved me,' Jaya said. 'That's why I followed him here.'

'Perhaps he did.'

'He certainly didn't act like it in the end.'

'It's hard to know, Jaya. People have dual natures. He may have loved you when you were alone together, but became someone different when not in your presence. People can do that.'

'Then,' Jaya sighed, 'it could not have been true love.'

'Just because you had only part of his heart,' Edith said, 'doesn't mean that the love between you both was not real.'

'But if the rest of his heart was divided,' said Jaya, 'then it does matter. It makes him a fraud. A cheat might believe his lies in the moment, but it makes no difference if he walks away laughing to himself.'

'I think people are more complex than that,' Edith said.

'No,' Jaya disagreed, shaking her head. 'I think people must find unity within themselves. What we say, what we think and what we do, must be in alignment. Otherwise, how will we ever find truthfulness?'

'But there is always dark and light in every situation,' said Edith. 'Shadings. Mysteries. We even have mysteries within ourselves.'

'Ah,' said Jaya, 'you are a wise soul. But if I ever give away my heart again, it shall be the whole heart. Not part of it. Not some of the time. And that person must do the same. It has to be all or nothing.'

'I understand. But after that day comes, you can rest assured that life will test you. Your heart will be disputed, and perhaps even divided. Because you are human, Jaya. We're all human.'

A gentle warmth spread over Jaya's cheeks. Edith was wise and insightful and her *friend*. She closed the book with the drawing of a juggling Krishnan and packed up her pencils and charcoals and put everything in her satchel.

'Our shift will soon start,' Jaya said.

'I thought you'd forgotten. That's why I came looking for you. I know how you get once you start with your drawing,' Edith said, beaming at Jaya.

They linked arms and walked toward the hospital.

***

When they arrived, the ship's guard rushed up to Jaya. She was not keen to see him. He'd proposed love to her twice before, once when he was drunk, and she was in no mood to put him off again.

'Jaya,' Bert said.

'Bert, we must rush. Our shift is starting,' Jaya said, pushing past him.

'No wait!' He followed quickly after them. 'A man was here to see you.'

'A man? What sort of man?'

'Yes, a man, an important one I think.' Bert nodded. 'He was quite forlorn to have missed you.'

'What was his name?' Jaya couldn't think which man would come to the hospital looking for her.

'William Edmundson.'

Bert said the name as if it was any other. But it took Jaya's breath away. Edith noticed the effect it had on her friend.

'Did he leave a note?' Edith asked Bert, while Jaya recovered from the shock.

'No note. Just a message.'

'What was it?' Jaya asked. 'What did he say?'

'He said that he's to remain in the neighbourhood for a single hour. Went to that pub, The Queen's Arms, down the road. Said he'd wait for you there.'

She knew the place. It didn't have a good reputation. In fact, it was known for being a bit rough, certainly not the kind of establishment that William was known to frequent. Unless, of course, he had fallen on hard times. She hoped that wasn't the case.

'How long ago was that?' Jaya asked.

'I would say,' he began, clearing his throat, 'fifty or so minutes ago.'

Jaya looked at Edith. 'Shall I go with you?' Edith asked.

'No,' Jaya said. 'I'd rather see him alone.'

'I understand.' Edith touched Jaya's shoulder. 'Good luck. I'll sort things out for you with the matron on duty. Don't worry. You go. Find out what he wants.'

Bert said, 'Time's running out.'

Jaya looked at him, and then kissed Edith's cheek and hurried out the ship's main door and returned to the street.

***

While making her way over to The Queen's Arms, Jaya understood why William would choose such an establishment. He ran no risk of running into anyone he knew.

That was disappointing. It was just like the old days; William still lacked the courage to be true to himself. She found that sad.

She heard her name as she stepped through the front door of The Queen's Arms. Turning around, she saw him, William. Her old love. Her first love. He looked as handsome as ever, yet leaner, more tired. He held out his hand to her and she took it. There would be no hugs then, she thought.

'This place is not very nice. Could we go for a walk? It's a sunny day,' William suggested.

Jaya nodded and followed him out.

Together, the pair made their way to the same park that she and Edith had left just minutes ago. They wove their way down an assortment of paths, and through a variety of trees, before settling upon a white bench which was adequately concealed.

Jaya was not sure of how she was feeling. It was odd that, in a way, she felt relief to see him again, though she wasn't sure where that feeling came from.

'So, you're a nurse now?' William asked.

'Yes,' Jaya said.

'That's good … I looked for you once, but I failed to find you.'

Jaya nodded and said nothing more about that. 'How are the boys? I think of them often.'

William ignored her question. 'I've missed you, Jaya,' he said to her. 'Have you missed me at all?'

It took her some time to think what to reply. But when she

did, she gave an honest answer. After all, as she had said to Edith, she wished for her inner and outer self to be in as much harmony as possible.

'Yes,' she said, quietly. 'I have missed you, William.'

He touched her hand and tears filled his eyes. He seemed to not only miss her, but to crave her. This touched her in a way she could not deny. And still, here they were. Hiding amid the foliage in a park. She pulled her hand away.

'How's Rebecca?' Jaya asked.

'I was hoping,' he said, 'we wouldn't speak about her.'

'Why?' Jaya asked. 'William, it has been over ten years since I left your home. Many things have changed for me, and I suspect many things have changed for you.'

William dragged his hands ruthlessly through his hair before staring back at her, his eyes wild as he searched for words. Words that he found hard to accept. That much was clear.

'Some things have not changed. Some things will never change, no matter how much I wished otherwise. Jaya, I think of you always. In my mind … and heart, you have never left.'

Jaya could do nothing about that. She would not say it was the same for her. Seeing him again confirmed that she was a vastly different person than the scared, lost, heartbroken ayah who had left his home so many years before. She had loved him, loved him desperately, but she didn't love him anymore.

'You and Rebecca are married,' Jaya reminded him.

'Yes. But does that matter?' William took her hand in his again. He tried to pull her closer, to put his arms around her, but she stopped him. He sat back and accepted her denial.

'Your marriage is not really the most important thing here,' Jaya said. 'Our love affair was a long time ago. I left your house completely ruined, and desperately sad. I felt stupid believing the promises you made me were contracts between us. You showed me that they'd been little more than whispers in the night to calm a child. For, indeed, I had been a child. I am a woman now.'

'Jaya. I'm sorry for how I treated you. I think about it constantly. I did many things wrong. I'll never be that way again, I promise. And I'm sorry. I really am.'

'I believe that you are, William. I forgive you.'

'You've changed,' he said. 'I read about you in the papers.'

'And?' Jaya asked.

'You've become political, then? It's true, what I read?'

'I don't think of it as political. I think of it as being human.'

'I did look for you, Jaya. I went to the Ayahs' Home. I even spoke with the matron there. Nobody knew where you were. Or nobody would tell me.'

'I haven't been living at that place since I first walked out of your door, William. Even then, I only stayed for one night. I was lucky really, with the way things have turned out.'

'You seem happy. I don't know … you seem content in yourself in some way. You look so beautiful. I can see why that man Rafik still loves you.'

Jaya was shocked to hear Rafik's name coming from William. 'Rafik? Do you know about Rafik?'

'No, of course not. You mentioned him once is all. Have you married anyone?'

Jaya could not remember having told William Rafik's name, but then a lot of time had passed. Perhaps she'd forgotten.

'No, I'm not married. I am happy, though. You know, William, women can be happy and not married. I finally have a purpose in my life and freedom over it as well. I've done good work with the movement. And now I'm a nurse at the hospital. With the war going on, I want to help.'

William looked at her with eyes full of sadness. 'Rebecca is insisting we move away from London for the war. We're going north with Christopher, and our daughter, Jane. Her family has an estate.'

'You have a daughter?'

'Yes, she's ten now. Surprisingly, she's very like me, much more than the boys ever were. They were more like Sara, I think.'

'Do they see Sara?' Jaya asked. It was odd to speak her name after all these years and feel nothing. She'd been so cruel to both herself and Sayida. She had loomed so large, but now she didn't exist in Jaya's mind at all.

William hesitated. 'No, they don't. Jaya, Sara died in the asylum. She killed herself; she got a pair of scissors and cut her wrists. She bled to death.'

Jaya's jaw dropped. The feelings she had on the day that Sara was committed to the asylum flooded back. 'Oh, my goodness, William. I'm so sorry! That's awful.'

'Yes … well, I'm to blame. She did it shortly after she was told about the divorce. I should have done many things differently.'

Not only did Jaya think about the deceit, but also reflected on her own experiences in the asylum, of being there when she wasn't clinically insane, of being drugged and the adverse effects it had on her, as it had on Sara. Would Sara have eventually taken her own life if she had remained at home and been drugged by William, or was it the unbearable life in the asylum that made her do it? Either way, Jaya still felt some responsibility, but did not voice this to William, as she could see clearly how much he regretted his past actions. She took small comfort in knowing that Sara was no longer suffering.

Jaya could see William carried many burdens in his heart and likely would until the end of his life.

'And Edward? Is Edward moving with you? I think of the boys often, you know. I loved them very much. Leaving them was difficult.'

'Edward has volunteered. He's at The Front. We've not heard from him for three months.'

Jaya's heart fell. How could her dear, kind-hearted Edward be at The Front? How had William allowed it?

'I'm sure he's fine,' Jaya said, more to calm herself than William.

They both knew that was a lie. Young men were dying by the thousands in the trenches at The Front. Jaya hoped Edward would be among the lucky ones to come home alive, not to be buried in a foreign country. She would pray for him.

'I must go, William,' she said, rising. She needed to get back to the hospital. 'I don't know why I rushed to see you. Bert, the guard, relayed your message. And I ran, William. I ran for you. But in truth, deep down, I don't think I ran to meet you. I think I ran to meet myself.'

William looked confused. 'Jaya, I know it's wrong, but could I see you again? Is there any chance you might ever love me again? In the way that you did?'

Jaya knew all of the power was in her hands. William was kneeling before her begging, if only in words. Her cruder self might have punished him. She would not allow that. He *had*

373

loved her. As Edith said, he had loved her with the part of him that could. She'd learned to accept that. And now the man she had spent so many beautiful nights with, the man who had taught her to enjoy her body, that man stood before her asking for mercy. She would give it to him.

She hugged William.

'William, I loved you very much. And I thank you for the love you gave me, and for everything you gave me. But I've changed. I can't be someone's mistress again. You go home. Love your wife. Keep our memories, but know that I will not be with you again. And we will both be fine.'

She walked toward the entrance to the park and then to the hospital where people were waiting for her. She didn't look back.

CHAPTER 33

The war continued to escalate as Christmas passed and the new year arrived. There wasn't much to be happy about in 1915. The casualties at The Front were high. Many soldiers arrived at Jaya's hospital already near death. There was little they could do but give them morphine to ease the pain, and sit beside them to help them die peacefully. Unfortunately, Jaya had grown used to death.

It was sad that these young men died almost always without a single family member nearby. That often made Jaya think about her own family. She'd sent two letters to Krishnan, but he never replied. Still, she wanted to know about them, so she decided to send her mother a letter. Despite the many problems between them, her mother replied to that letter, so they continued the correspondence.

The replies took months to arrive, and were frustrating in their lack of detail. Her mother had to pay a letter writer in the bazaar to write the letters since she was illiterate. Perhaps that was why the letters had so few details. Jaya asked about her brother in each letter, but her mother never mentioned him in her replies. Perhaps it was a punishment for Jaya who had left them behind. Still, it was good to hear from someone at home, even if the news was sparse.

On one cold January night with a lacerating wind beating against the hospital's windows, a dark-skinned British soldier named Corporal Ayan Miah appeared in her ward. Soldiers of Indian origin were not common, but not unusual. Jaya was always keen to talk to the ones who appeared on her ward.

Corporal Ayan Miah had come to England as a lascar, only to find himself on a troubled and winding path that eventually led him to sign up for military service. It was not unlike her own path, though he was quite a bit younger than her, only twenty-one. Jaya realised, by the way he spoke to her, that he thought they were of a similar age when, in fact, she was more than ten years his senior. He was not the first person to imagine Jaya was much younger than she was. Despite the rough life she had endured, especially since arriving in England, her face remained unlined and did not show the effects of the passing years.

Ayan's ailment was of an unusual nature. He had no wounds, but his superiors guessed that he had consumed some infected food that had been poisoned. His skin had developed boils and he needed a great deal of rest. Jaya knew that such an ailment could not be treated with medicine. The poison needed to make its way through his body, and it could only do that with lots of rest and plenty of clean water, both of which were hard to find at The Front. His body would either find its way to recovery, or it would not. It was a game of waiting.

So, that was exactly what she and Edith and the four other nurses on hand offered, rest and plenty of water. When the male doctor arrived to check on Ayan, he hardly gave him half a glance, knowing full well that, despite the care being given, the man was held in the hands of fate.

Ayan, when he was awake, was keen to talk to someone, and Jaya, if she was not busy, filled that need. He, like her, missed home. He also had a brother that he'd left behind, and who he thought about often. He intended to go back as soon as he could, and his wishes became Jaya's too as the days passed.

'No question about it, I'm going home as soon as I can.' Ayan's breathing was weak, yet the force of his words could not be ignored. 'We must all revisit the place from which we came. It is part of being human. Animals may stray, but human beings must reunite with their pasts.'

Jaya helped Ayan into his wheelchair and wheeled him outdoors where the air was nice and crisp. She pushed him off the boat and across to the park. She sat down on a bench next to his parked wheelchair.

'I'm not the person I was before,' she explained to her new friend. 'That person has vanished, like a ghost. Maybe no one in India will even know me.'

'How so? How have you changed?'

She shrugged. 'I'm stronger now. More confident.'

'Then bring your new self to your old land. Does no part of you crave such an experience?'

'I'm not sure ...' Jaya said.

'Why?'

'Because the place has nothing left to offer me. I left there in search of something different, something out of the ordinary. Although what I've discovered was not at all what I expected, I must admit that it all fits together. So what would be the point of going back?'

Ayan smiled, appreciating her candour. 'You seem to think that life is lived as a straight line with one thing coming after another.'

'Does it not?'

He shook his head. 'That's just an illusion. On some level, yes, we exist in linear time. One year follows the next. Each new event is stacked on top of some great big pile. But we also exist in our minds. And in our minds we are always looking in different directions: forward, backwards and sideways. Be that as it may, you never left your home. It still exists within you.'

'But I don't see why that means I must return.'

'That's just the thing, you can't know what such a journey will bring. There's no way of knowing. Only God is in possession of such knowledge. That is until you get there.'

'And supposing the knowledge is not worth it? Or the knowledge is painful? I love my brother very much. What if I go home and he has forgotten me completely?'

'You still live in his mind, too. I'm sure of it.'

'I don't know if I have the energy for that journey. Physically or mentally.'

'God only shares with us what we're ready to receive. Otherwise, the message would never penetrate our minds. I yearn for home, always, not only to check after my brother. I want to feel that heat, I want to see the plants and hear the birds from my childhood. I want to smell that spicy air. Something tells me that once my feet sink back into that land, I will have finally understood something about the shape of the journey that life has taken me on.'

'I wonder,' Jaya said.

Is that how life works? So tidy like a perfect little bow? She doubted it. Already she saw that life was far more disorganised and haphazard than that. She did understand about wanting to feel that sun, hear those familiar birds and see those trees of her childhood.

'Will you stay in India then? Maybe get married?' Jaya asked.

'I thought you were going to marry me.'

Jaya laughed. 'I'm flattered, but I doubt it.'

Ayan smiled too. 'As for staying in India, I'll know when I get there. I know somehow I'll get the answer.'

'You're very certain,' Jaya said. She conceded to herself only that the youth often were.

'You must want to go too; otherwise your thoughts wouldn't be haunted by the possibility. You know that something there is calling you as well.'

'Perhaps, but it's more complicated than I've admitted,' Jaya said.

'How so?'

She looked at her watch and saw that they'd been away for some time. She should get Ayan back. Just the same, she knew this conversation was rare and special. When would she ever again have the chance to meet a man with whom she had so much in common? If Ayan improved, he'd be back out at sea within two days of his release. If he did not, then another form of departure would claim him. Either way, their time together was limited.

'Remember I explained to you the conditions under which I left?' Jaya asked. 'How I was torn between two fates, two men?'

'Yes.'

'Well, the man, the British man, with whom I arrived here, well, that chapter is closed. But the other man is a different story. I had hardly met him when suddenly I was leaving for England. He was older than me, with children from his first wife who had died. He was an intellectual. I think we might have had a good life together. While I've been here, I've often thought about him. I've thought that maybe I made a bad choice. I would be very sad to go home and find he had married someone else, but it's almost certain that he has.'

'How will you know?' Ayan straightened his spine. 'Maybe he hasn't.'

'Perhaps. But it would be sad if he had.'

'Don't think of it that way. Life goes the way it goes. Jaya, this story of yours has not reached an end.'

'You mean my life story?'

'Yes. That too. But I'm referring to the story about this man. What's his name?'

'Rafik,' she whispered.

'Rafik, good. You have no ending with him.'

'I do. I left.'

'This man stays in your mind. Not because you feel a love for him, maybe you do, maybe you don't. But a connection is still there. I can hear it in your voice. Your reluctance to speak his name out.'

'I am comfortable here. I earn a living. I have friends. I am part of English life, of this city's goings-on. In fact, in many ways, I feel as if this is my nation now. I feel a freedom here that would not be available to me in India.'

'All very positive and noble things. I love England for many things, too. I've made a life here as well. But I appreciate the wonder of the path God has placed me on. Just the same, home calls to me. Do I know why? Not wholly. Am I convinced that I must obey the call? Not always. But I do know this, Jaya, it keeps on calling. Every day it calls, the call is stronger than the last.'

Jaya didn't say it out, but home called her, too.

***

Before Jaya finished her shift that night, she told Edith about the conversation she'd had with Ayan. Edith made it clear that she agreed with Ayan.

'So, you think I should plan a trip to India? I've been saving money, but I don't have enough. It would take me a few more years to have the right amount.'

Edith looked at Jaya. 'You must go. However long it takes to get the money.'

***

The next day, Jaya arrived at work early, eager to talk with her new favourite patient before her day began to get hectic and noisy. She went to his bed and found it empty. She slowly walked back to the nurse who was on duty during the night. She didn't want to ask for fear of the answer she might get, but she had to know.

'What happened to Ayan?' Jaya asked, her voice shaking. 'Did he pass away?'

'No, my dear,' said the older nurse.

'Where is he then?'

'We got word that we're getting many new wounded later this morning. We needed space for them. You will have a busy day.'

'Where did they take Ayan?'

'They transferred him to a local hospital since he does not require specialised care. He only really needs rest. He's nearly recovered. He might be discharged in a day or so, and sent back to The Front two days later.'

'Do you know where he is right now?'

Getting directions from the older nurse she left the ward, and on the way out she told the matron she had a problem and needed the morning off. She was allowed since it was unheard of that Jaya would take a day off. It must be something important if she was asking for time off when they were expecting new wounded.

She walked a half-mile to the place where Ayan had been transferred. It was a sort of rest home. When she got there, he wasn't in bed. He was dressed and seated at a table with four other patients, playing cards with one hand and holding a cigarette in the other. Though the four other players all had white skin, Ayan seemed entirely at ease. From his easy manner, his smile, his relaxed shoulders, she could see he was used to being in mixed company.

'Ayan,' she said, fearing that she would embarrass him.

When he looked up, he smiled. Right away, he abandoned his card game. The others did not seem to mind. A visit from a woman overtook a card game for all of them.

'Jaya,' he said. 'What a nice surprise! Come. Let's talk outside.'

'Our conversation yesterday,' she said. 'It meant a lot.'

'Did it? I'm glad. It meant a lot to me too.'

'I'll be going back to India. In the summer months. Next year.'

Ayan smiled, the sunlight painting his face. 'I'm envious of you.'

'You'll get back, too,' she said, with a firmness that gave it the weight of an actual promise. Ayan stayed quiet. He'd go back to The Front before the week ended. Nothing could be counted on after that.

'May I kiss you, Jaya?' he asked. She stepped forward and kissed him on the right cheek. He was the first man she had kissed since William.

Ayan opened his eyes and smiled. 'Thank you, Jaya.'

They sat on the nearby bench. Ayan took out a small piece of paper and a stub of a pencil from his pocket. 'Write your address, here and in India. When I get to The Front, can I write you? It helps to have someone to write to.'

'Of course. I'd like that.'

'And after all of this, we'll see each other at home.'

Jaya smiled, but said nothing.

Ayan's face got serious. 'Promise me.'

'I promise.' Jaya meant it. She would not forget Ayan.

They said goodbye. This time they stood in the foyer and the doorman looked on. She promised to visit him again the next day.

But as the night nurse had warned, they received many new patients that afternoon. A hundred and seventy-four soldiers arrived, but there were only thirty-five spare beds. Fifty-six had died the night before, and many were still on stretchers in the corridor. Many had grave and serious wounds. Very many more died in the course of that day. Jaya became so distracted by work that she could not lend much of her mind to Ayan that day. Or the next.

When she finally got back to the rest home, he was gone. Jaya wrote him four letters in all. He never replied to any of them.

CHAPTER 34

In her heart, when she did not receive a reply to her first letter, Jaya knew Ayan had been killed at The Front. She wrote three more letters, just in case. She'd spent only a few days with Ayan, and yet he had changed the direction of her thinking and of her life. She'd made promises to him, and she would not let him down. She would return to India.

She'd told him that she would travel in the summer of 1916, but the money was still not enough. That did not deter her. She continued saving. The war ended, and she got a job in a big hospital in the city. In the summer of 1919, she had finally saved enough money.

It was time for Jaya to go home.

***

Jaya was thirty-eight years old, and she had been away from home for eighteen years. She had no idea what she would find, or how what she found might affect her. But she believed that she was ready to find out.

With the war having just ended, the people of India desired their independence more than ever. Riots increased throughout the country, eventually culminating with the Amritsar Massacre, which claimed the lives of hundreds of innocent Indians. The friction between the British and Indian people had escalated. Many were flocking to get behind Gandhi, so taken were they by his vision of a nonviolent world where the people of India could decide their own path. Also, the Government of India Act had just been passed, allowing the opportunity for Indians to be represented in government, alongside the British. Change was happening with such rapidity.

Edith was married now. Her second husband was a soldier named Harvey Dawes. She'd met him at work when he was brought in on a stretcher. Harvey was missing his right leg, so he could no longer participate in combat. This was fine with Edith, as it meant she would not lose him in such a way. He made a good living behind a desk, still working for the army, like his wife. Harvey fell in love with Ruby and Madeline as much as he had with their mother. They were happy together. Despite that – and much to Jaya's delight – Edith decided that she would leave Harvey at home with the girls and set off with Jaya on a grand adventure. She would go home with Jaya. Jaya wasn't sure how things would go once she was home and having someone to lean on was going to be a big help.

***

With their arrival in India only a few hours away, exhaustion and seasickness had taken their toll on both women. It had been a long, rough trip, and Jaya sensed that Edith missed her family and regretted having joined her for the voyage, though neither of them mentioned it. Jaya was starting to think the entire trip might have been a mistake.

Jaya remembered her journey to England. How different that experience had been! She thought about Sayida. She wondered how different everything might have been if Sayida had not been killed by Komali. On deck, she'd often look out over the waves and think of her dear friend somewhere in that vastness.

As they approached the Indian shoreline, Edith became excited, asking Jaya endless questions. Jaya on the other hand became nervous. She only knew that her mother would be waiting for her when the ship made land. Would Krishnan be there? She'd never received a letter from him. Her mother never mentioned him. She feared for what awaited her.

When the boat docked in Calcutta, Jaya's eyes landed right on her brother though he was in a crowd of people waiting for their loved ones to arrive. Mosquitoes buzzed around annoyingly, and fireflies flitted around like tiny lights. The familiar smell of burning coconut oil made Jaya feel as though she had never been away.

As soon as Krishnan saw Jaya, he started moving towards her and Edith.

In a moment they were standing in front of each other. Jaya's heart pounded in her throat and her eyes filled with tears. Krishnan's beard had a few white hairs, but his eyes were young; they were her dear brother's eyes.

Krishnan spoke first. 'I'm sorry. I am ashamed of my behaviour. I wrote to you so many times … but I could not find a way to take my hateful words back,' Krishnan said. He spoke quickly, the words falling out of his mouth. 'Since you've been writing to our mother instead of me, I thought you were completely done with me. I hope I can make up for all that I have done to you.'

Jaya listened and said nothing. Tears poured down her face. When he finished, she threw her arms around him.

'I forgave you a long time ago,' she said. 'I know I disappointed you, so I need to apologise to you, too.' Although Krishnan had not said as much, Jaya hoped that he had forgiven her for her indiscretion.

Then a boy of about seven poked his head from behind. Krishnan didn't need to tell her who he was – he was his son in every way. It was as though she were looking at Krishnan as a boy: the cheeky smile, the mischievous twinkle in his eyes and the identical facial features.

'I am Chandran,' the boy said when his father pulled him to the front. 'You are my Auntie Jaya.'

He held out his hand to Jaya, a serious look on his face. Jaya took it. 'Yes, I am your Auntie Jaya, and you are my nephew Chandran. I am so happy to meet you.'

'Who is this then?' Edith asked, coming to stand next to Jaya. Jaya turned to her, her heart finally settled, overflowing with joy.

'This is my brother Krishnan and my nephew Chandran. This is my good friend Edith. She accompanied me on the journey.'

Edith shook Krishnan's hand. 'I've heard about you for years. I've seen so many drawings of you; I would have known you anywhere. I'm happy to finally meet you.'

'Come, come meet my wife. She's over in the shade. She was attacked by mosquitoes,' Krishnan explained. 'It's no good for her to be in the sun.'

Loki wore a big hat, and although Jaya could see the mosquito bites upon her face, the woman was still lovely, and clearly so to any onlooker. Jaya hugged her, calling her 'sister'. Edith, too, leaned in and hugged the woman. The malaise they felt on the ship, as thick and oppressive as it had been, now vanished and was replaced by joy.

It felt so very good to be home, Jaya thought. Ayan had been right.

*****

A journey on the new train and then the bullock cart to the village took two days altogether. Finally, they arrived in Khesar. Krishnan took Jaya and Edith to their mother's house.

'She is getting old,' Krishnan warned on the way.

'I thought that might be the case,' Jaya said.

Still, she had not been prepared for how old she was. Her age was clear, as her bones felt brittle in Jaya's embrace, and her face had changed completely, overcome by countless sags and wrinkles. It was hard to imagine that this was the woman that Jaya had been afraid of, who she ran away from nearly every day.

'You have returned,' her mother said.

They hugged and Jaya thought that it might have been the first hug she'd ever received from her mother. The years, and all that had filled them, slipped away. Jaya finally let go of what had caused the unease between her and her mother. She thought of Ayan and his idea that a circle would be completed once she was home. Perhaps she did not have any revelations about the life path she had followed but, at least, it allowed her to forgive her mother... and for now that was good enough.

At the rear of Maji's home, in the modest garden, Jaya and Edith, along with Krishnan and Loki and their son Chandran enjoyed a meal of squash and rice and endless cups of mango tea. Jaya laughed so much and cried so frequently that day that she fully forgot her shipboard lassitude until the sun went down, and she was suddenly exhausted. Edith too.

The pair were set up in a tiny guest room, so slender that one could walk across it in the time it took to complete a single breath. However, each of them had a bed, albeit a small one, in which it was unwise to turn over, along with fresh sheets and plump, warm pillows.

Before she fell asleep, she thought about the happiness she'd felt and witnessed since she'd arrived, especially the day that had just ended. She wondered if her family's apparent state of contentment was owed to her presence. Although she wished for nothing more than for her loved ones to be content, part of her hoped that her presence was contributing to their mood. She felt welcomed home in a way she never could have imagined.

***

With the first light of morning, Jaya was able to see the situation in her mother's home through clearer eyes. The truth was, though her family remained quite close and contented, they, like all others, were not without their problems. Over breakfast, while Edith still slept in the guest room, Maji explained to Jaya that there were several issues between Krishnan and Loki.

'She sees other men,' Maji whispered, teacup clutched in hand.

'No, she doesn't,' Jaya said.

'Ssshhh,' her mother said. 'Yes, she does.'

'Oh, you must be exaggerating. It must be a rumour.'

'It's a man down the street who owns a market. They flirt. I do not approve.'

'Oh,' said Jaya, with a wave of her hand, 'you're being dramatic.'

'In any case, it breaks my Krishnan's heart,' she said. 'He gets jealous. He tells himself wild stories.'

'And it's no help to have you fanning the flames of his imagination. Loki's a sweet lady. They have a good family. Leave them alone.'

'Mmm, well, she feigns sweetness, but I don't always trust it.'

Sipping her own tea, Jaya felt relieved to see the bubble of perfection pierced. Her relief instantly made way for guilt, but it did not evaporate entirely. Her mother was the same woman she'd always been. It was Jaya who had had the distance from her that allowed her to accept her mother's temperament. Jaya knew that being embroiled in such petty daily dramas would have made her crazy. She could feel the places where the puzzle parts of India no longer fit in the places that they used to.

Her mother continued to gossip about her daughter-in-law. About how she squandered Krishnan's money, how she spoiled Chandran. Jaya listened with one ear. She was waiting for a chance to ask the question she needed to. Finally, a break in the conversation appeared.

'Do you know where Rafik lives now?' Jaya asked.

Her mother hesitated, looked at her daughter, but somehow, against her nature, held her tongue. Jaya knew all the words her mother swallowed. All about the good husband Jaya had left behind. The shame the broken promise had caused her. The grandchildren she did not have. None of that was spoken of. Instead, she gave her daughter directions to Rafik's house.

***

She decided to send him a message so that they might meet

away from his house or the bakery. She wrote a note and sent it with a passing child. Later that day, they met at a teahouse in the village. It was agreed they would be there at three when the sun was less hot.

Jaya arrived early on purpose. Her nerves were a mess. Edith had asked if Jaya wanted her company, but Jaya refused. She needed to see Rafik alone.

She sat on a wooden chair in the shade cast by the building, and a young girl brought out her tea. Sipping her tea from a heavy clay mug, she saw him before he saw her. She set the tea down and waited for him.

'Good afternoon, Jaya. You have not changed a bit,' Rafik said. 'I would have found you on any busy street in London. I am sure of it.'

He held out his hand and she shook it. He looked around and noticed people were watching them. Jaya knew already that the two women from England were the big news story in Khesar. Now they could add this bit about Rafik meeting the woman who had left him.

'Let's walk to your river. I always think of it as your river,' Rafik said.

Jaya took the mug and chair back inside and thanked the girl. Then she and Rafik headed down the dirt road leaving the village. Jaya thought of the many times she had run down this road to get away from her mother. At that time, she knew every break in the forest that led her down to the river. Now, everything was grown over and unfamiliar. Still, they found a narrow path and followed it to the banks of the river, sitting next to one another on a boulder. They sat quietly for a bit, watching the river flow on its endless journey.

'Jaya,' Rafik said, 'you must know I am married.'

'No, I didn't know, but I am happy for you.'

'Are you?' he said. Did Jaya hear a tinge of sadness?

She nodded.

'My wife is a good woman. She has made my life happy.'

'I'm glad,' Jaya said. 'You deserve a good woman. You are a good man.'

They sat quietly for a bit. Jaya watched a lizard come down from the nearby tree and drink at the edge of the water.

'Do you still draw?' Rafik asked.

'Yes, I do. I paint, too. It gives me a lot of enjoyment.'

Rafik shifted. Jaya could hear there was something he wanted to say. She would not push him; he would say it when he could.

'So, about the letter …' he started.

Jaya looked at him confused. 'The letter?'

'Yes, the letter I sent, about a year or so after you left. Do you not remember it?' Rafik asked.

'I never received a letter.'

Rafik looked at her. 'I sent it to your employer, Mr Edmundson. It probably arrived there about a year or more after you left that position. I learned of your leaving quite a long time after it happened.'

Jaya had never received any letters, and a single letter would have been something to mention when he found her at the hospital that day. But he had said nothing, and he'd brought nothing with him. Then she remembered something he'd said that day. He said: 'Rafik, the man who still loves you.' He must have received the letter and read it. How else would he have known Rafik's name? How could he have done that? She became upset, near tears.

Rafik must have noticed the change on Jaya's face. 'What is it?'

'I think Mr Edmundson got the letter. I think he read it. But he never gave it to me. I'm only now putting the pieces together, now that you told me you sent a letter.'

Rafik did not become angry; instead Jaya could see only sadness. She felt that same sadness in her heart.

'I waited for three years for a reply. I'm such a silly old man. I nearly missed the chance to marry my wife. I kept thinking your reply must be on the way. I kept assuring myself that it was. But after three years it was foolish to keep waiting. I gave up. I married. I tried to forget about you.'

'I'm sorry, Rafik. I'm sorry that happened.' She was sorry and angry. William had committed a crime against both of them.

Rafik looked at the water passing their spot on the riverbank. 'Would you have come back? In the letter I told you how much I loved you. And how whatever had happened between you and Mr Edmundson meant nothing to me. That I would be waiting here for you. Would you have come back?'

At that time she had been in the asylum. What if William had come with the letter? What if he had managed to get her released? Would she have then chosen Rafik over William? Or would she have chosen herself over both of them?

Jaya nearly laughed. Suddenly she understood. Ayan had been right. This trip home had closed her circle; it did show her what it all meant. She looked up and hoped that somewhere Ayan was reading her heart.

'Rafik, I want to make my own way in this world, I have always wanted that. Even if I had received the letter, I would not have come back for you. I'm sorry if that's not the answer you wanted to hear.'

Rafik smiled. 'Actually, it's the exact answer I wanted to hear. It means the path was set for me to find my wife, no matter what happened with my letter. We will forgive Mr Edmundson. Carrying anger and regret is never good.'

Jaya agreed. She was tired of carrying such things. Rafik was indeed a wise and loving man.

They talked of other things for a while and then walked back to the village as the sun fell deep below the western horizon.

***

That night, before falling asleep, Jaya told Edith about the conversation she'd had with Rafik. She told her about his missing letter.

'William was wrong to do that. It was not his place,' Edith said.

'Yes, but it's done. In any case, maybe he did me a kindness. In my misery, I might have given in and come home to Rafik. It would have been the wrong choice.'

'Do you really think so?' Edith asked.

'Yes, my life is in England. I still have work to do there. It is there that I can live my own life, the one I want. That is all I ever wanted, Edith – a whole life.'

'So, I won't be travelling back on that horrid ship by myself?' Edith said with a laugh. 'I feared that, you know.'

Jaya laughed. 'No, we'll be seasick together on our way back to England, on our way back home.'

The End.

ACKNOWLEDGEMENTS

First and foremost, I thank Almighty Allah who has blessed me in many ways.

A special thank you to my publishers, Onwe Press, for taking me on this journey to publication. You've all been amazing. I am eternally grateful. Thank you to everyone who contributed to this book and allowed me to tell this story. I couldn't have done it without you all.

My family who have always supported me, and my four dear children who grow with me.

Thank you to the readers. I hope this story touches you in many ways.